Of Mischief & Magic

Previously published as
A Touch of Gypsy Fire

SHILOH WALKER

Copyright

Original title
A Touch of Gypsy Fire
Copyright © 2004 Shiloh Walker
Revised 2020
Edited by Pamela Campbell
Electronic book publication April 2004
Cover Designed by Shiloh Walker
Images
© Vladimirs Poplavskis | Dreamstime.com

This book is a work of fiction. The names, characters, places, and incidents are products of the writer's imagination or have been used fictitiously and are not to be construed as real. Any resemblance to persons, living or dead, actual events, locale or organizations is entirely coincidental.

All rights reserved. No part of this book may be reproduced, scanned, or distributed in any manner whatsoever without written permission from the author except in the case of brief quotation embodied in critical articles and reviews.

This title is licensed for your personal enjoyment only. This ebook may not be resold or given away to other people.

Please note that if you purchased this from an auction site or blog, it's stolen property. Thank you for respecting the hard work of this author. Your support is what makes it possible for authors to continue to provide the stories you enjoy.

Dedication

To my editor Pam, the Wondrous One.

To my kids, Diva, Guitar Kid & Brat—my world revolves around you two. I love you.

And to my husband, my real life fantasy…I love you.

Author Note

This book was originally titled *Touch of Gypsy Fire*. In 2004, when this book released, I was unaware of the negative connotations associated with the term 'gypsy'. Since then, I have become more aware of such matters.

While I love this story, I don't want insult a marginalized population that has already suffered far too much harm, so I decided upon another name for the race in this world previously called Gypsies and I've retitled the book.

The story has also been heavily revised with 20k worth of new material added.

Tyriel's World

High Barrow
Large province that separates elvish Eivisa from most of the human-populated provinces Zhalia, Nenu and Orn.

Wildlings
Nomadic people of the High Barrow Plains

Averne
The elvish kingdom inside Eivisia, ruled by Tyriel's father, Prince Lorne.

Eivisia
The High Kingdoms of the People, consists of four separate kingdoms, each ruled by a king or queen who are all distantly related, as the High Kingdoms were founded by a family of four, three brothers and a sister. The sister and youngest brother were twins. The younger brother Dyn and sister Ryn took over the northern and western kingdoms, with Ryn ruling the north because she had magic that blended well in cold provinces (ice, wind) and Dyn taking the western kingdom that would become Averne.

Estate of Hyra
Isolated keep along borderlands between Barrow and Eivisia. Tyriel lived there from the time she was eight until she left when she was thirty.

Nhui
Banshee-like creatures, they prey on the vulnerable. Existing in the twilight world, they manifest easiest in dusk and dawn, but can do so at other times to feed. They siphon off a being's will to live. They love preying on the fey because their energy is so powerful, but the fae are harder to catch, and know how to fight nhui so they generally wander around small villages, caravans or in areas where there is plague or war. Not common in larger towns. Spectral creatures, they are tall and thin, with spidery fingers they use to wrap around their victim's head as they feed.

Jiupsu
Early race of humans who settled in the plains of ancient High Barrow when wild magic still dominated much of the land. A nomadic warrior race, they were the progenitors of the Wildlings now seen in the world.

Prologue

A thin haze of smoke hung in the air, rich with the scent of tobacco and ale.

A sad-faced harpist played away by the campfire, his gaze distant. Voices were solemn, hushed, while outside the rain fell in a heavy downpour.

In one corner, behind a curtain hung solely for that purpose, a serving wench was servicing a handsome lieutenant from the city guard. She had considered herself lucky when he had smiled at her. He was clean, he had always tipped well, and he had kind eyes. When he had whispered in her ear, several other girls had given her very evil looks and as he took her hand and led her to the back of the room, she had merrily waggled her fingers at them behind her back. Occasionally, his grunts and moans could be heard out in the main room.

In another corners, one of the guard and his wench didn't bother with the curtain; he merely jerked her skirt up and pulled her down on his rigid cock, grunting and groaning his way to a record finish while the girl faked her way along. Neither of them were particularly clean or choosy. He wanted sex. She wanted money.

Ah, the ambience.

In yet another corner, two men sat, backs to the wall, facing the small crowd that lingered, waiting for the rain to let up. A mug of ale sat untouched in front of the swordsman. Though he slouched in his chair, his entire body was tensed, ready. His face, one unusually pretty considering his trade, was grim. Pale blond hair was secured at his nape, revealing one pierced earlobe, a single blue stud glinting there.

He had a thin upper lip, a full, sensual lower one. His long legs were sprawled out and covered from waist to ankle in supple, worn fighting leathers that allowed freedom of movement and light protection.

Across from him sat a gaily-dressed Wildling, his bright shirt the color of the sun the town hadn't seen in nearly a month. His breeches were red, cut full from the waist down to the knee, where they were tucked into high riding boots.

"Old Lita wanted us to pass the word along. She'd like to see Tyriel, while she's able. The lady doesn't have much time left, I fear." His black eyes—Wildling's eyes—were somber, sad. Very unusual for a Wildling.

Aryn had been hoping the Wildling had a message from Tyriel, a message, a plea for help, that she had landed her fine ass in trouble, something...but he barely had time to acknowledge the disappointment. His mouth went grim and tight as he closed his eyes. When he opened them, they were dark with concern, fear and rage as he straightened in his chair. Firelight glinted off the deep blue stone in his ear as he leaned forward.

"Kellen, I haven't seen or heard from Tyriel in nearly a year. We parted ways last winter," Aryn said, a frown darkening his fair face. His voice was low and rough, with the frustration he still felt over their abrupt parting. In the pit of his stomach, that gnawing doubt that something was very, wrong grew even larger. It had been troubling him for some time and now, he had concrete proof. Tyriel wouldn't have avoided her family this long. "She had plans to meet up with the family in Bentyl Faire."

Concern entered Kellen's eyes as Aryn spoke. Staring at the swordsman, the Wildling shook his head, frowning.

Aryn closed his eyes and rubbed them with his fingers, suddenly feeling unbelievably weary. "She never showed at Bentyl, or any of the other faires, did she?"

"We haven't seen Tyriel in nearly two years, Aryn, since we saw you both together at the faire in Kenton. Why did you break apart? Everything seemed to be going so well for the both of you."

With a restless shrug, Aryn said, "That's what I thought. We had a solid partnership; people asked for us by name, looked for us." He paused, glancing at his blade, an enchanted sword that had once been such a burden. "It's...complicated."

"Complicated," Kellen said slowly, the look in his eyes saying he wasn't buying the horseshit Aryn was selling. Nor should he—Wildlings were excellent purveyors of horseshit and Aryn was barely adequate.

Annoyed, Aryn snapped, "Aye. *Complicated.* I never planned on either of us going our own way. We worked well together. We suited each other."

At least until the last day, he thought darkly, grimly remembering that day. She had left one morning after saying things the night before that had knocked him flat off his feet, storming out of the room before he could take it in. And that night—a night that was mostly list to him.

He had Irian to thank for that, he had no doubt. He cursed silently at the sword, a sword that had remained all but silent for many months.

Bloody hunk of enchanted metal, I ought to throw you in the fires of Itherri Bogs.

Not only had his best friend up and left him, the Soul inside the enchanted sword that had become a companion who had all but ceased talking to him.

If there wasn't a job that needed doing, Irian was nothing more than a brooding silent presence in the back of Aryn's mind.

As if summoned by Aryn's thoughts, the enchanter stirred, a low, husky chuckle escaping him.

It was the most Aryn had heard from Irian in months outside of their work.

"So she just left? Didn't say anything other than she'd meet up with us in Bentyl?" Kel raised and lowered his ale without drinking, his black eyes serious and concerned. "If Tyriel had said she was going to meet up with us, she would. Something must have happened."

"I know. That's my fear, too. Tyriel being who she is, only the Lost Gods only know what sort of trouble she found—or what trouble found *her*," Aryn said dryly, using humor to cover his very real fear. "Why don't you spread the word through the caravan? I'll ask around and we can meet up in Bentyl. Somebody surely has seen her."

When they met at the Bentyl Faire some weeks later, it was with grim faces. Nobody had seen or heard from Tyriel in months.

Word came winging in from Wildling clans scattered far and wide. Tyriel seemed to have dropped off the face of the world.

If a Wildling hadn't seen her, then she wasn't around to be seen.

Clad in somber browns, his fair hair secured in a queue at the nape of his neck, Aryn listened as Kel finished talking. Absently shifting the sword harness he wore, Aryn rose to pace the confines of the small tent.

"Now what?" he asked.

"You don't need to concern yourself, Aryn. We're her family and—"

"Don't." He turned on his heel and advanced

on the shorter man, backing him up against the wall. In a low threatening growl, he repeated, "Don't. We were partners for six years; we shed blood together, nearly died saving the other countless times. Anything that concerns Tyriel concerns me. *Everything* that concerns her concerns me."

Not bothering to hide his small, pleased smile, Kel relaxed. "I'd hoped you would say that. Something tells me Tyriel is going to need all the help she can get." Rising, Kel wandered over and picked up his harp, absently strumming a somber tune. "The best thing to do is go back to where you two were when you split, since that seems to be the last time anybody saw her. That would be the first place we ought to try."

"The first thing we need to do is contact her father," Aryn contradicted, turning to face the suddenly still Wildling.

"Her father."

"Can you think of a person better equipped to find her?" he asked dryly.

"Her father." The forced laughter didn't quite hide the nerves in his eyes as he ran a hand through his short cap of black curls. He offered, "We could just send him a message through the courier guild."

"Since when did Wildlings trust the guild?" Aryn asked. "Send one of your own."

"Right." Rubbing his sweaty hands down the sides of his saffron trews, Kel tried to figure out if any of his kin would look upon it as an adventure. How many Wildlings got to see the enchanted kingdom?

Thousands, probably, he thought, sighing dramatically. And none lived to tell the tale.

"And maybe we will be lucky. Maybe Tyriel has been with him all this time," Aryn offered, trying to cheer up the younger man.

Not likely though. The elvish kingdoms would drive her mad within a month. Be her father a prince of the elves or no.

Aryn tossed restlessly, tangled in the rough linen sheets. He'd gone to bed wearing his leathers, ready to leave at a moment's notice, save for his boots. It was a muggy, humid night and the summer air coming in through the open window barely stirred the air. The sheets clung to him, twining around him like ropes as he fought the scenes playing out inside his head.

Trapped in dreams, he flung his arm out. "Tyriel."

Irian, the Soul within his enchanted blade, surged to violent wakefulness with Aryn's fingers brushed the hilt.

Their souls merged and Irian reached out, pulling on the powerful magic that had let him bind himself to the sword.

"Come," Irian said, taking control of the dream and dragging Aryn along with him as he flung himself into the dreamscape.

In a blink, they were somewhere else.

They were with Tyriel.

He could see her.

They could see her.

Gods, what's happened to her? Aryn thought, hardly able to believe the slumped still figure was the bright laughing woman he had spent six years with.

"She is a prisoner," Irian said, his voice echoing inside Aryn's mind. "Someone has taken her and holds her in this hole."

Aryn didn't snarl at the arrogant prick for pointing out the obvious. He was too enraged to form words.

A sob shimmered in the air, coming from the woman standing across from them, near the wall of the small cell. She turned toward them, eyes skating dully across the space where they stood without stopping. Her lovely features were covered in bruises, her eyes sunken and dull.

There was no dancing, vivid light in her eyes.

The sharp blades of her cheekbones, once so stunning, now looked almost violent, as if they'd cut through her skin. The hopelessness that hung around her filled him with impotent rage that only worsened when Irian said, "She's been raped. Beaten. Likely often."

Aryn didn't want to look, but he refused to avoid the horror, wouldn't turn away from it and forced himself to memorize dried blood, and bruises in varying stages of healing on her thighs, torso, breasts and wrists. Scars showed on her belly and legs.

The rage exploded into a wildfire when she went to move and collapsed, her too-thin legs not supporting her.

Forgetting he was here on in a dream, he lunged.

And several feet from her, he was slammed into a wall, unable to reach her.

"We can't help her from within a dream, Aryn," Irian said from behind her. "Wake, Aryn. You must *wake*."

Furious even though he knew the enchanter spoke the truth, Aryn shouted out her name.

It was his own voice that woke him.

Hair, face and torso soaked with sweat, Aryn sat up in the bed, his breath sawing in and out as he scrubbed his gritty eyes. A misty form shimmered into view and a large brooding figure started to pace, his eyes glowing red with rage, echoing the red that still shimmered around the blade.

This was Irian, a long-dead warrior of the plains, a nomadic race that had been the progenitors of the Wildlings, thousands of years gone from the land.

"Tyriel, what happened?" Aryn muttered, shaking his head as Irian prowled the room, swearing in a language no longer spoken.

"Does it matter? *We* never should have let her leave. I warned you." Irian continued to pace as Aryn brooded.

"What did you want me to do? Hold her prisoner?" Aryn snapped. The second he said those words, he wanted to yank them back.

Irian whirled to face him. In a blur of speed that made it seem if he disappeared, the warrior crossed to him and caught Aryn by the throat. "You see what's happened to her now that you didn't listen to me. Arrogant pup."

Although Irian's form looked misty and insubstantial, the hand on Aryn's throat felt all too real—and the pressure definitely was. But Aryn had fought with this warrior inside his skin. Freeing himself with a violence that spoke of temper, he said, "If you want to waste time fighting, that's fine with me, you useless hunk of metal. Or we could be smart and start looking for her."

Irian looked as he wanted to give into the violence he felt. Long dead he might be, but his soul was bound to the blade Aryn carried and he felt the same emotions he'd once felt, emotions familiar to Aryn.

"We find her." He gave a sharp nod and began to pace, his form flickering in and out as he brooded.

Aryn dropped down on the bed and stared at the floor.

What in the world could have happened between the four weeks between her leaving Ifteril and the Bentyl Faire?

Where could she be? And would he find her in time.

"*We* will find her, Aryn," Irian said, his voice fading. The primitive power in the enchanter was vast, but he had to hold it in check or it could overwhelm his bearer. Doing so for a long period, Irian had said, could be taxing.

"We?" Aryn asked, tossing the enchanter a look. "Or you, after taking me over?"

"We. Tyriel is yours, not mine," Irian said. But his voice was no longer the steady cadence it had been, rather an insubstantial whisper. *"After all, my body is long dead."*

Sadness filled the man's eyes, and grief.

Irian faded from view, and then a door shut inside Aryn's mind.

The swordsman knew Irian would respond to nothing else.

Even Aryn's response that Tyriel didn't belong to Aryn.

* * * * *

The pain, nauseating as it was, no longer kept her awake. Lost in a tumbling maze of dreams, the pain lashed at her out of the darkness. Flinching, she shrieked and tried to pull away from it, to hide.

But it merely found her again, and tore at her repeatedly.

When the pain did little to jar her out of her daze, the things came. Wet, spongy beasts from the underworld, crawling over her, invading her, ripping and biting at her helpless form.

The things weren't real, a construct created by her captor, but she feared them the most.

Her captor fed on that fear and she hated him all the more for it.

Once, she would have battled them, banished them as the illusions she knew them to be.

But there had also been a time when she would have lashed out and destroyed the man responsible.

In despair, she curled in on herself, to wait it out. It would fade. It always did.

And it would come again.

It always did.

Chapter 1

Six Years Earlier

Gay, cheerful music poured from the flute she held to her lips.

Eyes ever watchful, she played on with a scrap of attention on the music while she studied the crowd in front of her. She kept her hood over her head and her eyes low. In a place such as this, nobody thought twice of such things. Many people here were criminals, thieves, trying to hide themselves. They would think the same of her.

The innkeeper was a slovenly thing, Tyriel thought. But he was no worse than the rest in this city. How had it changed so much? It had only been a few years. Or had it? It was easy enough to lose track of time when one had lived so many years, and lived a great number of them alone.

No longer were men expected to take a wench upstairs. Now they simply retreated to the shadowy corners, engaging in oral sex for the most part, holding the wench by the hair or shoulders, tossing her a few coins when he was done. But one or two over the past few hours had actually pushed the woman up against the wall and fucked her right there.

Since the wenches seemed to enjoy the money, and the attention, Tyriel turned a blind eye. And a deaf ear when need be. Pity she couldn't turn her nose off. The scent of unwashed bodies and copious sex, stale beer, burnt food—she longed for the mountains, the plains, the green of the wood.

Her eyes closed and she briefly thought of home, longed for it—not the wagon trains of the Wildlings, but home—the Four Kingdoms of Eivisa, and the sprawling valleys and towering peaks of Averne, her father's realm, to walk among the woods and feel the magic of it seeping into her bones, to lie down on the mossy green grass and feel the hard, powerful body of a warrior over her while the magic mingled and their bodies—

Boisterous shouts intruded on her thoughts. She opened her eyes, torn out of her fantasies.

One lout, in particular, was annoying the hell out of her. He had made several lewd comments in her direction the night before, all of which she had brushed off and ignored. But he was already drunk and getting drunker, and the night was still young.

Turning her attention to the rest of the crowd, she dismissed him from her mind and looked for a likely mark with full pockets. The one she found was already nodding happily to her music, a sweet-looking old peddler, prosperous from the looks of it. What in the name of hell he was doing in this dive, she couldn't understand.

And even as she changed her music to match the emotions she sensed in him, he tossed two silver marks into the open case at her feet.

She nodded at him in thanks, pleased. Those two silver marks would let her leave a few days earlier than planned.

There might be more where those came from. It wasn't exactly the most honorable way to play, but she was not using magic. Just playing to suit his moods. What he gave was of his own free will.

A few coppers joined the scattered coins but she didn't even notice as a loud crash, followed by a bellow, echoed through the tavern.

The guard, an overgrown hulk of a man, looked at the spreading patch of wine that soaked the front of his already filthy uniform. The serving boy, no older than nine, stood on weak knees, his face pale, too afraid to even dodge the blow sure to come.

Behind the bar, the innkeeper did nothing, merely filled mug after mug with the disgusting ale. Her flute landed on the ground before the cup fell from the boy's trembling hands. A growl rumbled low in her throat as she crossed the room quicker than human eyes could follow. Another man was moving, a dark cloaked figure, but Tyriel moved far quicker.

The small boy stared at the guard, so pale as he cowered there, obviously awaiting a blow he knew would come. But the huge fist never landed. She grabbed the boy, shoving him backward before turning to face the guard.

"I doubt anybody is going to notice one more stain on your uniform," she said softly, her husky voice carrying through the suddenly silent inn as she pushed her hood back.

She'd kept it up out of a need for privacy as much as anything else. Unless she used magic to conceal her appearance, it was hard to hide who—and what—she was. Now, as the hood fell back, the people around them reacted. Whispers and gasps, plus a few curses, rippled around the room, spreading from those closest to them until even those in the farthest reaches, hiding in the dark shadows, were now watching.

She'd confined her dark hair in complicated braids that left the soft point of her ears partially obscured.the ears weren't the most obvious sign of her heritage, not for those who knew what to look for—that lay in the luminous glow of her topaz eyes, even now holding a warning as she eyed the guard.

A guard who, clearly, was too stupid to see that warning.

"Mind your own business, bitch," he growled, looming over her, going to knock her aside.

He failed.

When she stood there, immovable as a rock, the guard's face twisted, growing redder with anger.

"I told you to piss off," he snarled, placing the flat of his hand on her chest and shoving.

Tyriel, though nearly as tall as he, was reed

slender. Had she been human, like the guard, she would have stumbled back onto her tail, likely taking the boy with her.

Unnoticed in the crowd, a patron went still. He'd been halfway to intercept the guard, ready to bloody him if he struck the poor, clumsy child, but the minstrel had moved from the stage where she'd been playing with such relentless cheer, it had almost driven him back out into the dark, cold night.

Now, hand still resting on his blade, he observed as the guard's hard shove failed to make her moved so much as finger's width.

Concealed in the shadows of his hood, he watched the woman smiled tauntingly at the guard.

The fool might be half-drunk, but something resembling sense had finally penetrated his ale-addled mind. That, or he noticed the danger lurking in her smile, for he fell back a step to give her a narrow-eyed study.

Nonchalantly, she gathered her braids into a thick tail, using a tie she produced from somewhere to secure the mass at her neck. All the while, she held the guard's gaze as that taunting smirk widened.

It couldn't even be called a *challenge*, the man thought, watching with growing interest—and amusement. The guard was no threat to her, even had he been sober. He'd counted a solid ten guards in the inn and all *ten* wouldn't be a challenge for this woman.

"Elf."

"Look there, see the ears? Oh, my stars, see her eyes?"

The voices blended into the background as she stepped closer to the guard.

All the blood drained from the man's face and his next breath came out a high-pitched wheeze.

Inside the confines of his hood, the human, a swordsman known only as Aryn, chuckled. Movement out of the corner of his eye caught his attention. He slanted his gaze without moving his head.

It was so quiet, one could hear a bloody mouse fart.

Or the faint clink as a pickpocket made his way around the room, so brazen even the presence of a high-magic user didn't deter him.

"Shall I continue to mind my own business?" the minstrel asked.

Aryn stayed tuned in on the conversation as he circled the room, keeping to the shadows, as he went about his task.

"Perhaps...perhaps it was my own...my own fault, milady," the guard stuttered, his booming belligerent voice now a mumble. "Seein' he jes' a kid, after all. No harm done."

"None at all." An agreeable smile lit the minstrel's face and her eyes all but glowed, making everybody watching her feel warm, welcome...*loved*.

Well, almost everybody. The guard and his

cohorts were scared shitless, having barely avoided slaughter.

With a near-audible *pop*, the tension drained out of the room and the guard turned on his heel to return to his seat.

Aryn, task completed, watched the players in the odd little scene.

As if fearing to attract her notice, the guard's companions and other various miscreants hurried away from the fae female. Others remained standing, gathered near the minstrel. They didn't quite *surround* her and none actually approached. But their awe and interest was visible. For some, it wasn't just *awe* or *interest*, but outright worship.

Aryn wasn't surprised. He doubted the minstrel was, not considering how far from her people's lands. Zhalia, far from the Four Kingdoms, called the enchanted kingdom by the human races, was a superstitious land and had been for generations.

Magic and its practice wasn't forbidden in the province, at least not anymore, but outside the larger cities, few used it openly and races inherently magical, like the elves, were nearly on the same level as angels—or, depending on who you asked, demons—and only a mere step below Nominu, or the Nameless One, among some peoples, the deified, sacrificed God recognized in this part of the world.

As she returned to the corner where she'd been playing for much of the night, Aryn watched as she tugged her hood back up. Her hand hovered over her chest but she didn't rub the area where the guard had shoved her. She might be stronger than two or three average humans, but he suspected the guard's attempt to knock her back had hurt.

The moment lasted barely a heartbeat before she lowered her hand and her facial muscles didn't change. That, too, was unsurprising. He'd seen no sign she had any companion and it didn't take more than a few days or weeks of lone travel in this world to figure out that it was best to never show if a hint of weakness.

She bypassed the low stool where she'd sat to play, closer to him now. Unable to hold back the curiosity now, he spoke. "Interesting reaction there. Does that happen everywhere you go?"

Chapter 2

Tyriel was irritated now—and tired.

Also, very hungry. She'd planned on staying at this inn for a few days, but likely needed to reconsider that decision. Not in the mood to play word games, or any much of anything, she looked toward the speaker and found herself staring into a pair of blue eyes—very beautiful blue eyes.

The shadows cast by his hood would make it hard for a human to notice that fact. But elves weren't human. According to her father, a fae lord who had lived for more than two thousand years before he fell in love with Tyriel's Wildling mother, both of them had often debated about whether Wildlings were, in fact, still human themselves.

Wildlings had lived for millennia in areas where the wild magic had flowed freely, refusing to flee to human villages and cities, hiding by tall stone walls with iron gates where they bedded down at night and prayed no magic creature would find their beds.

Wild magic had a...curious effect on people after a time. After generations of living in areas rife with wild magic, Tyriel wouldn't be surprised to learn the Wildlings weren't human anymore.

Like her deceased mother, she had her own suspicions on the subject, leaning toward the likelihood that the Wildlings had veered from simple humans to something more complex several centuries back.

Tyriel certainly wasn't human.

Her vision had always been keen, keener than any she knew from either fae or Wildling lineage. She appreciated it yet again as she took in the blue irises, a nose that had been broken at least once, but set with rather admirable skill, and a mouth almost ridiculously pretty for a man.

Well, hello, lovely man.

His brows rose and she reminded herself—*he asked a question, silly chit.*

"It happens often enough that I'm used to it." She considered that a moment before adding, "Mostly."

"Used to grown men nearly piss themselves when they see you while others look at you as if they can't decide if they want worship you or hide before you notice them? Used to them sighing in rapt devotion all over a smile from you?"

"All of that." She winked at him. "The fae eat babies at breakfast, didn't you know? Mere humans should know better than to anger us. That's why they sigh—it's not devotion. It's relief."

"Babies for breakfast." He chuckled as he pushed his hood back. "All the elves I've ever known were vegetarian."

Now able to see him completely, she had to wonder at some of her fae cousins who never left Eivisia, convinced they'd never find a lover or mate among the mortal races.

How wrong they were.

This man's face could have been carved from alabaster—*should* be, forever captured by an artist's hands so future generations could gaze upon the elegant perfection, the only imperfection that slight crook in his nose.

Just *how* did he know that little fact about the People?

"Are you going to give me away? Let them know how meek and cowardly we really are?"

"I didn't say a thing about meek or cowardly." Gesturing to the seat at his side, he said, "I'm impressed, though. Even as drunk as he was, I didn't expect him to show much in the way of common sense. Zhalia's not a bad province, all in all, but this particular town? You rarely seen a guard back down from anything short of a fair fight."

"It wouldn't have been fair. I could have taken down a man like him when I was barely old enough to pick up a sword."

He grinned at her. "Well, there is that. I imagine you already noticed the other guards in here. It was still a risk, confronting him."

"Hardly." She sniffed. "Zhalians are notoriously superstitious—it will take generations for their distrust of the magickers in this world to fade, even though it was the People who aided them when they finally decided to overthrow their oppressive rule. They still believe that we lurk around in the shadow world, waiting for people to displease us so we can haul them away to harvest our mines for us."

"I doubt you'd let anybody not of fae blood into your mines," the swordsman said. "Not as protective as you lot are of your treasures. Speaking of which..."

He tossed something at her feet.

Tyriel heard the clink of coins and narrowed her eyes. "What's this?"

"Your coin." His eyes slid past hers before moving to the inn's entrance.

Her sensitive ears caught the sound of movement, even above the normal noise — furtive and fast, somebody fleeing. Sighing, she scooped up the coin purse and glanced at the cap she'd put down to collect any money that might come her way while she played. "Pickpocket?"

"Aye. Can't decide if he was stupid or bold as brass, stealing from you once he knew who you were."

"Bit of both, most likely." She opened the coin purse and transferred the funds from it into hers, then tossed the emptied bag to the swordsman. "If you haven't eaten tonight, I'll buy your meal to thank you for your trouble."

"I've eaten. But I won't say no to company as I finish my ale, since it seems you're done playing."

Tyriel glanced around. "Oh, I'm done."

Once they were at a table, closer to the door and far from the guards, the swordsman lifted a tall, pewter mug in her direction. "To interesting nights."

She inclined her head, watching as he drank before shifting her attention back out over the crowd. She'd been in this inn before, had rented a room in the inn on her last trip through.

The town hadn't been like this.

"Can I buy you one?"

"I'll pass." She glanced at him a serving wench put another mug on the table in front of him. She shuddered in distaste, remembering the one taste she had taken earlier. He took another drink, licked foam from his lower lip. Her belly tightened as she imagined echoing that movement herself, licking his lower lip. For that pleasure, she might even torture herself with the taste of shitty ale, if she could taste *him*.

But there was no sign of interest in his eyes. At all.

There goes my pride, Tyriel thought.

"You seem to know quite a bit about the kin," Tyriel said after declining the offer of ale. "How is that?"

He flashed her a grin. "I get around."

"That knowledge doesn't. At least not easily." She ran the tip of her finger idly over a scar in the worn table's surface. "You've already mentioned two things about the People that some of my family might consider worth killing over."

"Some… but not you?"

The blue of his eyes didn't darken the way a fae male's would, but Tyriel felt his interest sharpen all the same. She told herself she should get and walk away from this intriguing man now.

Right now.

"Call me...*undecided*."

"Very, Lady Undecided. Tell me, did your eyes truly glow earlier? I'd swear they did, but I'm not entirely certain if I saw what I think I saw or if it's another myth about the fae told to scare bad little human boys."

Tyriel laughed.

Around them, a brief lull in the conversation fell, eyes drifting their way and lingering on her before conversation slowly resumed.

"Be good, little boy, or the elves will sneak into your room like a monster and snatch you from your bed?" she said, a smile on her face as she looked him over.

"Just so. And…you have not answered."

"What do you think?" When he merely arched a pale gold brow at her, she sighed. "Swordsman, you might have pried certain secrets from a fae or two along the road but that doesn't mean I'll tell you more."

"Fair enough. You know, you saved that boy from a sound beating." His eyes drifted over to the guard who sat staring sullenly into his wine. "The guard will forget by morning, but that wouldn't help the boy. He would have been hurt badly enough to not work for a day or two. If he can't do his job here, he would likely be sold."

"Sold." She spat the word, bile coating her throat. She looked around the inn's public room and shook her head. "Slaves. That's one of the reasons I head out this week. There was a time when slavery wasn't lawful here. I didn't believe it when I was first told some fool lord had pushed for it to be legalized. Barely out from under an oppressive rule a century and already the monied and privileged seek to oppress those beneath them."

Her eyes drifted over to where the serving boy hurried back and forth between the kitchen and the tables. Often, he cast grateful eyes her way as he carefully avoided the area around the surly guard. A handsome child, if you could overlook the overly long, tangled hair and obvious malnourishment.

More than one patron had overlooked.

Body slaves were bad enough. Forcing a child into that role was unthinkable. And it wouldn't be long before the innkeeper did just that. Tyriel had noticed the appraising looks the innkeeper gave the boy when a particular customer would stare at him overly long.

"I've only been here a month myself. Hired on for a job. Once the contract is up, I'm northbound." Sympathy darkened his eyes as he watched the boy.

Yes, a handsome child.

At his back, his sword seemed to weigh

down heavily on him for just a moment. Automatically, he shifted the harness as he turned his eyes back to the elf. "I'm Aryn. May I ask your name?"

"Tyriel," she murmured, dragging her eyes from the child and studying the outrageously beautiful man in front of her. Over the morass of scents in the inn, she could smell him, and he smelled delicious...warm, male, clean. The sword strapped to his back was harnessed across what looked to be a lusciously powerful chest.

The sword...it drew her eye, flashing far more brightly in the dim light than it should have. The carving in the pommel was scrolled and marked, letters—familiar, they seemed to move and twist, and call—

Tyriel shook her head slightly as Aryn shifted his shoulders once more. The movement distracted her, drawing her attention away from the sword's hilt and pommel, and back to him.

His shoulders were wide and strong, arms were long, lean and muscled under the clean cotton of his shirt. The sleeves of that shirt were rolled up to his elbows, revealing muscled forearms, thick wrists, long-fingered hands with wide palms. And his scent—

It was *maddening*, how good he smelled.

A small hand appeared on the swordsman's shoulder. Turning her eyes upward, Tyriel watched as one of the serving girls lowered her lips to speak quietly into his ear.

Tyriel tuned the words out, although she could have listened in—and was tempted.

She already knew what was likely to be said and when Aryn gave the woman a slow smile and short nod, Tyriel felt an unwelcome twist in her belly—envy.

How odd. She couldn't remember the last time she'd felt *envy*.

The girl, well, woman had large breasts, a narrow waist, and full hips. Exceptionally clean, which was unusual in a dive like this. Her gaze landed on the brand marking the young woman's wrist and the pieces fell into place. It was the shape of a quarter-moon—the girl was an indentured servant. She could work off her five years here, or be bought by a willing party and work off the time with another. Once her debt was paid, that quarter moon would be filled in and people would know she was no longer obligated by some law or another to work off whatever sentence had been placed on her slim shoulders.

So young, Tyriel thought. So, *so* young.

Had the mark been an 'X,' it would have meant she was a slave and she'd never know freedom, not unless something extraordinary happened.

An 'X' encircled meant a body slave, basically a body whored out at her master's pleasure, with no choice in his or her bed partners, or any say in where he or she bedded that partner. Tyriel had seen body slaves who knelt in alleyways in broad daylight to service or be mounted.

Judging by the look in her eyes, this girl likely sought a new keeper.

Tyriel recognized the satisfaction in the serving girl's eyes as she strolled away, hips swaying subtly beneath the plain blue wool of her skirt.

Ah, well, Tyriel thought, *too bad*.

Damn it all.

* * * * *

Aryn the swordsman at least had the decency to take his tumble upstairs. The girl was clean and soft and sweet-smelling—looking for a way to a better life.

Aryn couldn't, and wasn't interested in, offering that, but a soft female beside him for the night wasn't a bad thing. He'd leave some extra money with her so she could stash it. Most indentured servants skimmed a little money here and there, hoping to earn enough to buy their freedom a year or two sooner.

Barely clearing the door, he turned and grabbed her, pinning her against the wall and lifting her skirt to close his hands over naked hips.

"Why, you naughty thing, no undergarments." He shifted his hands to her butt as he nibbled his way down her neck.

She hadn't accepted another man's favor all night, or the past three, waiting for this one. He was clean, he was handsome, and he had kind eyes. Since she did have some say in whom she spread her thighs for, she had waited and watched him.

With a smile, she pulled her linen shift up and over her head, freeing the large breasts that had teased and taunted Aryn half the night. "Not a thing, sirrah," she replied. "I was hopin' you'd like some company after all. And I wanted nothin' in y'way."

It had been nearly four months since Aryn had been around a woman clean enough that he didn't fear some scourging dick rot if he bedded her.

His need for a woman was powerful. Without another thought in his mind, he freed his cock, then lifted her and drove into her, the soft, silky fist of her sex closing tightly over him.

"Sweet little thing."

She gasped at the penetration, wet and soft, an eager moan falling from her lips as he lowered his head to catch a nipple between his teeth. He surged inside her, gripping the full, round curve of her ass.

Aryn held back until he felt the orgasm rippling through her, and then he rammed into her repeatedly, until his own climax broke free.

He then took her to the bed and guided her head down until she could wrap her pretty mouth around his cock, groaning with delight as she set to the task with obvious, unfaked pleasure. Her round, firm ass stayed high in the air as she worked him. Aryn cupped one soft white globe, massaging the flesh while his other hand wrapped in her loose hair. Occasionally, because that pretty butt just seemed to want it, he would give it a sharp little smack with the flat of his hand.

Her soft curls tossed over her shoulder, she stared at him through her lashes. Pulling away to swab the head of his penis with her tongue, she paused momentarily to grin at him. Going back to her task, she moved down to suckle and nibble on his sac before taking him into her mouth again. Moving slowly down the thick, rounded head, she took as much of him into her mouth as she could, falling into a slow steady rhythm that soon had Aryn lifting his hips to her caress and moaning.

The ruddy flesh of his cock gleamed wet as it slid in and out of her mouth, her hand gripping the base of his shaft, holding it steady as she moved. She slid the other hand under his hip, gripping a firmly muscled buttock and massaging.

"Oh, that was tasty," she murmured after he came in her mouth. Swallowing it down, licking her lips, she stroked his penis lovingly as she sat down next to him. "Should I be goin' now?"

"Hell, no." Her eyes widened in surprise as he pulled her down onto him, guiding her legs to either side of his hips, then pushing inside her yet again.

Aryn thought later that the little servant had been the answer to a prayer.

He spent the night ridding himself of the desperate need to ride a woman and come inside her warm body. And she was tempting. Tempting enough that he found he had a bit of regret when he denied the silent question in her eyes before he ushered her out of the room.

But, no, he wasn't letting her stay, would not wake and ride her one last time before he headed out.

Alone, he washed up, using water from the basin that had already gone icy, ignoring the chill out of years of practice.

Once clean, he dressed in a clean set of trousers and shirt, leaving his boots by the bed before stretching out.

As he drifted off to sleep a little later, he wondered one last time about the pretty, wild-eyed elf he had seen.

* * * * *

The wild-eyed elf had paid for the room and used a touch of the elemental magic most fae had to rid warm the water in the basin before washing, then again as she swept the room for signs of vermin.

Discovering only a couple of small mice, she left them alone and lay down, her body weary. The bed was lumpy but she'd slept on worse. The room was warm enough since she had chosen the one right over the kitchen.

And she had been serenaded by the sound of various couples fucking.

Unfortunately, her sensitive ears had made it possible for her to even pick out one set of voices—the ones right across the hall. It seemed Aryn the swordsman had the room across from hers and he'd spent half the night bedding the serving wench.

Not that Tyriel was jealous. Exactly. But the man wouldn't have had to *pay* for sex. Tyriel would have been happy to join him in bed that night. Had even been working up to extending such an invitation. At her age, one might think she'd be skilled at it, but the truth was, she seldom had to practice.

Usually, men made the offer before she even decided if she was interested.

And yet, here she lay, her bed largely empty because the man she would have liked to have next to her chose to while the night away with a woman who took coin for the pleasure.

She didn't begrudge those who chose to make a living in the flesh trade, as long as all parties were consensual—and no children were involved. But that envy rubbed her raw, her own vanity and a wounded sense of female pride.

Judging from the sound of it, Aryn's companion came out with the better part of the bargain. More than once, soft feminine squeals of pleasure drifted past the door.

It made for a very, very restless night on Tyriel's part.

* * * * *

"Of all the damned fools." Tyriel faced down the guard who stood at the gate, attempting to bar her way out of the city. He continued to stand there, one grimy hand extended. "Taxation for leaving the city?"

How had this town slid so far downhill in the few short years since she had visited last? Mentally, she counted back and was somewhat disconcerted to realize it had been nearly fifteen years, not the two or three she had thought at first. Sighing, she shoved her hair back.

When you traveled alone, time had a way of slipping by with little notice.

"I was taxed when I entered, when I contracted a short job as bodyguard, when I paid for my room and board, and whenever I made a purchase. And you expect me to pay more simply for leaving?"

"Pay your dues, milady," the guard repeated. "O'course, iffen yer short money, we kin work it out." His eyes landed on her mouth, letting her know exactly how she could work it out.

I'd rather bite it off than suck it, nasty little man.

Instead of saying that, she pursed her lips and pretended to think.

"No. No, I don't think so," she said slowly. "Perhaps I'll go make my complaints known to the constable and have him explain this new tax to me. I'm certain he's meant to get a percentage of it, as the collector of such taxes. And of course it goes on to the town's coffers. I'm certain he can help me better understand this issue, as well as explain exactly I am expected to pay it off. Then, perhaps I'll pay." She turned and studied the street behind her, frowning thoughtfully. "I believe his office is at the town center, just to the right of the rather gaudy and filthy fountain. Is that right?"

Swinging around at the guard's strangled intake of air, she smiled brightly. "Is that a yes?"

His eyes, now wider and slightly panicked, guard's eyes answered her question. There was no taxation. But few people thought to question it, she supposed. Even fewer would think to mention the constable. The damned guards in this town grew worse every trip.

There had been a time when this had been a decent city, with good decent folk, honest servants. No slaves.

"What? No response?" she asked dryly as the guard's hand fell. He offered only a sullen glare in response. "I'll just take my leave then."

With a smile, she led her horse through the gate and off the road, pausing just long enough to check the riding gear and her own supplies. Then she swung up on the horse and offered a cheery wave before nudging Kilidare onto the road.

Her nearly empty coin purse slapped against

her hip as the horse took off at a ground-eating gallop. Good thing he hadn't pressed the issue. Tyriel doubted she would have bothered with going to the constable and this morning's purchase had near emptied her resources, for the time.

She could always change that. Her father would be more than happy, even rather insistent on changing that.

And she was rather insistent that he not.

She had made it by on far less than she had now. She could do it again.

* * * * *

"Sold?" Aryn repeated, staring at the innkeeper with shuttered eyes. By the gods, he thought angrily. One of the patrons that had kept shooting the boy looks the past night, no doubt.

Pretty child slaves didn't last long in places like this. They usually ended up in private homes or whorehouses. How could such filth be legal? Why was it allowed? His gut roiled and his hand ached for his sword.

He would find him.

That was all there was to it.

Shifting the harness at his shoulders, he closed his eyes. A headache pounded behind his eyes, a familiar one. The blade at his back had that odd heavy feel to it.

West, they had to ride west, find the child...soon, no, not soon, now.

Of Mischief & Magic

They had to go *now*.

He shook his head as the odd spell of dizziness swarmed up.

Shoving it back, Aryn clenched his hands and focused. The boy. He had to focus on the boy.

Damn it! Had he seen to it last night instead of having his cock ridden—ah, but it was too late now.

No. He'd seen what was done to too many of the slave children.

If he could help just *one*—

Aryn had no idea what he would do with a small child while he traveled, but he would come up with something.

With a flat stare, he looked back at the innkeeper. He drew the long-bladed knife he wore at his hip and gave the sharp edge of it a slow stroke.

"To whom?" He offered the innkeeper a slow, cold smile.

Nervous now, the innkeeper licked his dry lips and shot the knife in Aryn's hand a quick look. "The elf las' night. Didn't know she was fae 'til then, but it was 'er. The one that saved 'is lazy arse last night, see. She up and paid for 'im afore headin' out this mornin'."

A smile spread across his face. Aryn's rush was relief was unreal. "Any idea where she was heading?"

The smile had the tension inside the innkeeper's chest loosening, turning to greed. "Mebbe."

Aryn turned the knife, letting it catch the dull light as he cocked his head and studied the innkeeper. He arched a brow, waiting.

"Maybe?" he repeated. When no answer came, he slammed the knife's tip into the bar, reached out, snagged the innkeeper's filthy shirt and dragged him closer. When they were nose to nose, Aryn said, "I suggest you remember, and remember fast. Else you are going to have a difficult time running this sorry inn—because I am going to cut out your tongue and shove it down your throat. And if I'm still feeling edgy, I'll chop off your dick as well."

Rapidly, the innkeeper said, "M' boy saw 'er loadin' the boy up w' the caravan that was outside t' wall las' night. Right happy, the boy looked." His face was pale, save for two spots of color high on his cheeks. "The Wildlings have him now. And I did not lay a hand on t' boy. Gave 'er a good price, I did."

"There is no *price* on a life," Aryn said in disgust. He dropped him abruptly and shoved. "Perhaps I should take your boy and let the Wildlings have him as well. And you could buy him back, for a price. But then, he would know true happiness, and he would never want to leave them for you."

Gaping at him, the innkeeper said, "You can't do that! He's my boy! My son!"

"That child you sold to the elf is also somebody's boy, somebody's son. Didn't keep you from buying him like he was a shirt or a pair of shoes, did it?"

Disgusted, Aryn left, grabbing his pack and hitting the streets. His contract to the wagon train was up and he was free. If he didn't get away from this blasted city, he would go mad.

Chapter 3

"Eh, thas jes' a bloody girl."

Oh, isn't he a bright one?

With some amusement, Tyriel watched as he scratched his head and eyed her dubiously. Putting down her gear kit, she rose to her full height and studied the big man.

Fighter, she decided, but nothing more than a muscled grunt. A guard who relied on his brawn and not much else—likely because he had little else to rely on.

Gerome, the man who'd hired her for a rather princely sum, gave the big man a dark look. "Benjin. Be silent."

But, no. Benjin would not be silent. Tyriel decided she'd be amused rather than insulted, though. Her gear kit, a rolled-up piece of leather that held the tools she used for polishing and cleaning her weapons, and sharpening her blades, lay in plain view on the stone she'd used as a work surface, and anybody with sense would have noted that, or the sword at her back, the knife at her waist. Not Benjin, though.

So, his next comment didn't even surprise her.

"Y' takin' to bringing whores along?" the dunce asked, too stupid to recognize the warning in his boss's eyes.

Whore, am I?

She had no ill will to those who sold themselves—*assuming* it was a choice. Tyriel sold herself as well, although what she sold was skill with a blade and magic.

So she kept her voice mild as she said, "I'm not here to whore for anybody."

"I've not seen many her equal when it comes to a sword," Gerome said, stepping forward and meeting Benjin's eyes with a sharp look. "Since Dheo is no longer traveling with me, we're short—and all my guards could use with some sharpening of their skills. Tyriel can help with that *and* keep the wagon train safe. I don't care if she's one of the exiled if she can handle you lot and keep my people safe."

"I don't need no handlin'." Benjin's face folded into surly lines and he gave Tyriel a dismissive look. Crossing his arms over his massive chest, the surly fellow looked Tyriel over with derisive eyes. "I ain't workin' alongside no bloody girl. Unless'n I kin be putting her under me."

Gerome eyed the fellow with pursed lips, then shrugged his shoulders. "All right. Aldy, get Benjin's wages together. He gave me three days of work."

"Huh?"

Aldy, the spry little man who had brought Tyriel the work contract the previous night, scurried over to the hulking idiot who stood staring at Gerome as if he had grown a second head.

"Wages? I thought we got paid at the night before each stopover." The dunce reached up to scratch his straw-colored hair a second time.

"The trip is done for you. You won't work beside a...girl." A glint of amusement lit the wagonmaster's eyes as he looked at Tyriel and she knew then he hadn't made the mistake many humans did, assuming her youthful face meant she *was* young. "Since I have no intention of passing by an excellent swordsman and mage in favor of you, you are done here."

Effectively dismissing Benjin, Gerome gestured to the other two guards who'd come along with him.

"This is Vjorl." Gerome gestured to a tall, wraith-like man with skin the color of soot.

Tyriel recognized the man's appearance, if not the man himself. "You're from the Burin lands."

Vjorl dipped his head in acknowledgment as he pressed a hand to his chest, the People's way of showing respect when meeting an equal from another race, dignitaries and such, since no elf ever would bow before *anybody.*

Smile breaking out across her face, she returned the gesture before moving to him and offering her arm, a gesture more recognizable in the lands outside her own, a warrior greeting another.

"Lady Tyriel," Vjorl said in High Elvish, as he wrapped his hand around her forearm, squeezing slightly before ending the clasp.

Her eyes widened before she replied in the same tongue. "Just Tyriel, Vjorl. Here, it is just Tyriel."

The Borinian inclined his dark head. "If that is your wish." He hesitated a moment before asking, "When next I see the prince, am I to withhold mention of this meeting?"

"Heavens, no." She broke into laughter. "Although what a small world it is. Few who know him travel so far west."

"The same could be said of those who are of the People." He smiled easily and dipped his head once more.

She caught sight of the smooth, bare skin of his scalp and noticed the fine lines of the tattoos there, marking him as a sojourning warrior-priest.

"How did you come to meet my father?" she asked, still speaking in her father's tongue.

"We had chance to meet when on a hunt."

The emphasis he put on the final word had her brows rising. Her father was a prince and sat as guardian to the Western Gate, the mountainous range that separated Eivisia from the human lands, and one of his duties as guardian there was protecting that land, and those surrounding territory from any and all threats.

He was also one of the High King's most trusted warriors, dispatching threats to Eivisa and the lands beyond.

Although it wasn't often, Prince Lorne did

leave the lands of the fae to hunt down threats that came too close to their borders or were deemed to be too much a threat to ignore, regardless of where they were.

There were always those bold enough, or desperate enough, to push for power beyond their control. Lorne, with his elite unit, had eliminated more threats to the peoples of their world than Tyriel could fathom over his centuries.

She recognized the look of a similar warrior when she studied Vjorl. "Knowing the kind of hunts that might lead my father to cross paths with a warrior priest from Burin, I won't ask any more then."

"It's actually an interesting tale." Vjorl's lean face lit with a smile. "But not one I'd care to share when there are prying ears to overhear."

"Vjorl, I'm getting my feelings here hurt."

Tyriel looked at the second man, a stout redhead with a warm, wide smile that twisted on the left, thanks to a vicious scar that bisected his cheek. He nodded at Tyriel before looking at the warrior priest.

"Nine years, I've known you and it took you four of those to say half of many words to me," he said, pointing a finger at the taller man. "For all your preaching on celibacy in service to your god, you're easily turned by a pretty face."

"In my defense, old friend," Vjorl said. "Her face is far, far prettier than yours—even after that scar. You're the only man I know that actually had such a scar *improve* his appearance."

"Oh, so harsh." But the redhead's grin widened as he turned to Tyriel.

The wagonmaster had stayed silent as Tyriel and Vjorl spoke but now he cleared his throat. All three warriors looked at him.

"Chastin, this is Tyriel, the warrior and mage I told you I'd be bringing on." His brows arched as he looked between Vjorl and Tyriel. "Clearly, you will have no trouble settling in."

"It may be a struggle but I'll try to get by."

Gerome snorted. With a nod, he indicated a figure off in the distance, approaching on horseback. "There's another one of my men. One of my best. Aryn. Between the four of you, I will sleep much better at night."

* * * * *

"You."

Tyriel raised her head, one hand holding a suede cloth, stroking it up and down the length of her blade.

The man in front of her stood with his back to the sun, towering over her. Raising one hand to shield her eyes, Tyriel made out the features of the swordsman from the inn she had met the previous fall.

"Yes, me," she replied evenly.

"I wondered if the Tyriel Gerome told me about was the one I had met a few months back."

"Looks like it," she said cheerfully, sliding her blade into its sheath. "Aryn, is it?"

"I didn't know the Kin hired themselves out to wagon trains," Aryn said, squatting down beside her. Damp tendrils of hair clung to the sides of his face and neck and his bared chest glistened with sweat. And it was every bit as fine as she had imagined it would be, wide, sculpted, muscled. His arms were roped with muscle, but not overly so, his shoulders wide and powerful, and she imagined, would cradle a woman's head perfectly.

After.

Oh, yummy.

Hmmm. Maybe, just maybe, this trip could turn out to be rather pleasant. Very pleasant. If he would just...cooperate.

Since the day was rather cool, Tyriel guessed he had been practicing. Nodding at the shallow nick on his forearm, she asked, "That happen in practice?"

Glancing at it, dismissing it, Aryn said, "Yes. The short, stocky redhead. Chastin. He's got a fast hand. How did you end up hiring your blade out? I've never known a lady of the elves to want to leave the wonder of their lands for ours."

"I'm a breed, Aryn," she said shortly, sliding into her harness and rising to her feet. "You know what that means? I don't belong with the People. And as much as I love my mother's folk, I can only take so much of them at a time."

"Who are your mother's folk?"

"You're not as closemouthed as I would have expected," she mused with an arch of her brow. And then she reached up, grabbing a hand full of springy black curls. "With hair like this, who else? The Wildlings, of course."

A laugh tumbled from Aryn's unbelievably beautiful mouth as he dropped to sit beside her, mirth making his eyes dance.

"Oh, bloody hell. That is rich. The Wildling lady and a lord of the kin—I'd think an angel and an incubus would have made a better match."

"Quite possibly. And you're not the first to make such a comparison." A sad, bittersweet smile tugged at her lips and her exotic eyes took on a faraway look. "But we'll never know. My mother died in childbirth. If she hadn't been with the Kin when she went into labor, I wouldn't be here." Shrugging her slim shoulders, she said, "I can say, without hesitation, I had an interesting childhood."

The amusement faded from his eyes and he bowed his head. "I'm sorry."

"No reason for you to be. My father loved me, as did his family. They couldn't have predicted my mother's death." She hesitated before adding, "Childbirth is a dangerous business."

"Your father raised you then?" He drew one knee up, resting his elbow on it as he studied her.

Such a simple, innocent question. No reason for to cause such a volatile surge in her emotions.

And yet...

Tyriel rose and eyed the swordsman, her eyes narrowing. Emotions swirled within, surging with the violent power of a storm.

Aryn uncoiled and got to his feet, hands out in front of him in a conciliating manner. His blue eyes widened, growing shades darker as nerves spiked.

Her sharp ears picked up the erratic trip of his heartbeat.

Tyriel blew out a soft, control breath and pulled back on the magic that had built inside her, causing her skin to glow and her eyes to spark.

Such uncontrolled spikes of power hadn't happened in ages.

Closing her eyes, she pulled the power back inside her and turned from Aryn.

She walked away, his unanswered question an echo in her mind.

Hours later, that question still sounded in her mind.

Who raised you?

The wagon train left in the morning at first light. If she had any sense, she'd be in town, getting a decent meal at some fine inn, the last she'd have for several weeks, if not more. Instead, she sat by the creek near where the wagon train encampment, her leather leggings shoved up to her knees and her bare feet in the chilly water.

Lowering her eyes to the cold, clear water, she tried to figure out why Aryn's question had upset her so much. She had loved her father, still did. She'd never once questioned his love for her. Keeping her isolated from her mother's family had been a misguided attempt to protect her.

Da was a good father, had always been kind, loving, generous, unafraid to show those emotions. Not exactly a commonality among the high fae, especially the High Royals.

Not that her aunts and uncles hadn't been kind, hadn't shown her love.

But it had been a distant thing, their many years of life engendering a remoteness that even the bonds of family couldn't break.

Outside the family, others hadn't been so kind.

More than a few had found themselves bloodied by her father, one of his fighters, even by aunts, uncles and cousins.

Being a member of the High Family didn't protect her from the prejudice too many elves carried. Being a half-breed was a step up from being a dog in the eyes of some.

By the time she was ten, her father had retreated with her to one of the most remote estates the family owned and there she stayed until she almost thirty—still a child in the eyes of the people but in reality, she'd been on the cusp of adulthood, thanks to her mother's more mortal bloodline.

There, on the Estate of Hyra, a large piece of territory that had once been a fortress stronghold for the fae armies who guarded Eivisia from the wild magics that had nearly ripped their world in two, Tyriel learned her own magic under the tutelage of Eivisia's greatest mages. She'd learned to fight and swing a sword under the tutelage of the land's most fearsome warriors, her father's own men, the legendary De Asir.

Her father had allowed every request, denying her nothing when it came to honing her skills with both magic and blade.

Many elvish princes and princesses barely trained their magic for anything more complex than lighting a fire or pretty little displays that might make a suitor laugh at court.

Tyriel thought the idea of court sounded terribly dull.

Her father had never cared for court himself and had long been a warrior. With countless enemies both inside the fae realm and without, the idea of his daughter knowing how to protect herself was a comfort.

He hadn't realized she'd been training for the day when she'd slip away.

He'd loved her dearly, still did. His people were the same and every time she returned, it was to tears and laughter and celebratory balls that lasted for days.

She loved Averne and the lands of Hyra, but

she'd been suffocating there.

Her father hadn't realized he'd been stifling her.

That he'd done what he had thought was best, what he had thought was right, she'd never doubted. Keeping her isolated from all—the Kin and the Wildlings—trying to protect what some of his own cousins had deemed a 'mongrel child'.

He couldn't have known, or understood, how easily and deeply Wildlings gave their love. Not when the elves rarely gave anything easily, and loved nothing deeply, save themselves and their own.

So different from her mother's people, the Wildlings of High Barrow.

When she had arrived among them forty years earlier, she had been welcomed with open arms and happy hearts by her mother's family.

They'd thrown a weeklong celebration. There, she'd laughed, sang, played and danced with dark-eyed men with bold smiles and hot eyes.

Everything the Wildlings did, they did with passion and life—so very different from the People.

Absently, she fingered the elongated curve of her ear, so much longer than that of her human kin, yet it was remarkably dissimilar from her elvish cousins.

*You should have died...*she'd heard the whispers in the years since she'd forced her father to acknowledge she was no longer a child he could protect by locking away on a lavish estate.

Instead, because of her father's love and her determination, she thrived.

After spending a decade with her mother's Wildling clan, learning more about the magic her human mother had possessed and why her own was so different from other fae, she'd traveled farther west, into other mortal lands.

Five years at a school for assassins, another five at a school of higher learning where she studied the history of all the people of this world instead of just the elvish, and learning nearly thirty languages—within the first two years. The third year, the headmaster had said there was nothing more they could teach her so she could either become an instructor herself or she could leave.

She'd tried her hand at instruction which was great fun the first year, entertaining enough the second, and awful the third. After that, she left and went back to her father's side for a decade, this time, insisting he live his life as he had before he'd retreated from elvish society to care for his little halfling daughter.

He'd been wary, but he'd relented.

He'd taken her with him to the first court ball only because she'd said she'd come to experience life at court.

Moments after their introduction, as they descended a grand staircase of pure *Stefini* marble, there had a titter in the crowd, followed by a low male whisper and laugh. Tyriel, without a blink, had dropped a blade into her palm and threw it. The man who'd laughed had screamed like a young child when it buried itself in his shoulder.

Nobody else had laughed as one of the footman rushed to retrieve the blade and bring it to her, after carefully cleaning the gleaming steel.

She'd accepted it and returned it to its place, while her father had said, tone bland, "The next time, she has my permission to use an iron blade. Insults to the royal families are punishable with any punishment we see fit to dole out."

After that, she was treated with a wariness that wasn't quite respect, but was far from the disdain she'd glimpsed on the faces prior. She could slit their throats while they drank their wine and they would never know it until they fell down dead.

Her father would stand by and applaud.

Averne was the largest and most powerful of the elvish realms and it spanned nearly the entire western border. For over two millennia, it had belonged to the ancient family of Dyn, her father's forebearer, who had protected Eivisia against any and all who'd dared threaten the People.

Save for their cousins in the north, descendents of Prince Dyn's sister, none of the People had ridden into battle for centuries. Under the steely look of smoke-gray eyes, none dared to challenge him even now.

They might think the Prince half mad for falling in love with a Wildling—she might have been a little more than mortal, but she could still die so easily. And she had, taken in childbirth. But that love had changed him. Losing her had changed him even more. For their daughter, he'd lay waste to the world.

"I miss you, Da," she whispered, reaching up to stroke the amber-colored moonstone beneath her jerkin. It lay side by side with another chain, this one bearing a pendant from the Wildlings, a stunted tree, a symbol that represented the Nameless One, the sacrificed god, lost so long ago few beyond the Wildlings and the Kin still remembered him and ever fewer still lifted their voices in worship.

It had belonged to her grandmother, a woman Tyriel had never known—she'd passed away a few years after Tyriel's mother had lost her life. When Tyriel finally found her mother's people, the pendant had been gifted to her by an aunt, her mother's oldest sister.

She found comfort in the two simple pieces of jewelry most times, a connection to the two unique people who had created her.

But not tonight. Tonight, she felt oddly hollow...and more lonely than she'd felt in a long, long time.

Chapter 4

She came back to camp later that night—much later.

Aryn shifted on his bedroll to watch her wind through the sleeping bodies on the ground.

She was unbelievably quiet, gliding on feet so silent she didn't even disturb the animals sleeping throughout the camp.

She paused a few feet away, and though Aryn could barely make out her form, much less her face, he knew she was watching him, that she could see him clear as day. He didn't have to see her to recall that form, those wild black curls, her large eyes, tilted up at the corners, winged black brows, a red kissable mouth and that tiny mole near the right corner of her lips.

Tall, reed-slender, small-breasted and slim-hipped—she shouldn't have been so enticing, he knew. Oh, but he was enticed. Those long legs, that smile. Her hair, her eyes...and the utter perfection of her bottom. Every damn time she bent over, he saw the tight, rounded ass and wanted to grasp her hips and pull her to him.

He had fantasies of tugging her to the ground and pushing her trousers down just enough so he could drive into her, feel her close around him, tight and snug, wet as the rain.

Other times, he imagined the pleasure they'd both derive if he took his time, stripping her naked, peeling away every stitch of clothing—and one deadly weapon—slowly, piece by piece.

He swallowed a groan and fisted his hand as he willed her to walk on by.

He burned...to know if the fire he saw in her eyes, sensed beneath her skin was as real as he suspected it was. Ached, so badly his cock throbbed every time he caught a breath of her intoxicating scent.

Her eyes had started to haunt him at night, and her low, husky laugh, the way her magic seemed to shimmer in the air around her.

But it was more than that. She had something that drew words from him, something that made him open up.

Aryn was rarely open.

What is it about you?

She continued on past him without speaking. He was closemouthed, or had always thought himself to be, until just a few marks earlier. How had she frozen him in place with simply a look? Why was it his flesh prickled every time she was near?

Not his cock. That did not prickle—it stiffened, hardened and ached.

But he wasn't a slave to his desires. He'd

long learned the dangers of intimacy—physical intimacy was simple enough and easily obtained with a whore or barmaid. He never had to worry about anything beyond satisfying his body's demands and once morning came, it was over.

The Wildling called to him in ways he knew would demand far more than a night of hard, sweaty sex.

Those demands were something he'd have to ignore, because they came with expectations and promises. He had no desire to give those to anybody, not even a woman who fascinated him.

With a sigh, Aryn flipped onto his back, flung his arm over his eyes and ordered himself to sleep.

God above knew, sunrise came awful early to a mercenary.

* * * * *

Though she had slid into her bedroll far later than the others, Tyriel was the first to rise. Thanks to her elvish blood, she needed little rest most nights, unless she was ill or was coming up to a magical surge—a leap in magical power.

Outside the elvish races, she didn't think magic worked that way, but, perhaps because they were so long-lived, elves continued to grow in power with their magic for centuries— the strongest of them having surges well into their first and second millennia. Da had explained it was like the stages of growth in children or adolescents, periods of little change followed by a sudden spike of growth that came seemingly out of nowhere. The surges were a drain on the system and required more fuel in the form of food and sleep.

The fae were vulnerable during those periods. Tyriel always traveled to the Wildlings clan of her mother's people or to Averne when she sensed a surge coming. She'd trust no other when she was in a period of such vulnerability.

Stretching her arms high overhead before bending over to touch her toes, loosening muscles stiffened from a night on the cold ground. Rolling her head on her shoulders, she eyed the sleeping camp.

Rain was coming. The damp, earthy scent was faint on the wind. The rain probably wouldn't hit until later in the day; with hope, it would even hold off until they made camp tonight.

Grabbing her pack, she headed to the stream for some privacy.

A short time later, Tyriel wound her wet hair into a braid and flipped the long tail over her shoulder. Stuffing her clothes and soap into the pack, Tyriel rose with a smile and an appreciative sniff. The cook was up and had cava going.

The thick, rich scent of it had her mouth watering. She was almost able to ignore the heavy, greasy scent of bacon. Poor little pig, she thought sympathetically as she made her way back to camp.

But that was the way of it. And even if the thought of eating meat turned her stomach, it didn't bother her if the humans ate it, providing it didn't come in contact with her own food.

Few people, very few people, outside the Kin knew that meat was akin to poison to an elf. The proteins found in meat were far too strong for an elf's system and if ingested in large enough amounts, it could cause the body to fail. The heart couldn't beat right, the blood thickened as the reaction strengthened, and eventually, if not treated, the elf could die.

Which was why so few people knew.

With such a strong weakness, if their enemies knew, it could prove fatal. Foods could easily be tainted in ways that would be unnoticed.

The enemies of the Kin were many, coveting their wealth, coveting their mines, coveting the magic that flowed so easily from one generation to the next.

"Good morning."

Turning her head, she smiled at Aryn as he stepped from the trees, a pack like her own hanging limply from one hand. "I'm done. It's all yours."

"I believe that. I doubt the majority of our fellow campers have ever heard of the concept of regular bathing," Aryn said wryly.

Remembering the oily stench of unwashed bodies, Tyriel adopted a horrified expression.

"Bathe? As in regularly? But baths cause the pneumonia," she said, adopting a falsetto squeal while fluttering her hands in the air.

"I've heard that." A wide grin lit his lean face. "I guess I'll just have to take my chances."

Waving to the stream with a broad gesture, Tyriel offered, "Go ahead. Dunk yourself—commit suicide. I'll tuck the blankets around you when the pneumonia has its hold on you."

"How kind." His eyes lingered briefly on the damp tunic that clung to her before he turned away.

The hesitation was enough. Her highly attuned senses could pick up the sound of his heart when it sped up a tiny bit, the scent that spilled out of his pores when he was aroused.

Tyriel was proud to admit she was only slightly tempted to linger in the trees and spy on the blond swordsman as he washed up. Just a little tempted.

As she turned, her eyes landed on the sword he took off. Still in its sheath, it leaned up against a nearby stone, within easy reach. Even as she turned to walk down the path, it seemed to draw her eyes again. The runes and marking on the hilt were...familiar.

That temptation was even stronger than the one to play voyeur while Aryn bathed.

If honor didn't run so strong in her blood, Tyriel might have tried to take the blade, just for.

The blade seemed to call her, all but whispering her name and she had to force herself to turn away.

* * * * *

New moon.

Lying on the ground, listening to the silence, Tyriel studied the star-studded sky overhead. They were even brighter than usual without the moon's brilliance.

The air had a heavy feel to it. Almost sticky. Very odd, considering how cool the night air was. Rolling on her side, she stared into the fire, hardly even aware that she drifted into sleep.

When she awoke a short time later, the camp had grown quiet, abnormally so. Was it her imagination or did the breathing of the mercenaries around her seemed quieter than normal?

Closing her eyes, she slowed her own breathing and reached out with her senses.

What she picked up sent a chill through her blood.

It was *far* too silent.

Nor was it her imagination that the rhythmic, familiar music of heartbeats and breaths that surrounded her had slowed.

Dropping her shielding, she let her sense of self flow into the ground beneath her. In just a few heartbeats, she sensed it and came fleeing back inside herself as she sensed a dark, fouled magic.

There was mischief and magic afoot. Bad magic. Slowly, she looked around before she sat up. They were all sound asleep. Unbelievably sound.

Rising, Tyriel took her sword in hand and slid it out of its sheath. Turning in a circle, she studied the camp, counted bodies. All were accounted for, save the guards and a quick study revealed each where in their place—but they *slept*.

Not likely, she thought darkly.

Her ears pricked and she turned, cocking her head, staring into the woods that lay just to the east of their camp. A threat. Her own heartbeat kicked up and her breathing became softer, shallower as she struggled to pin down what had alerted her instincts.

Her eyes were drawn to the woods and the warrior inside her whispered this was where the threat lay hidden. But the other half of her, the guardian, commanded she stay.

Slowly, she lowered herself to the ground, her long legs folding beneath her. She put her back to the fire, lay her blade across her lap, and stared into the woods.

The threat, whatever it was, would go through her first.

It was a very long night. The first of many.

* * * * *

Of Mischief & Magic

"I tell you, I'll do nothing as long as she is within the camp," the first voice repeated.

"A deal was made," a second, softer voice refuted. "You'll abide by it, or else."

"When the deal was made, there was no elf bitch within the camp. If you think I'll take on the likes of her, you are sorely mistaken."

A growl rumbled from the other's throat. "What if she isn't within the camp? Can you do it then?"

Head tilted to the side, the first pursed his lips and pondered. "If given enough time, I can do it."

"Then do it. I must have it."

"And the mercenary?"

Skinny shoulders rose and fell in a disinterested shrug. "Whatever is easiest for you."

* * * * *

The sleepless nights were taking their toll. Even though her elvish blood made it possible for her to go days on only the bare minimum, she eventually would falter if she didn't rest. And it had been nearly three weeks since Tyriel had gotten a good night's sleep. Every time she drifted close to sleep, somebody woke her, purposely or by accident.

The feeling of being watched never lessened.

"You're not looking well, Tyriel."

Looking up, she met the gaze of the healer contracted to ride with the caravan. Clad in robes of gray, signifying his school in the gray arts, Michan stood watching her with concern on his bony face.

"I'm fine, Healer." With deliberate care, Tyriel slid the stone up and down the length of her blade.

"You're tired."

In a cool tone, she said, "As I said, I am fine."

"I do not mean to overstep, lady." With a gentle smile, he dipped his head. "I may come from the gray schools, but my healing ability works like any other healer's. I can feel your exhaustion. There have been nights when your restlessness has disturbed my own slumber."

"My apologies." She gave him a disinterested look.

"No need...I simply speak out of concern for you." He hesitated before saying, "Perhaps I could offer you a tonic?"

"Most of the tonics made for humans are either worthless on my kind, or deadly. It's kind, but unnecessary," she said, concentrating on her sword.

"I've studied with the elvin kin. I know some of the remedies used by them. I've moonwart and polyseed."

Simple herbal sleep remedies, commonly used among the kin. Studying the nondescript brown eyes of the healer, Tyriel gave him another, longer look. Gray-robed or not, he did know his healing. She'd kept an eye on him from day one, leery of the line he walked that was sometimes so close to the blacker arts.

But—call her paranoid—she wasn't accepting even a cup of water from Michan, or anybody else on this train. She trusted very few, and he certainly was not on the list. She'd even begun to source her own food.

"My thanks, Healer. But I will be fine."

It was late that morning, just before the midday break when she acknowledged that she was not fine. Lack of sleep was making her feel dull-witted. She had to rest.

Seeking out a familiar face in the wagon train, she waved Chastin down and made a request.

When he nodded and gestured to the wagon, she gave him a grateful glance. "Just a nap and I'll be well."

Of the sixty-odd members of the caravan, Tyriel trusted only four. Chastin, who was as honest as the day was long, Vjorl, who was committed to his god and order and wouldn't betray anybody out of loyalty to that oath, Aryn, with those sinful eyes and Gerome, who was too damn greedy to do a damn thing that would endanger his caravan.

Of those four, it was only logical to approach Chastin and Vjorl. They were long friends who shared a wagon where they bedded down at night.

It had been Vjorl, though, who had approached her, rather than the other way around. He had been watching her for a couple of days and just a short while ago, he'd approached her and asked why she wasn't resting at night.

She hadn't given him a direct answer, but he'd sensed what she hadn't said.

"You feel it, too."

His softly spoken comment had unsettled her until she considered who—and what—he was. The warrior-priests of Burin communed with the earth for the first three years after taking their oaths, learning to read the subtle cues the land gave, and for some, they learned how to read the earth's energies and manipulate it to perform small magics.

The darkness she'd sense first came to her through a disturbance in the earth, so it was little wonder Vjorl's instincts had been alerted.

When he offered the protection of his wagon should she desire a rest a nap, she'd agreed.

Now, inside the secure space that smelled of herbs and dry goods, she dropped to the small cot, stretched on her belly and folded her hands under her head.

Knowing the caravan was safe, she was asleep in less than a heartbeat.

* * * * *

"Where's Tyriel?"

Vjorl glanced down at the blond swordsman who had guided his horse to the side of the wagon.

"She's resting." He nodded to the back of his wagon to indicate where the woman had taken refuge against the sun's bright rays.

"Resting?" Aryn repeated, his brows rising. "In the middle of the day?"

"She's exhausted. So I told her to rest."

"Why is she exhausted?"

"If you want to know that, you should ask her." He lapsed into silence for a moment, then added, "She's gone without sleep for nearly a week. I've noticed her awake and on watch twice now." He slid Aryn a pointed look. "She'll share when and if she's ready, but if something had alerted her elvish senses, I'm going to listen...and watch. I want her rested if there's danger afoot."

A new voice called Vjorl's name in the distance.

Through the dust stirred up by the wagons and beasts of the caravan, they could both make out the Healer's gray robe.

Sliding Aryn a glance, Vjorl said, "Say nothing."

Aryn cocked a brow but said nothing as he, too, shifted his attention to the robed figure of the healer.

"I was wondering, have you seen Tyriel?" Michan asked. "I've been trying to watch her for the past few days. She doesn't look well."

"She's off doing an errand for me," Vjorl lied. "She'll catch up with us later."

Bushy black brows rising, Michan asked, "But isn't that her horse?"

"I sent her on my horse. Her steed picked up a rock last night." Vjorl didn't even look at the big stallion. Called Kilidare, the steed had tossed his head, then bared his teeth at the gray-robed healer. Now, from the corner of his eye, Vjorl watched as the damned intelligent thing actually began to walk as if he was favoring one foot. He'd always suspected those beasts were far too cleverer than the horses they looked to be at first glance. "Her mount will be fine, but he doesn't need to do any heavy work for a day or two."

Aryn frowned but kept his gaze focused ahead even as he listened to the grey-robed healer talk with Vjorl. Once the healer rode away, Aryn asked, "What is going on? Why didn't you tell him she is sleeping?"

"Do me a favor, run and set my horse loose. He's in the back with the rest. Slap his flank and tell him to get feed." Vjorl's gaze was still on Michan's back. "My boy will know what that means, and he'll come back when he's through. Be quick, and be back fast. Don't let that healer see you, either, else I'll slice your pretty face up."

Chastin had sat in silence throughout this, but now he rose. "I'll keep watch on Michan, make sure he doesn't double back too soon. See to that horse, Aryn." With that, he jumped easily from the wagon bench seat where he'd sat next to Vjorl and took off at an easy jog.

Aryn frowned, eyes on Chastin.

"Aryn." Vjorl's voice pulsed with intensity and he waited until the swordsman looked at him. "She doesn't want anybody to know she's resting. Please."

Aryn's brows lowered, but with a sigh, he nodded. Saying nothing else, he brought his horse around. Clicking to the large bay, he said, "You heard the man, Bel. To the back of the train."

He didn't like not having more information, but he trusted his gut and his gut said Vjorl and Chastin were good men, while his skin crawled any time he was near the gray healer.

Aryn turned the matter over and decided that the tattooed warrior scribe had best be quick to offer an explanation—and if he wouldn't, then Aryn would be having a talk with one long-eared lady this evening.

Vjorl's ugly beast, a Borinian-bred gelding, took off eagerly, his intelligent eyes wide and bright as he clambered up the hill that bordered the side of the trail, nimble-footed as a mountain goat. Once Harfax, Vjorl's mount, was out of sight, Aryn brought his own horse around and returned, the questions burning in his mind.

"I don't trust him." Vjorl didn't even wait for Aryn to demand an explanation when he returned, just opened his mouth and baldly stated those four words.

"He's a healer." He didn't mention his own feelings of misgiving about the gray-robed Healer.

"Bah." Vjorl snorted, the expression at odds with his lean, dark elegant features. "He might wear a Healer's robes, but I don't know that I believe his claims of being a Healer. Even if he is, he's from the grey arts, so any covenants he made when he took on his robes are subject to his own approval. He may not violate the laws of nature when he heals, but he doesn't have a problem violating the laws of man."

He lapsed into silence for a moment, clearly considering his own words before continuing. "It isn't just that she's not sleeping at night. Something has her on edge, keeps her awake so that she can guard the camp. I've never met anybody with instincts to rival the fae. If she feels a need to be on guard at night, then there's something unpleasant watching us."

"Have you sensed anything?" Aryn asked, well aware that a Borinian warrior-priest had keen instincts, honed to a razor's edge.

"Two nights ago," Vjorl said softly, his gaze on the wagon some distance ahead of them. "I awoke in the middle of the night. There was a...strangeness to the night. Tyriel was awake. The guards were awake. No one else. I said nothing, just sat under the wagon and kept watch. But the feeling didn't leave. And last night, I couldn't even close my eyes without feeling a wrongness in the night. Whatever it is, she's been aware of it for even longer and she's kept watch. But she needs rest."

Aryn had been alive too long to ignore the prickle of unease as it raced down his spine.

"So. We've got problems coming." The blade at his back became noticeably heavier. Warmer, too, and as he shifted the weight of it, he could have sworn the blade started to pulse. He frowned, a flicker of memory rising in his mind, followed by a sharp flash of pain, gone as soon as it started.

Then he forgot the sword's weight, the odd sense of déjà vu.

"It would seem so. But Tyriel would know for certain." Sliding Aryn a glance, he said, "But I've known many a fae in my life. And when they are uneasy, we'd all be wise to remain on alert."

"I know what you mean, old man."

"We'll handle it," Vjorl said, his eyes flicking to the man riding along side one of the merchant wagons just ahead of them. It was Chastin and the two of them had already discussed the odd sleeping—*non-sleeping* patterns of the fae guard. "Chastin is on alert and now you as well. We'll talk to Lady Tyriel when she wakes and see what happens."

Chapter 5

Tyriel awoke feeling sluggish.

Bracing her hands under her, she pushed up from the small cot.

My head.

Reaching for it, she cradled it between her hands and concentrated, trying to clear the haze. How long had she slept?

That was when she realized night had fallen.

Cocking her head, she peered through the small opening in the rear of the wagon.

It couldn't be that late. But there was no movement in the camp, no sound.

Vjorl had promised to wake her before they stopped for the night.

Silently, she rose, blinking her eyes rapidly and taking slow, deep breaths. As she breathed, the cobwebs cleared from her mind much slower than they should have, a sticky film that felt wholly unnatural.

She did a quick self-assessment, already suspecting a source, but sensed nothing. It didn't matter. She was awake now and *that* was what counted.

Sliding from the wagon, Tyriel peered around and what she saw filled her with dread.

They hadn't stopped for the night. It was as if they had just stopped for the afternoon watering and not moved since. *Unable* to move.

Creeping around to the front of the wagon, Tyriel peered into the still frozen face of Vjorl.

For one horrible moment she thought he was dead.

Reaching out, she placed her fingers on his wrist, felt the slow pulse. Dangerously slow, especially for a human. His eyes were wide-open and frozen, his mouth open as if about to speak.

Hissing, Tyriel jerked her hand back.

Mind magic.

One hand moved in an age-old symbol of protection as she faded back into the shadows cast by the wagon. There was no moon and the night was eerily silent. No sounds of a camp settling down for the night, no birds calling, no horses snuffling in their feed.

Silently, Tyriel moved to the next wagon and stared into the face of another frozen man. The cook and his wife sat staring at each in other in a bizarre moment of affection they would never let the rest of the camp see.

Each wagon, each horse and rider showcased another frozen statue.

Only two were missing.

Mouth drawn back in a snarl, she searched the camp a second time, trying to find them. But they were not there.

Both Aryn the swordsman and Michan the Grey were missing.

Reaching up, she closed one hand around the pendants at her neck. "Be with me."

Then, going to her knees in the dirt, she drew a small knife from the belt at her waist.

First, she carved a circle in the earth.

Then she spat into it. With the knife, she cut the tip of her left index finger and smeared her blood into the saliva and dirt.

Rearing up, she held the knife high overhead, chanted under her breath and drove it into the earth.

Moments later, the earth shifted and a small sphere rose from the circle she had drawn in the earth.

After murmured words from Tyriel, the sphere cleared...spinning, waiting.

Another whispered order and now it showed the faces of several men. Most, she had never seen before, but she recognized them from the looks in their eyes, the cut of their clothes. Mercenaries.

Bandits would be a better word. Their type rarely worked the way a mercenary did, preferring to hide and attack and pilfer.

One man, though, she knew.

Michan.

"Where?" she whispered, rising to her feet.

As she rose, the sphere drifted in an eastern direction. Toward the woods. To the west was the Shojurn River. The caravan followed the path that headed north, to Shojurn City, still nearly three weeks away. If she remembered correctly, and she was certain she did, the nearest village was a good three-day ride, not even equipped with a militia.

But where was Aryn?

The globe went blank, saying Aryn wasn't anywhere that her power could locate.

So, like Tyriel herself, Aryn was shielded.

Tyriel gestured fluidly to the camp. *"Ay vern noi."* *I cannot see you.*

She murmured quietly in ancient elvish, "May the darkness protect and hold you."

And that simple, the camp was gone—or so it seemed.

Illusion. A simple shield, but the sleeping people in the camp weren't the ones in danger.

Prowling through the woods, sword in hand, Tyriel searched. Countless circles, countless deer trails. She had already spied where the others were, the ones who hunted for their prey, and dodged them easily as they also prowled the woods.

When a hand shot out just behind her, Tyriel didn't hear or see anything until a blade was pressed to her throat, held by a very knowledgeable hand, with the sharp edge just to the right, where the large vessels lay. A bit different on an elf, but eh, she could still bleed to death if he cut deep enough.

She murmured under her breath, lifting one arm to plow back behind her when he started to speak.

"Hmm. I can tell you aren't here t' cause harm but know this—I go to none but the one who already bears me." The voice was Aryn's but the cadence, the rhythm, was not.

She lapsed into silence, releasing the magic

she'd been calling to her in preparation to fight.

"Fae magic," he whispered against her ear. "I know the taste of that."

She shivered, the brush of his mouth against her ear unbearably erotic as a new magic, wild and potent, somehow primitive, filled the air and began to swirl around her.

She'd been right. Aryn's blade was enchanted.

Heavily enchanted.

And there was something else—the magic in the sword had started to settle inside the swordsman. He was no trueborn mage, but in time, he would be a mage, or enchanter, all the same.

"I mean no harm to him or the others. Only the ones who cast the sleep spell," she said slowly, lowering her sword and simply waiting.

"Hmmmm." The hand around her throat urged her back, back against his body, until she was flush against him. His other hand stroked the moonstone at her neck, then stroking the pendant of the stunted tree as the moonstone glowed in recognition at his touch—how odd. Last, he slid his hand along her neck to the curve of her left ear. "You're fae."

"Aye."

"Hmmm. Not just elf. Blood of my kin as well. Jiupsu," the deep guttural voice said, one hand stroking over her dense black curls. His other hand went from her throat to trail down the center of her chest, down her torso to spread flat over her belly. The knife was suddenly just gone as his hand spread wide open over her stomach, pressing flat and holding her flush against him.

Against her back, she felt his cock swell and throb. "Jiupsu. Warriors who sing and dance—"

Jiupsu. Wildling...the race her mother's people descended from, thousands of years ago.

Tyriel's head spun at the realization of just *who* had bespelled Aryn's sword.

More...now, she *ached*. Ached for the touch of the man gripping her in her what she realized was complete and utter possession.

Oh, no...No, no, no...

Grabbing onto her sense of self with everything she had in her, she said coldly, "Release me *now*."

Her power cracked in her voice, resonating. No true magic escaped her, but it was a clear warning to the man behind her.

The unbelievably strong hand fell from her belly and she whirled to face him, raising her sword. In those dark-blue eyes, she saw the shadow of something very ancient lurking. Possibly even more ancient than the history of the People.

The hair on the back of her neck stood on end in response to the power she sensed inside him.

Damn. This...*being* was living inside Aryn?

Conversationally, hands held up with palms

out, she said, "I'd really like to know more about how you landed inside Aryn's body, but I think that needs to wait." Her eyes drifted to the east, deeper into the woods, and she said, "It's you they are searching for, isn't it?"

"Aye." A smile—a slow, sensual curl of his lips—appeared.

Tyriel had the disconcerting image of another man, taller, broader, with wind-tossed black hair that fell in waves to his waist, black Wildling's eyes, and a wicked, wicked smile...then sadness, deep and bitter.

"I doubted he was just looking for the sword. It's the power inside he seeks. To get that, he must forge a bond. With *you*." The being controlling Aryn turned, studying the direction Tyriel's eyes had gone. "And to get you, what will have to be done with Aryn?"

"My bearer must die before another can bond with me."

Blowing a breath out in a rapid whoosh, Tyriel said, "I was afraid you'd say that."

Those dark, familiar, yet unfamiliar, eyes turned to her, puzzled. "Why? I won't let tha' happen. you Won't either. And he's a powerful warrior. Why else would I have chosen him?"

Tyriel silently made a note.

Ancient beings take things very literally.

"No. I won't let that happen."

She shifted, slid her sword into its sheath and dropped to her haunches.

Cocking his head, Aryn/Ancient One studied her. "What are you doing? This is hardly a time to rest."

"I'm not resting." The blood on the tip of her finger had dried, and it was already tender, but again, she pierced it with her knife. "Most elves have at least some elemental magic." Tyriel had more than *some*. "Some have just enough to light a fire, while others are true elemental mages. We draw our strength from the elements, we use the earth as our eyes, the wind as our ears, the trees and grasses can be our hands."

One fat crimson drop of blood fell to the earth and soaked into the soil.

She flicked a look at the man who wasn't Aryn.

"The earth will be my eyes." With that, she focused on the dirt where it had accepted her offering of blood. Without her having to ask, it offered up the answers she sought.

"Ten men, eleven if you count Michan the Grey. I hate to point out the obvious, but the healer *really* wants to get his hands on you."

"No healer. Healing ability, perhaps. Knowledge of herbs, aye. But no healer." The heavy brogue of his words had smoothed out the more he spoke, making his words easier to understand, almost as if he had fallen out of the habit of talking and was relearning it. "Are you as...capable as Aryn thinks you are?"

"More." It was her turn to smile now. She turned his words over in her mind consideringly and decided he was right. She'd misjudged Michan, seen his healer's robes and dismissed him as a threat.

That was a problem she'd rectify very shortly.

Rising, she met his gaze. "Well. Let's go take care of him, shall we?"

"Yes." He gave her a savage smile and turned. "I'll try not to kill all before you catch up."

She might have laughed—there was no way a human could outpace *her*.

But then the swordsman *moved*.

Well. She might have to reevaluate.

She caught up with him with little effort, her senses attuned for danger. Aryn, or, rather, the being inside him sensed the first attack, surprising Tyriel. With a single brutal swing, the swordsman relieved the filthy bandit of his head.

But she sensed the second—and third.

All three were hired swords and all brawn, no brain, out on a patrol, guarding the tiny camp Michan's bandits had set up. Tyriel had disemboweled one as the other went after the tall blond. She saw the bandit's head roll to a stop near her would-be killer as he went to his knees, hands reflexively going to his gut.

Two more saw them just outside the camp, so close, Tyriel heard the snores coming from somewhere near the fire. One lunged at her while the other closed in on Aryn.

Tyriel struck swiftly, sword raised, all but bisecting him from his right shoulder to left hip before he got even a whisper of warning out.

He fell and she turned but the second guard was already dead.

She had no idea what the being within him had done, but when she saw the gore staining Aryn's clothes, she decided it was better that way. She had no problem killing her enemy—had just done that very thing, but she had a practical outlook to it. They had come to harm people she'd pledged to protect and unless she stopped them—permanently—they would do just that. But she took no pleasure in the kill.

This ancient creature, though...the bloodlust she saw in his eyes was enough to make the skin on the back of her neck crawl. Power hummed in the air between them and it all but left her nerves burning.

How does Aryn live with this being inside him?

Pausing, she wiped the blood from her sword on the tunic of the fallen man, studiously avoiding what remained of his partner.

"Five down," she murmured.

* * * * *

"Where are they?" Michan growled, staring at the leader with smoldering eyes.

"I don't know," Elkir replied. "The elf wasn't gone as you said she was. The gods only know where she is lurking and nobody has been able to find the swordsman. Your spell didn't so much as touch him."

"Your paltry magic has done little good," Michan said. "Don't dare mock mine."

"If you'd used a bit o' yours, we mighta already found him," Elkir snapped as he started to turn away.

"A bit?" Michan replied silkily.

Elkir's legs were frozen to the ground. Unable to move, he looked up at Michan and said, "Let me go."

"A bit more, perhaps?"

An unseen hand closed around Elkir's groin, and twisted. The bandit paled, his eyes bulged.

"Watch your step, Elkir. And find that man," he snapped, flinging the bandit to the ground with a mere flex of his mind. "I will have that sword."

Crouched in the shadows, Tyriel glanced over at Aryn/Ancient One. Unease filled her. The power rolling from him unnerved her, and that was saying something.

That she hadn't sensed it until he'd manifested it was even more befuddling.

Elves were inherently magical. Her mother's Wildling ran thick with magic as well and she was no green youth. What kind of power and skill did it take to hide from somebody like her?

And what could a man like Michan do with access to that level of power?

Not that it would happen.

Even if Tyriel wasn't in the equation, Michan had no chance in hell of severing the bond she sensed between Aryn and the being bonded to his blade. Whoever he was, he'd said he *chose* Aryn. Chose.

As men moved in the shadows, Tyriel forced herself to focus. She could satisfy her curiosity later.

"You take the leader and these men," she signed in the trader's hand language, indicating the ones she wanted down. Hopefully, he'd learned that basic language as well as the others he seemed to have picked up from Aryn.

"I want the gray, as well," he signed back, gesturing with one hand over his head to indicate the healer's robe.

It was her instinct to argue. She knew her own skill, had no doubt she could bring down a human of perhaps four decades. But Michan had targeted Aryn.

She gave a grudging nod before continuing.

"I take the rest. Draw them out." She beckoned for him to pull back with her, putting distance between them and the camp. When they were some distance back, she deliberately snapped a stick in two with the heel of her boot.

As expected, two of the fighters were sent into the woods. The one Tyriel came upon was just a boy, really, the unease in his eyes striking her in the gut. When she emerged from the darkness and he laid eyes on her, his mind went blank with terror.

"Idiot child," she muttered as she made a decision.

Instead of killing him, she left him tied to a

tree, unconscious and certain to sleep until dawn. The knots would be easy for him to deal with, given time. To insure his path didn't stay on this road, she left a glamour spell that would trigger the moment he woke, and a warning. "Continue this path and you'll die before you have your first woman. I'll make certain of it."

When she came upon Aryn/Ancient One with his victim, Tyriel wished she had taken more time. Both the Kin and the Wildlings tended to make their kills cleanly. She'd wager Aryn did too. When Aryn was in control.

But in ancient times, when this being actually was a living breathing...whatever he was, she imagined life was more savage, more brutal. And messy.

Tyriel imagined if she were to ever find any scrolls on the Jiupsu, she would learn they had been very creative and visceral warriors.

The eviscerated corpse slid to the ground while Tyriel turned away.

"Soft stomach?"

Tossing him a glance over her shoulder, she said, "Absolutely. That's more meat than I care to see in a month, much less one night."

Down to three—and the gray.

After another man sent out didn't come back, those left remaining gathered around the campfire with Michan shooting fulminating looks into the darkness.

Finally, he shouted, "Come out, Aryn of Olsted. Must you hide in the shadows like a coward?"

When the being next to her tensed, Tyriel reached out and clasped his arm. "Don't give him the satisfaction. We can take them easily but we're not going to react to his stupid taunts."

"He questions our honor. Our courage."

Tyriel wondered at the 'our' but sighed. Men thousands of years ago were essentially just like men now, it appeared. Senseless. "He is baiting you, drawing you out to kill you—or rather Aryn—so he can take the sword and you. Is that how you want to prove your honor and courage?"

"Is this how the chieftain and your father raised you, Lady of the Jiupsu?" He loomed over her, his eyes narrowed and menacing, his body all but vibrating.

Tyriel cocked an eyebrow. "The chieftain is rather proud that I have a brain that I use. I'd bet he'd suggest you do the same. Let's think—not kill each other and the body you are wearing."

It took some convincing, but Tyriel was the one to leave the safety of the tree first, while her prehistoric counterpart made his way to the opposite side of the camp.

Tyriel simply sheathed her sword and walked out of the woods, well aware of the eyes drawn to her, one by one. When Michan turned and saw her, she smiled and waggled her fingers at him. "I decided I could use some of that moonwart."

She saw the thoughts flickering through his eyes.

Lie or not? Play dumb or attack?

She gave him her best smirk, letting her amusement at the situation shine through in her eyes.

Michan decided on attack. Launching a volley of energy bursts at her, he shouted an order at the others.

A flickering shield rose from the earth, deflecting them easily.

Before they could work up the nerve to move on her, she glanced at the logs they sat on, the vines and weeds beneath and whispered the final words to complete the spell she'd laid in the earth only moments before entering the camp. Her right hand up, flaring bright as Michan flung another volley of wild energy at her, Tyriel squeezed her left fist, then opened it and flung the last drops of blood to the ground.

"No!" Michan screamed as he saw what she was doing.

But it was too late. Vines, roots and long grasses erupted from the earth. Between one heartbeat and the next, the vegetation had trapped the guards on the sidelines. Aryn and his magical parasite erupted from the darkness, bloody smears on his face. He wrapped both arms around Michan and heaved, wrenching Michan's feet from the vines that had started to wind around the healer.

A guard exploded from a tent, bare-chested but wearing his boots and trousers. He was massive with a thick neck, arms thicker than Tyriel's thighs and legs like tree trunks. He looked around, tired eyes clearing rapidly.

"They killed Elkir," a thick, wet voice said from the perimeter of the camp.

Tyriel didn't take her eyes from the giant but she could see the other in her peripheral vision—a woman, tall and stocky, with short red hair, wearing a sleeveless tunic under a leather jerkin. She was pale and the blood trickling from the corner of her lips looked almost garish. "Toma, they killed Elkir. I just..."

She collapsed without finishing.

Toma swung his head around and his eyes landed on Tyriel.

"Fuck," she muttered.

A muffled shriek came from Michan.

She darted a look toward the gray practitioner and saw that Aryn held him in a bear hug from behind still, the muscles on his arms bulging, blood vessels prominent. And Michan's face was an ugly red.

The giant bore down on her. Swinging her blade in front of her to loosen up her wrist, she curled the fingers of her other hand. "Come, giant. Let's see what you're made of."

"I'll rip your head from your shoulders," he said, baring teeth gone black. "Then piss on your corpse."

"Nice. Let's see you try."

He lunged, moving rather fast considering his size.

But not fast enough. She waited until he was too close to stop his own momentum then darted away. He stumbled and tried to turn. She was already whirling. Blade lifted, she slashed.

For a moment, nothing happened.

Then a thin red line appeared at his throat. His corpse tottered, then fell, going left, while his head went to the right.

A sickeningly wet *crunch* filled the air and she spun in time to see the ancient thing inside Aryn's body release Michan's broken body. It was little more than a fleshy sack above the waist, ribs, arms and spine shattered.

For a moment, they both just stared at Michan's sightless eyes, bloodshot now, and gazing overhead at the lattice of tree branches.

"You are a worthy partner, elfling. He'd be wise to keep you as a friend."

Tyriel looked at the swordsman, saw his wicked smile but before she could respond, he turned and took off at a run, disappearing into the woods faster than any human she had ever seen.

Chapter 6

Tyriel bided her time, made sure the other had left Aryn's body.

She also made sure she had her own wits about her before she approached Aryn nearly a week later.

His sword rested against a rock while he knelt beside the creek, splashing his face with cold water.

Dragging her eyes away from his bare chest, she reminded herself she was here to discuss a matter of importance, not to ogle his physique, fine as it was.

But bloody hells, it was so fine—sculpted, lean, muscled. With water trickling down his skin, dampening the waist of his drawstring trousers, he looked like every wicked dream she'd ever had and every precious wish she'd never dared to ask.

"Would you mind telling me about your sword?" she asked when he turned questioning eyes her way.

With a frown he said, "Not much to tell. It was left to me at my mentor's death. He'd gotten it from his. I've had it more than thirty years now."

"Long time."

Aryn shrugged, drying his face on a coarse

cloth before reaching up and securing his damp hair with a leather thong. The blue stone in his ear flashed and winked at her.

Thirty years of bearing that heavy piece of metal might have something to do with that chest, she mused. Mentally, she slapped herself, dragged her eyes away from his chest, focused on the extraordinary blue of his eyes.

"Did your mentor tell you much about it?"

"Other than where he'd gotten it, I don't think there was much to tell," Aryn said with a shrug. Reaching for his shirt, he tugged it over his head and tucked the ends of it inside his breeches before fastening a thick heavy leather belt around his waist. The harness he slid into, shrugging his shoulders automatically until the weight of the sword was right.

"Another question." She looked him up and down, measured the *feel* of him against what he'd just told her. She'd estimated him to be perhaps just entering his third decade. Had his mentor given him this blade when he was still a boy? Perhaps...but... "Would you tell me how old you are?"

"Now that's a personal question." Amusement lit his face as he crossed his arms over his chest. It was a position that had his biceps bulging.

Tyriel had to work to keep her attention on his face. His open amusement, the way he smiled, that warmed her through.

"Are you going to answer?"

"I will." He shrugged. "I don't know that

Of Mischief & Magic

you'll believe me, though. I'm less than a year from my fifth decade."

Whistling under her breath, she gave him another once-over and decided she'd been right that about his blade—the magic within the blade was settling inside the bearer. "If I didn't know better, I'd think you were a mage yourself. Or perhaps had an elvish ancestor in your family line."

"Not a mage," he said with a disinterested shrug. "And if there are any long-ears in my family, I have no way of knowing. I was a foundling, left in the streets of some village in Nenu by my mother—I assume. A priest took me the nearest orphanage and there I stayed for some years."

"I'm sorry."

"There is no need." With an easy shrug, he shifted his gaze away from to study the terrain. "He wasn't a bad sort and the priest apparently felt responsible for me, stopping to see me once a month on his trips to the city. He gave the mistress of the home extra coin to make sure I had lessons and before I turned five, he took me out of there and signed me over to apprentice with his brother, the leader of the village guard. His brother and wife couldn't have children and the priest decided he'd make me a gift to them."

"Like a stray pup?" Tyriel struggled not to gape.

"I wasn't much more than that," he said gently. "Us mere mortals don't have the resources elves have and many don't have the communal families like the Wildlings. It was a good life. My adopted mother loved me and my adopted father had a boy he could train, who'd help care for him and his wife as they grew older. They were good people."

Her heart softened as the note she heard in his voice. "You loved them."

"I did." He looked away, a muscle pulsing in his jaw. "They've been gone almost twenty-five years, him first, her a week later."

"Is he the one who left you with the blade?"

"What's this curiosity about my blade, Mistress Tyriel? You have a fine one yourself." He made a point of looking at the hilt of her blade, worn in a sheath at her hip, as opposed to his. "And it's rather grand one—I imagine that's a moonstone in the pommel, a powerful deterrent against those who might use enchantment in a swordfight."

"You've picked up interesting knowledge."

"Some. And yet I'm still wondering why you're so curious about my blade." He held her gaze with a flat one of his own.

Tyriel made a decision. He wouldn't like what she had to say, but he would listen. Somewhere inside, he already suspected something was amiss. She'd seen it in his eyes the day after the attack, had sensed it, felt it. A few times she had sensed him questioning himself, then his eyes had gone dazed, and she had felt a rush of magic rise up.

The enchanter within that blade was

blocking him.

Well, perhaps it was time for that to stop.

"May I?" she asked, holding out her hand.

Silently, Aryn reached behind him, drew the sword from its harness and handed it to her.

No wonder the script on it had looked familiar. The words were a very, very ancient form of the old Wildling tongue—one that hadn't been spoken in probably two or three thousand years.

"Irian." She traced the script on the blade, studied it again and compared it to her knowledge of what she'd learned of her mother's people. Yes. *Irian*. Raising her amber eyes to his, she said, "That means enchanter. This is very old."

"What else, lady?" Aryn asked, his eyes dark and turbulent. In them, she saw the knowledge he'd been struggling with, the understanding that the blade was more than just a fine piece of weaponry. "I doubt its age means much to once such as you."

Magic pulsed within the blade. She could *feel* the enchantment now, feel it pushing at her, trying to usurp control over her and force her to surrender the blade back to its owner—no, *his* owner. His master—the man the enchanter had given his loyalty. She had no problem with that, except this enchanter was taking control of Aryn's mind.

That bothered her.

"The age of the sword doesn't matter all that much, except its age is part of what it is.

Your sword is enchanted, Aryn. Or maybe I should say, possessed."

He stared at her as if she had lost her mind.

Tyriel sighed and stroked her brow. She most likely had. It was his fault—he was too bloody distracting. Long, lean, those broad shoulders, those deep blue eyes...*ah, Tyriel, focus—focus!*

But it wasn't just the way he looked, or the way his fine backside filled out his breeches.

He *called* to something inside of her, something she had never felt in all her years.

A smile tugged at the corners of her mouth and she handed the blade back to him. As she did, she made certain their hands touched, and she closed her other hand over his, focusing, whispering silently to the one inside his mind, as the clouds tried to take him over and wash away his will.

I am telling him...he will know the truth... and know it today. Now go away.

There it was...that first sign of surprise, and then disgruntlement. Then outright refusal.

Tyriel tried again, reaching out to that ancient being alone who shared Aryn's skin.

I am not a mortal creature like the body you now inhabit, Jiupsu warrior. You try to enslave this man—I do not care for that.

And now she felt his shock, then silence.

No, he had never seen it that way, had he?

"It hides itself very well," she said, letting go of Aryn's hand, and the sword's hilt. Meeting his eyes, she studied him and saw the understanding in his blue eyes. Yes, she thought. He already suspected something. "Maybe, though, I should say *he* hides himself very well. If something hadn't happened last week, I may not have known. He certainly doesn't want others knowing."

"He?" Aryn repeated, staring at the sword he held in his hand for a long moment before slowly lifting his gaze to hers.

A grim resignation filled his eyes.

Too many odd things had happened since he had first taken the blade, she suspected, for him not to realize there was truth to her words.

"Hmm. Definitely a 'he,'" Tyriel said. "He's taken control from you before, hasn't he?"

Those blue eyes darkened as Aryn stared at Tyriel, while she watched memories flicker through his eyes.

Then his gaze became shuttered and he lowered his lashes until only a sliver of blue remained visible.

"What have I done?" he asked, his voice rough.

Tyriel's heart broke as she saw the horror in his dark blue eyes begin to grow...she suspected he feared that he had committed atrocities while unaware.

Gently, she said, "I don't think you've done anything wrong, anything you wouldn't have done of your own free will, if you had been given the choice. He was protecting you, and the camp, the night I realized what was going on. There's a warrior residing inside the blade, make no mistake of that, Aryn. A man with a soul much like your own, I would imagine."

She relayed what she had awoken to that night a week earlier.

"So there wasn't something odd in the food that had us all feeling like shit the next morning. No bad meat or aught else. It had been a spell." He lowered himself to a crouch, balanced on his heels, hand gripping the blade's hilt as he studied the weapon.

"I imagine you were the one who gave the cook the idea, aren't you?" He glanced up at her but it was clear he had little interest in her answer. "And...Michan. He didn't disappear while seeking help. I killed him."

"Yes. I...suggested it, rather strongly. I don't want the camp knowing..." her voice trailed off as she attempted to explain why she had concealed the truth.

"You don't want the camp to know how powerful you are," Aryn supplied, looking from the sword to her. "And you didn't want them know about me."

Meeting his eyes, Tyriel admitted, "Yes."

"Tell me all of it. Now."

"So...you believe me."

With a hard sigh, he dragged a hand down his face and looked away. "This isn't the first time I've woken with blood on my hands and no knowledge where it came from."

* * * * *

Of Mischief & Magic

Sometime later, Tyriel leaned forward in her saddle and stroked the side of Kilidare's neck, promising the bored elvish steed some excitement soon. What exactly, she didn't know. She'd conjure up some mock battle, if it would spare her the woebegone looks he kept giving her.

Not a pack horse, his sullen thoughts kept telling her.

"I know," she crooned, rubbing the strong neck beneath her hand.

"Frequently talk to yourself?"

Turning her head, she caught Aryn's amused eyes on her.

"Yes, I do. But this time, I was talking to Kilidare," she told him, nodding at the stallion. The gray ears flickered and he turned his huge head, regarding Aryn with intelligent, and very bored, eyes. "He doesn't approve of this trip. Not a pack horse." She poked out her lip and affected a sulky tone, mimicking the elvish stallion's mental tones as he bemoaned his plight.

His eyes lingered, very briefly on her mouth before he smiled.

"Bored, eh?" Aryn asked. Running an admiring eye over the lines of the steed, he agreed, "He's definitely no pack horse. That's one of the finest animals I've ever seen."

Kilidare preened, tossing his head and lifting his feet high, prancing along the roadside as though it were a stadium.

"That'll keep him happy for a while," Tyriel

said, laughing as Kilidare's neck arched. If he were a man, he'd be flexing his muscles about now.

"Tyriel."

She looked up, and nodded as Aryn gestured to the side with his head. Sometime later, they rode at the back of the train, far enough back that dust didn't disturb them, but close enough they could be seen, if they were needed.

"I want to know more about...Irian," he finally said, scowling. Aryn had never been one for naming his sword, or anything other than his horse. And now, he was talking about the damn sword as if it were real.

"It is real. He is real."

Aryn's head flew up, eyes narrowed. "I don't care for anybody's hands inside my head."

"Neither do I. And you needn't worry on that level—I can speak, in a way, to those I've established bonds with, and only for short periods and over short distances. I can, however, speak easily with most animals—that's a gift many Wildlings possess. As I have no bond with you and you are clearly not an animal, you needn't worry. I wasn't in your head. I knew what you were thinking just from the look on your face."

There was skepticism in his eyes.

"Hells." She lifted her eyes heavenward. "Give me patience, Nameless One. Aryn. How old do you think I am?"

When he didn't answer, Tyriel took care to blank her features. She didn't care for the odd twinge of...hurt.

"I'm nearing my first century, Aryn, and for the past four decades, I've spent the majority of my time in human lands. You don't spend that much time around humans without learning to read their expressions. I don't need to go poking into their minds; their thoughts are usually spread all over their faces."

He frowned and she suspected he didn't like the idea of being easily read.

"What sort of bond?" he asked.

"Familial ties are the strongest." She shrugged. "But I can forge bonds of friendship that allow for such a connection over time. Or..." Feeling wicked and rather out of sorts by that odd jolt of hurt, she added, "Of course, if you'd like me to join you in your bedroll tonight, I've forged surface bonds with men after a good fuck."

His face, tanned a soft gold from the sun, flushed pink, and he quickly looked away.

"Is that a no? Ah, well. Then you can relax. I have no way to get inside your thoughts. You're not kin to me, you've no desire to be a lover and you're not a dumb animal. Your thoughts are your own, but I can't help the fact that I've years of experience at reading faces. Now that we've established that, what do you need?"

"I've offended you," he said, voice stiff. "I...My apologies, Tyriel. My temper is short today. I find myself at very conflicted—and rather brassed off."

"I imagine so. Finding out you've lost

control of your body and thoughts to an enchanter...even if he seeks to do good deeds, well...I'd be brassed, too." She nodded her understanding and told herself to shelve her personal feelings. He wasn't interested. That was fine, truly. "There's nothing more I can tell you, though, at least now. I'd have to talk with the enchanter to know more. It's my guess he either forged his soul into the blade, or it was trapped there. He may not even know the answer."

"How do you know it's old?"

"He, not it." Nodding her head to the forest to the east, she said, "I know he's old the same way you know those trees are old. Age leaves a mark, a feeling. And he is ancient. He's a predecessor of my Wildling kin, a race who called themselves Jiupsu—when he spoke to me, he recognized me, called me Jiupsu, the warriors that sing and dance."

"I don't want anything controlling me, ancient or otherwise."

With a smile, Tyriel lifted her face to the sky.

"How did I know you were going to say that?" Her long braid trailed down her back and a tiny smile curved her lips. "How did I know?"

Aryn eyed the blade he held with acute dislike. He had a gut instinct that the feeling was mutual. Heaven and hell, he'd gone crazy. He had acknowledged, if only to himself, this

Of Mischief & Magic

hunk of metal had feelings.

Worse, it had a soul.

No...*he*.

Aryn could sense it, just the way he could sense the being's displeasure at not being able to prod Aryn into blind obedience whenever he felt the urge.

Hopefully, the miserable bastard had gotten the point.

Aryn wasn't sure if he could take another morning like the past, should the blade not have gotten the point.

The bloody sword had almost made him in a liar, had almost made him into a man whose word couldn't be trusted.

Hours earlier, Aryn had been packing his gear. For no reason, he'd found himself fed up with the wagon train, the job he'd signed on for, tired of Tyriel's instruction, bossy shrew that she was, and tired of sleeping on the ground.

He'd wanted a warm meal, a warm bed, and a warm woman next to him that night. He'd needed a fuck, a drink, and away from fools who thought to order him about.

It wasn't until Tyriel had appeared at his side while he packed up his supplies that he had questioned that nagging voice in his head.

"You signed a contract, swordsman. Doesn't that mean something to you?" she'd asked in a low voice.

He had snapped at her, but then, her hand had landed on his arm and he had felt compelled to look her in the eye.

When he had done that, when he had looked into her oddly glowing amber eyes, the other compulsion shattered and fell apart. She had waited until the anger gathered in his eyes before she had stepped back.

"He's done this to you before, I think," Tyriel had told him.

Now, after the wagon train had pitched camp for the night, they were in the small clearing across the stream, within sight and sound of the camp, as she helped him work on controlling the blade's control over *him*.

"You're his only link to the world now. He lives through you," she told him, holding the blade to keep him from hurling it off the cliff as they passed. "Throwing him off the cliff may work for a little while...but all it will do is have somebody picking him up long enough for the blade to drive that person insane while they deliver the blade to you. And you'll pay the price meanwhile. You're soul-bonded."

Through gritted teeth, he asked, "Is there a way to keep him from taking over? *Those* weren't *my* thoughts, damn it. Yeah, a fuck would be nice, and so would a nice soft bed. But I've never neglected a contract and I'm not starting now!"

Her strong, deceptively slim shoulders raised in a shrug. "Only one way to find out."

She returned the blade to him.

The moment she did, the urging was on him again. And when he resisted, it hurt. Like a fire was burning inside his head.

Irian wasn't happy at being refused.

His refusal didn't come in words. It was another compulsion, stronger than the last, emotions burning hot inside him.

Anger, frustration, need, impatience. They were real—and yet, the more he resisted, the more alien they felt.

Tyriel chuckled sometime later when Aryn nearly collapsed onto a fallen forest giant, sweating and exhausted. Taking pity on him, she had taken the sword, chiding the ancient being to be kinder to his wielder.

The 'answer' she received came in a rush of sensuality and images, so blatantly erotic, it left her blushing all the way to the roots of her hair.

If she ever had any doubt he had once been mortal, all doubts died in that very moment. The force of he enough hoped to have Tyriel yearning for a cold bath.

The moment she laid her palm on the sword, touched her flesh to the metal oddly warm, pulsing as though it had a heartbeat, a wash of desire poured over her, a man's desire, and her mind was flooded with images.

A man—the flickering image of that warrior, tall, rugged, with windblown black hair that tumbled down his back in heavy waves and wicked black eyes—laying her down on a pile of furs and pillows, crushing her beneath him as he lifted her hips and buried his cock, thick and long, deep inside her.

Oh, my.

It was an erotic, visceral image and she was damn glad Aryn was too busy dealing with his exhaustion and a likely headache to notice her for the next few minutes.

* * * * *

Aryn followed her into the woods later that night.

She'd been unable to sleep and had only been gone a few moments when she heard him on her trail.

A prickle of magic rolled over her skin and she blew out a breath, amending her thoughts. It might be Aryn's *body* but it wasn't *Aryn*. After the swordsman had laid down for the night, exhausted by his lessons in learning to control the blade, the enchanter had taken advantage and pushed his way to the fore.

When he caught her arm, she looked at him and sighed. "Irian, you know, you don't *own* that body you're—*oh*...."

The rest of the words were caught by his mouth as Irian the enchanter pressed her against the bulk of a massive oak and kissed her. It was Aryn she scented, Aryn she tasted—and it *was* his taste, for he tasted the way she'd known he would, of life, of the wild, of smoke and man and strength. The hands on her hips were Aryn's, the fingers sliding under her tunic were Aryn's.

It was Aryn's fists tangling in her hair,

freeing it from the confining braid as he licked his way into her mouth and feasted on her like she was some fine confection.

But it wasn't truly Aryn kissing her—it wasn't truly Aryn giving her what she'd hungered and needed for months, until it was an ache inside.

She shoved her hands between them and tore her mouth away. "Wait..."

"Why? You hunger. I hunger. *Avet*, Tyriel, so sweet, so hot, I ache."

She knew that. It was why he was here. But she couldn't do this...

Even as she tried again to gather her scattered wits, Irian had her trousers unlaced and she cried out as he thrust two fingers inside her. She gasped, arching into his touch.

"Tight. You're tight, lass. You've an ache, too, haven't you?"

The words—the cadence of them, it was wrong. She tried to think past the haze of lust clouding her brain, but he was already kissing her again, those two fingers pumping inside her, his thumb circling her clit, while he used his free hand to strip her trousers away. Once she was bared from the waist down, he stopped, but only long to whip off his shirt, then hers, tossing the clothing down on the hard-packed earthen floor.

Tyriel gripped the rough bark of the tree behind her, her eyes watering as she stared at the naked back of the man in front of her. Her vision wavered, magic unfolding between them. Another man superimposed his form over Aryn's and she gasped as his magic released, twining with hers.

Too much magic, too wild and held in check for far too long, circled and eddied around them. She felt drunk on it and when he turned back to her, hauling her close, she forgot she was supposed to be arguing.

He spun her around, pivoting them both simultaneously so her back was to his chest and they were facing the mat formed of their clothes. Palming her breast in one hand, Irian bit her neck. "I want to sink m' cock inside ya, feel your wet cunt wrap around me."

Tyriel whimpered, her head falling back against his shoulder.

"Look...your magic, it comes to me."

She only barely registered what he said, watching as he traced a hand over her skin and lifted it, his fingers glowing with a soft, pale white luminescence—her magic, set aflame by her need and now rising for him.

In seconds, he had her on her knees, her head bowed low as she waited.

The first press of his cock had her going rigid. He was big, thick, and it had been years. *Many* years.

"Shhh...I know you're tight, lass. If I hurt ya, it will only be the sweetest kind of pain. You'll whimper and beg for more by the time I'm done."

That was what she feared.

"Irian—"

He pushed inside and her thoughts splintered into a thousand fragments, forever out of reach. He caught her shoulders and pulled her up so she straddled his lap, back to his chest. Before her weight could force her farther down on his hardness, he grabbed her hips and lifted her—slow. So *deliciously* slow. She trembled as he stopped, only the flared head of his cock inside her. The length of him pulsed and every sensitive nerve ending there flared to raging awareness.

She moaned and jerked, thrashing impotently against his hold as she struggled to take more.

He chuckled, arrogance underscoring his amusement. But he gave her what she wanted and urged her weight down on him, giving her more this time before dragging her back up. She was so wet, she was slippery with it, but it still wasn't an easy fit, the spasming muscles of her sheath gripping and fighting him.

And it wasn't *enough*. The ache inside her swelled, expanded.

"Please," she begged.

"I'll please you, my beautiful, wild little elf," the deep, husky voice promised. "But...say my name. Let me hear you say it as you break."

She shuddered, grabbing his wrists in her hands to brace herself as he rocked up, pulling her down simultaneously.

He filled her. Completely.

Tyriel moaned.

"My name," he demanded, reaching around

to flick her clitoris.

She broke apart around him, shaking and rocking, riding him as his cock pulsed and hardened.

"Say it!"

"Aryn..."

He swore.

She didn't care because she was *flying*.

Irian didn't give her a chance to come down before withdrawing and flipped her onto her back. "*My* name," he growled, staring at her through Aryn's eyes, his impatience clear. He shoved her legs wide, held her at the knees and drove into her with rough passion, filling her with one stroke this time. "Say *my* name."

Tyriel closed her eyes and arched, twisting with pleasure and need and an ache that would follow her through her dreams and waking hours.

"My *name!*" Irian demanded. And this time, he brought his hand down on the exposed, vulnerable flesh of her exposed butt.

She jerked, staring at him with stunned eyes. Pleasure and shock ricocheted. He'd...had he just...he *had!*

"Do not look so shocked," Irian murmured, stroking his hands along the inner faces of thighs, along her calves, rocking his hips now in slow, torturous movements. "You're no new babe, scarcely a year from the Plains. Give yourself to me. Let me have you."

He wanted more than this. Tyriel could feel it.

But she wouldn't yield any more than she already had.

He sensed it and increased the sensual assault, tangling a hand in her hair before tugging her head back. "Feel how good we are, sweeting...yield to me, darling girl. Yield. Say my name."

She bit her lip until she tasted blood.

"Stubborn thing." Irian shuddered. "I'll win you yet."

He rolled against her, hitting a different spot inside her vagina and she moaned, her hands falling to her sides to curl in the clothing beneath them. Irian chuckled, clearly pleased with her response. He caught her right ankle and brought it up, then brought it over her body to join with the left, her thighs now pressed tightly together.

"Ohhhhh*hhhhh*...." She twisted and squirmed, so full of him now that she could barely stand it.

"Perfect," the man above her rumbled before swatting her rump again.

She jolted again but didn't protest, stunned by the sharp pleasure that sliced through her. She was no green youth, unaware of the varied ways one could find sexual pleasures. But she'd never imagined *she* would find pleasure in... this.

"Your cheeks have gone pink, lass. I think

you like have your ass spanked. Say my name and I'll turn your bum as pink as your cheeks while I fuck you."

But looking into blue eyes that weren't *his*, she couldn't. She couldn't force words past her throat now—it was tight with longing, regret, need. Averting her gaze, she reached for the strength to call a halt to this.

"Hells." Irian brought her right leg back up and bent over her, crushing her, hooking her thigh over his shoulder to open her completely...fully. "You're with *Irian* now, lass. I'm the one fucking you and making you squirm while your wet cunt grips me so hot and tight."

He drove into her. Again. Again.

The climax hit hard and he came in the next moment.

Breathing hard and fast, Irian eased away from her and flopped onto his back.

But when he tried to pull her against him, she resisted, laying on her side, facing away from him.

You stupid, silly fool.

Tears wanted to come but she held them back.

"Look at me, lass."

She resolutely faced away from him, scanning the darkness. Her trousers were a few feet away, along with the simple, close-fitting tunic she wore to support her breasts. Her shirt was still trapped beneath their bodies, but she had shirts a plenty. Her boots...there.

She rose, not bothering to hold back on the speed of movement natural to her. Grabbing her clothes and the weapons that had fallen when Irian recklessly stripped her naked, she started for the path.

He was behind her and moving fast.

But not fast enough.

The moment she stepped into shadows formed by the thicker trees, she took off at a run only possible because of her fae heritage. No human, even one possessed by a long-dead warrior enchanter could catch an elf in the darkness.

She was ashamed for running, almost just as shamed for letting her needs blind her. That hadn't been *Aryn* in control then. Aryn barely seemed to notice she had tits. But Irian had taken advantage of her need—and likely Aryn's want for a soft woman, then used it against them both.

Bloody bastard.

Chapter 7

Morning came and Aryn had no memory of it.

She didn't know whether to be frustrated or thankful. Clearly, Irian was *letting* Aryn remain in control during their sessions each evening, otherwise Aryn would have taken control last night. Unless he was acting now...

But, no. She didn't think that was likely.

There *was* something amiss—it called to him. Or rather, to Irian, pulling him to the surface so they both looked through Aryn's eyes.

Something called Irian, something on the other side of the chasm that lay just to the west as they left the woods of Morstia. Something more than the whim to live vicariously through Aryn.

But the blade had to learn a better way of communicating his needs and wants. He could do it—she knew that without a doubt. The enchanter used words now instead of taking over Aryn—a first, she suspected.

It wasn't always so simple, though. There were times, like now, when she contacted him, Irian could not tell her what drove him.

As she watched, the snarl faded from Aryn's face and he looked at her, that slight grin tugging at one side of his mouth. "He backed off. And what the bleeding hell do you know? The bastard can speak. Seems like he's in a foul mood, too. He told me to go fuck myself, and a bloody-arsed goat. They made them sick and twisted then, didn't they, elf?"

With an answering smile, she said, "Why doesn't it surprise me that you're just as stubborn as an ancient sword?"

The wagon train contract ended.

Tyriel wasn't surprised when he came to her room at the inn that night. Although she was hungry, she'd stayed in her room, checking her gear and repairing what needed repairing, admiring the pretty new shirt she'd bought with some of the bonus she'd earned and...waiting.

When the knock came, she answered. Aryn stood there, his pack in one hand, Irian sheathed at his back. Before he could ask, she said, "Yes."

"I haven't asked yet," he replied.

"You're going west. You want to see what is calling you—what's calling your blade and you want me to come with you. The answer is yes."

"I need a partner," he said bluntly. "I've lost jobs because I'm a solo contractor, or because I've no magic in me. The few times I tried to make a go of it with some magic-user I'd met along the way, the bastard annoyed me too much. But you...we work well together. I thought this could be a trial run, see how we do outside a caravan contract."

Something told Tyriel she should say no, that she'd only go with him for this. She already felt too drawn to him; spending more time with him would only make it worse.

But she didn't.

"Do you have a room for the night?"

Head cocked, he said, "Not yet. This bloody hunk of metal has been chattering like a magpie in my ear, telling me things I must have for the journey. I've been in the market since collecting my pay and buying supplies."

"You're not likely to find a room this late. You can stay with me. I can sleep on my bedroll—"

"No." He shouldered inside, edging past her. The doorway was narrow and his bicep brushed her breast.

Tyriel felt that contact to the tips of her toes, both nipples contracting and tightening as if he'd touched his mouth to her flesh, rather than an accidental brush of his arm.

Her mind stupidly blank, all she could do was stand there, gripping the door and trying to get her burning need under control.

"No?"

He glanced back at her before moving over to the empty space by the window. "No. This is your room. I'll not steal your bed. I can sleep on my bedroll easy enough."

"Aryn—"

"Just stop arguing, Tyriel. Haven't you

learned yet? I'm easily as stubborn as you and it in no way makes sense for me to steal your bed when you were the one who paid for the room." Face twisting into a scowl, he looked at the bed before adding, "Besides, that bed will fit you—barely. I've a couple hands on you so there's no way I'll manage."

They followed the call that was still only a whisper to Aryn, but as the hours turned into a day, then two, that whisper became a song, then scream.

He was almost mad when they finally reached a small border village. The hand-lettered sign on the outskirts read *Morstia*.

Eyes glittering like he had a fever, Aryn looked around.

The small town was picturesque in its perfection, with brightly colored cottages with thatched roofs on the outskirts, bricked buildings in the central section. Boys and girls were busily cleaning up the streets and guards were professionally friendly and courteous.

Such a far cry from the town where the two of them had first met.

"And something is wrong here, 'ey?" Aryn drawled, kicking one long leg over Bel's back and sliding to the ground. Booted feet planted wide, he crossed his arms over his chest and surveyed the village once more before looking at Tyriel. "What problem had that useless hunk of metal dragging us across the countryside?"

"Perhaps not so useless, my friend." She suppressed a smile as she continued to look around.

The village *was* a peaceful one, out of the way and not used to new faces, but they all seemed friendly.

And yet...

Tyriel lifted her head, scented the air. Yes. There was something amiss.

Death lingered here.

Not a normal death.

Bad death.

"You owe your useless hunk of metal an apology, Aryn." She looked once more and found her gaze falling on a wooden board posted outside a large pub. A message board — she'd seen the like in several towns and villages.

In the middle of the board, a hand-lettered post stood out.

Missing
17 summers, Girl child
Elsabit Minsa
Last seen at the Square near Sundown
Summer Solstice Eve
Reward

Centered in the poster, a hand-drawn picture of a young girl, the bloom of innocence still on her face, perfectly caught by the artist's

Of Mischief & Magic

hand.

Tyriel dismounted and stroked her hand down Kilidare's neck and gestured to the hitching post. "On with you, my boy. Wait for me."

He whickered and did as asked.

Tyriel heard the surprised murmurs from the curious villagers as her elvish mount followed orders, but she paid little heed, drawn to that picture.

Aryn finished tying Bel off and moved to join her, the two of them studying the girl's face as a breeze tugged at Tyriel's hair.

It stirred the worn pages pinned to the board and Tyriel glanced at Aryn before moving closer, carefully peeling up the notice for Elsabit.

Beneath it, there was another notice, this one for a boy, a year older, gone missing the night of the winter solstice.

There was another under that one, a girl, fifteen, disappeared near the summer solstice.

Then another...and another.

Chapter 8

The constable studied the woman in front of him.

"Why should a Wildling and a hired sword care about our troubles?" he asked wearily, rubbing his grizzled face.

Aryn opened his mouth, but Tyriel laid her hand on his arm. Aryn lapsed into silence and let Tyriel speak.

She stepped closer to the desk. "I see the blood of the Wildling in you, Constable Chatre."

"Blood calls to blood?" He snorted. "Don't bother with that tripe. Yes, there's Wildling up the family tree some generations back, but that's not why you're here."

"Don't be so dismissive of blood loyalties," Tyriel said softly. "Have you heard of a *geas*?"

His lids flickered, eyes widening slightly as he looked form her to Aryn, then back.

"Which one of you?" he asked.

Tyriel saw the flicker of hope in his dark eyes.

"I am." Aryn had heard of the magical compulsions before, but was only coming to understand them now, thanks to his odd half-elvish, half-Wildling friend. "But even without a *geas* compelling me, the thought of lost children would drive me to act, Constable."

"Why?" Chatre looked unimpressed.

"Are you saying you wouldn't act to help a child in need?" Aryn asked. The look on his face said he already knew the answer.

Chatre flushed and looked away. "It's my job. 'Tis what I was hired to do."

"And if you were a baker or a miller...you'd ignore a child in need."

"Fuck me," the constable muttered under his breath before looking at them both dead on. "Aye, I'd help. I became a deputy of the previous constable when I was still a green youth, because I wanted to help." A thin smile curved his lips as he glanced at Tyriel. "Perhaps *that* is in the blood."

Before either could respond, though, Chatre continued. "But I was raised here. It's not the same for me. A family's home catches fire, the village helps rebuild. A mother dies in childbirth, we help the father until he's through the worst of the grief. But this is *our* home and you are strangers. Why would you care about our missing children?"

"Because they are children—they could be *my* children, the children of my cousins, or a friend's...had the Nameless God not been merciful, it could have been any of us. So, because we are able to help, we do that, in hopes that when the time comes and those we love are in need, there will be one there to offer them in aid."

Long moments passed while Chatre sat in silence and studied them.

"Very well, my lady," he said quietly. "Sit, please, and I will tell you what I can. For a while, the disappearances only happened on a solstice—twice a year. But another street child went missing just a few weeks back and my gut tells me her disappearance is connected to the others. And that leaves me cold, deep inside."

* * * * *

"It's as though something swooped down out of the sky and made off with them."

Hours later, the constable's words still lingered with her, the awful mystery a pulse in her brain.

It was someone in the village or someone familiar enough with the villagers to go unnoticed when he's here to select, then steal his prey.

The children were likely close, she thought. If it wasn't a local, then whoever it was would have been noticed by now, if he came only at the Solstices. No, this would be a traveling merchant or a wandering priest in and out a few times each moon. Often enough he could watch the children, even get to know them so he could select his mark.

And they might not even be dead.

There had been at least six taken. Perhaps a few more. This was a small village—their last census had their numbers at just under fifteen hundred, but even with those small numbers, the constable admitted there were always a couple of youth who ran wild in the streets, either after their parents passed or because they ran away from a father with a heavy hand and cruel belt.

"There were three alley brats I haven't seen in a while...two brothers and a girl they kept an eye on. Treated her like a sister. I tried placing her with a family after her mum died, but she wouldn't stay. The Tipali boys were little heathens but had good hearts—they thought I didn't know they'd bed down in the constable stables on bad nights, but...well. I didn't leave extra blankets in there for the horses to use, now did I? But one day I realized I hadn't seen either boy or Demetra in near two weeks. Could be they left, but my gut tells me otherwise. It took me a year, though, to see the pattern—they'd disappeared on Winter Solstice, six months before Leeni Halder."

After one or two children went missing, and always near a solstice, the guards would be vigilant. Wagons would be inspected. It was possible a guard had been bought off, but her gut insisted they start the search *here*.

"Do you think we should search here?" Aryn's voice was tight with strain. "He...Irian thinks the children are here. But this isn't a large village. Where could they be hidden?"

"I don't know. But I think he's right." She eyed his face, jawline taut. "He's pushing you hard now, isn't he?"

"Yes. He says the voices are too loud, screaming for help." His mouth twisted in a scowl and a dark, awful rage filled his gaze. "I can almost hear them myself. We have to do something."

"I know." She brushed his arm with her fingers, withdrawing almost the second she made contact. "We'll help them. Come. Let's find somewhere to stable our mounts and find a place to stay ourselves. We won't find an easy answer here, so we need to stow our gear."

The village wasn't large enough to support a standalone inn—the only regular visitors were a couple of wandering priests who came through twice each season and two merchants.

However, the constable had given them the name of a pub—a large one near the village center, *Spindle and Shrew*. The pub had a couple of rooms on the second floor the owner let out to travelers for a coin or two. One was already taken, but there were several others still available.

The pub owner was a wise man and furnished all but two of the rooms with beds built as slabs jutting out from the wall, supported by ropes and sturdy pillars. There were four beds total, each one long enough that neither Tyriel or Aryn would have to worry about their feet hanging over the end. Each bunk sported thick mattresses stuffed fat and full.

Choosing one such room, Aryn paid coin to secure their beds for three days.

The pub owner assured them they could

Of Mischief & Magic

have the space as long as they needed. Fortune was kind and there was a stable in the back where they could put up their rides for only a bit extra.

"They'll be safe there, my word on it," the pub owner told them with a firm nod. "I pride myself on runnin' a clean place, a safe one. No thievin' or other foolery allowed, else I send your rump packin' and nobody here wants to be barred from the best pub in the village." He grinned broadly. "Or the second best—it's closer to the outer wall on the north side, and owned by my brother. He won't take no thieves in, either."

"Best not to cross your family, then." Tyriel saw a resemblance between the pub owner and the constable, suspected they were cousins.

"Indeed." He gave a short nod. "Your coin will pay for feed and groomin', too."

"Let your stable boy know that I'll handle my own grooming." Tyriel gave the man a kind smile. "Kilidare's an elvish mount. They don't tolerate the hands of strangers and I'd hate for your boy to lose a finger—or even a hand."

"'Is my daughter who watches the stable, lady." His eyes widened only a little. "And I'll let her know meself. She'll likely as you a hundred questions, mind. She's a fiend for a good ride. Had a few of the People travel through last season and she was thunderstruck by their mounts. One o' them, the youngest lad, I think, let her take a ride around the village with him. I half-feared she'd try to sneak away with him."

Soon after, rejuvenated by a quick repast, Tyriel and Aryn left the pub behind to explore the village. The market was the busiest area and Aryn followed Tyriel in silence as she moved from one stall to the next, buying a trinket here, a woolen blanket there, sweets from a sad-eyed older woman who gazed at the board holding Elsabit's picture.

Her eyes seemed to follow him. Aryn told himself it was only his imagination, but in the back of his mind, he could almost hear her begging him for help. Another voice, too, but this one was male, rough with impatience and pushing Aryn to find the girl.

He used one of the mental tricks Tyriel had been helping him develop, slamming a 'wall' between his conscious self and Irian, muffling the enchanter's demand.

That done, he concentrated more on his companion. She had a method to her madness, that her seemingly aimless wandering around the market wasn't aimless at all.

As the sad-eyed candy maker talked of her missing son, gone nearly three seasons now, Tyriel listened and nodded, but said little.

"Enough," Tyriel said after they'd moved on. Nodding to Aryn and indicating an empty area, free of stalls and villagers, she started in that direction.

Her eyes were grim when she finally looked at him, but she said nothing and her expression was too guarded for him to read.

That didn't keep him from studying her, though.

The past three months had been...intriguing. It had been a long time since Aryn had worked so easily without another. And someone who meshed so easily into his life? That had never happened. Most of the time, when a job came to a close, he was ready to leave any acquaintances he'd made behind and lose him out in the wilderness for a while, perhaps a trek into the Reval Mountains, or south to the Enny Plains, a few weeks to clear his head and be alone and away from everybody.

But not now, not with Tyriel. Even if it hadn't been for the sword's urging, he imagined he would have approached her about a possible partnership. A *work* partnership—something the baser part of himself couldn't seem to comprehend.

She caught him staring and arched her brows in question.

"You have heavy thoughts," he said, leaning against the solid wall that surrounded the village. "They weigh on you."

"Yes." She joined him at the wall, turned to face him, her shoulder close to his, close enough that if he shifted just so, they'd touch. "A friendly village, even with their grief. But they share little of their pain."

"We're strangers," he pointed out.

Tyriel's lips twitched in a faint smile and Aryn told himself not to think about how soft they looked, how lush they'd likely feel under his.

"Yes," she said. "And perhaps it would be different if *you* had been asking the questions. But you weren't. I was. And I...well, it wasn't anything untoward, but I *might* have used a bit of power to suggest they share their ills. Few did."

"Power. You mean magic," he said slowly, narrowing his eyes as he studied her. "As in you used a spell to try to get these people to talk to you."

She sniffed. "Hardly. I'm half-elf, Aryn. I *am* magic. I don't need to grind out wyrmwood and cast bones to focus my magic and make it work. And I didn't do anything that would cause harm. I simply *impressed* the fact that if any of them were to share information with me, I might be able to help."

"Hmmm." Not sure how he felt about that, Aryn looked away. "It doesn't seem like anybody took the bait."

"No. At least not yet. Sometimes, it can take time for the suggestion to sink in. Especially if the hurt is carried deep." She shifted her gaze toward the market and sighed. "These people have been carrying their hurts for quite some time."

"Pushing them to talk to us won't help."

"No. We need to wait until they're ready...or until they relax enough to talk freely around us."

Something in her voice had him studying her yet again. "And you have an idea on how to make that happen."

"An idea...perhaps." She batted her lashes at him, all but oozing female charm.

Instantly, Aryn felt wary. "What?"

"I know the perfect way to have people relax." She leaned closer to him, clutching at his arm while her face softened until she looked like some dewy lass, gazing up at her first love. "A way for us both to listen, learn...if you think you can carry your part."

"My part?" His voice came out scratchy and rough while his blood heated. In the back of his mind, he felt Irian stretch, the enchanter's awareness growing.

"Yes." Her voice dropped. "We're being watched. Two men, walking toward the market, coming from my side. Likely harmless, but we don't want anybody aware we're here for a specific purpose, do we?"

The constable was already aware, but Aryn doubted the man would tell the villagers that two mercenaries had offered to find the youth missing from the village.

Understanding Tyriel's intention now, or part of it, he pushed off the wall and turned, pinning her against it in one smooth movement.

Her eyes widened slightly as he left his back exposed and he smiled, tucking a strand of hair behind her ear. "If you can hear people approaching, and deduce that it is two men, before I even realize we're being watched, I trust you can warn me should I need to guard my back. What's this idea of yours? Are we to play at being lovers? For what purpose?"

"Two mercenaries in such a small village would raise questions otherwise. But if we were thought to be lovers, simply taking a rest after a long job, or during a long travel, fewer questions arise."

"We've already mentioned that we are passing through, had just finished a contract." He dipped his head, as if to nuzzle at her neck. Doing so let him glance to the side and he could see them now, two men, just as Tyriel had said, neither of them so brazen as to call attention to it, but both watching Aryn and the woman he had pinned against the town's protective outer wall.

She shivered as he skimmed a hand up her arm, the lower half bared, revealing taut, firm muscle. He felt that nearly imperceptible reaction all the way to his toes and before he knew what he was doing, he moved closer. She smelled divine and felt even better, lusciously female but supple and strong.

He'd been telling himself for weeks that he'd only been craving a taste because he'd gone too long without a woman, but now that he had his hands on her, he knew it for the lie it was.

But Aryn didn't fuck sword mates.

Oh, but he wanted a taste of her.

Another taste...the gruff murmur came from the back of his mind, a mind now overflowing with images of them together, bodies naked and entwined, her dusky skin glowing in the firelight as he kissed a path down her torso, all the way to the curls to that would guard the sweet, wet delights between her thighs.

She felt *right* in his arms, familiar even, like he had lain against her before, scented her skin as arousal burned hot within her, tasted her mouth as she cried out her need, held her quivering body against his while she dug her nails into his flesh.

"What all does your plan entail? We split up? Look for short contracts or daily work?" He forced his mind to think about the task at hand.

"No. We stay together."

He turned his head toward hers and their lips brushed. Aryn barely held his composure, fisting the hand braced on the wall near her head as she continued to speak. Averting his head slightly, he waited. This was bloody torture.

"If we're thought to be together, most of the people here will assume I follow your lead. That means they'll be more likely to discount me. The less they think about me, the better." The warm caress of her breath on his skin felt almost as intimate as if she had run her hands over his body.

Aryn gritted his teeth as his cock swelled in response.

"Excellent point," he agreed, straightening and trying to think in logistical terms instead of lustful ones. If they kept her gifts quiet, that meant a weapon none knew about. She had wrapped and stowed her blade, and none could possibly imagine how many numerous weapons she had hidden on her person.

Aryn swore silently.

He imagined he could find them—piece by piece as he stripped her naked. The dusky gold of her skin gleamed richly and she winked at him before nudging him back.

"I thought perhaps we could talk to the pub owner. I play rather well. See if he'd be open to me put out my cap for a few nights—I can play for coin while you have your dinner. We could have a few days to rest before we continue on our journey west." Her eyes told him what she held back.

She would play. He would listen. And they would see if they couldn't unearth the secrets in this village.

Still close enough to feel her body weight, Aryn nodded. "A good plan. When do we start?"

"Now." Her cheeks were flushed. Lifting her hands, she braced them on his chest.

Aryn caught her wrists and held them, gaze riveted on her face.

"Pretty thing, the Jiupsu women have always been lovely."

Irian's presence was unwelcome and Aryn floundered, caught in a web of desire. *Be silent*, he thought.

But the enchanter wasn't in a mood to listen. *"Take her upstairs, touch her, taste her."*

"Shut up, you hunk of metal," Aryn warned,

putting more weight in his warning. "Or I will wrap you in silk and stow you under the bloody bed."

Irian laughed. "Won't do you much good now. You've opened your mind to me. Close me out, you can, but removing me from your body does nothing," the ancient one said, his voice rich with amusement. "You've been too long without a woman, Aryn. And you've never known one like her, addictive as mead, rich as honey, spicy and hotter than fire. Let's have her now."

Aryn's blood pounded heavily in his cock, his head. He already ached, but Irian's seductive voice was making it worse, and Tyriel wasn't helping, leaning against the village wall and watching him. He still held her wrists and they felt bewitchingly delicate, skin soft and smooth under his touch. Her eyes burned as they stared into his.

Aryn took back the distance he'd put between them, looming over her now and breathing her in.

"She will taste so much better than she smells, brother of my soul," Irian promised. "Taste her..."

Taste her. Just a taste. That was all he wanted.

Dipping his head, he closed one hand around the thick weight of her hair and tugged.

Just before his lips would have brushed hers, Tyriel stiffened. The glint in her eyes faded and she shoved him back, this time with force and

Aryn felt back several paces, the strength in her undeniable.

"You are not yourself, Aryn," she said, her voice ragged. Her nostrils flared.

Aryn could scent of her arousal, knew she could detect his.

"I am." His head did feel a bit...crowded, but he had wanted her for weeks, months, a lifetime.

When he would have come to her again, Tyriel held up a hand, staying him. "Enchanter, you hold much sway over his mind right now. I feel it."

Aryn shook his head in confusion as she lapsed into a lyrical tongue—Wildling—but too archaic for him to follow and the ghost that lived within him wasn't in the sharing mood.

He felt Irian's rage, his refusal, his will trying to rise up. Pictures that didn't make sense filled his mind—Tyriel, lying on the forest floor while he spread her thighs, her woman's flesh, and tasted her. Him moving to cover her, riding her hard as she whimpered her pleasure.

Over it all, the ghost of another man tried to superimpose himself over Aryn's body, as if trying to take Aryn's place entirely.

Why did it feel like memory and not fantasy?

Irian reared up, tried to force his will onto Aryn and the bastard almost won—not because Aryn couldn't fight him, but because they both wanted the same thing. To take Tyriel, haul her back to their room over the pub, lock the door behind them before stripping her naked.

Fighting the will of the enchanter was never easy, but now, when what Irian wanted so perfectly aligned with Aryn's own desires, it felt almost impossible.

His cock still ached, but a vicious pain began to pulse inside his head as he battled Irian back.

"Stop fighting, brother," Irian said coaxingly. "Let us touch, taste..."

Aryn clenched his jaw and fought harder as he tried to retain control over his body and his mind.

Tyriel's voice cut through the dull roar of blood.

"Eyastian, Irian. Myiori, tymio efavo."

"*You would not dare,*" Irian growled, surging up to take control, forcing the words out through Aryn's mouth even as Aryn seized control over his body and backed up, putting enough distance between them so her scent no longer flooded his head.

Irian continued to use his body like a bloody puppet, words he barely understood flowing from him as he glared at Tyriel.

"You break our law by even speaking to me so, woman. I am Irian Escari, High Priest of the Jiupsu, Enchanter, Swordsman. You would not dare—"

"Oh, please." Tyriel laughed.

That enraged Irian even more and his control over Aryn faltered, giving the swordsman a chance to seize the reins.

"You have no idea how much the world has

changed since you walked the earth," Tyriel said. "You can't compel *anything* from me. I am not of your clan and I owe you no fealty. More...if that's how you try to claim bedmates..." A smirk lit her face and she flicked her hand dismissively. "Really, Irian. I'd have thought better of you."

Aryn shoved the enchanter down, slammed the door in the other's face mentally and finally, *finally* felt alone in his head. But the echo of Irian's anger and embarrassment burned inside him.

"I can fight my own battles," Aryn growled, his cheeks flushing red.

"True. Although you're not used to fighting them with an enchanter who has seen millennia pass—one who has planted himself inside your own mind and tries to use your own body against you. It's not like the playing field is level."

"You taunting him isn't going to help."

"I didn't taunt him." She smoothed her shirt and the leather jerkin before glancing at him. "I just made him aware that if he keeps trying to overwhelm you, I had access to magic and a weapon that could rid you of him."

Cutting around him, she said, "We should go, have word with the pub owner before the night gets too busy."

"Wait." Aryn caught her arm and immediately wished he hadn't touched her again. He could still scent her, could imagine the taste of her on his tongue. "What weapon?"

Tyriel didn't answer as she tried to tug free of his touch.

"Tyriel..."

"You're like a dog with a bone, Aryn." Sighing, she lifted her eyes to his. "Myself. If you choose, I could break the bond between you."

* * * * *

Aryn settled into a corner, looking foreboding and somber, his pale hair pulled back in a queue, Irian strapped at his back, a sleeveless leather jerkin revealing the muscles of his arms and shoulders.

Occasionally, he would glance at Tyriel and smile, or glare at the men who slid her long, lingering glances, but mostly, he was silent. Looking grim, possessive, and serious was his role.

Playing pretty music on her flute and smiling sweetly was Tyriel's.

Both were doing a very good job.

This was the second day and the frustration ate at Aryn like a tumorous growth.

Although it *felt* like they were going nowhere on this, Tyriel's face was less animated today. He doubted anybody else noted, but the shadows under her eyes spoke of her restless night and he could feel the uneasiness within her.

Something will happen soon, she'd told him as they journeyed down the steps to the pub earlier in the evening. *I can feel it.*

She had sensed something the past night, slept poorly. Several times, he'd woken to hear her mumbling in her sleep. He'd wanted to demand she tell him what was amiss, but didn't feel right in pushing. She'd come to help him—she didn't have to be here.

He, on the other hand, did. Irian no longer compelled him. Even if the soul in the sword suddenly disappeared, Aryn wouldn't leave her until he unearthed whatever foul magic plagued this seemingly idyllic village.

"*Stop it, lad.*" Irian came to awareness on a quiet sigh.

Aryn had the disturbing image of another man, a bit taller, broader, thick dark hair and black Wildling's eyes—the man seemed to stand beside him, watching Tyriel as intently as Aryn did. *"She does have t' be here. She feels the same gnawing in her gut that you feel right now. Her heart compels her t' be here the same as does yours."*

Aryn shifted against the wall. "I liked it better when you were just a sword."

Irian laughed. *"Never was I just a sword, Aryn. And well you know it. Part of you has always known."* The ghost-like image of Irian that lingered in Aryn's mind seemed to shift and he propped one fur-lined boot against the wall, watching as a man lifted his mug of ale to his lips and drank while watching Tyriel as she left the stage. *"He is wondering if she's for hire. Not from here. Getting ready t' toss some coin her way for a quick fuck."*

Aryn had noticed the man earlier—he'd been here the previous night and had spent much of the night staring at Aryn's partner then, too.

"Is he now?" he murmured. "Apparently my possessive act needs a bit of work."

"Lad, if you only knew—he's a bloody fool. Everybody else knows t' whom she belongs." The ghostly image slid him a narrow look. "Well, almost. But he's daft and stupid. Thinks Lady Tyriel is a lovely, hot young thing with naught much between her ears, a woman good for no' much more than a hard fucking. And he's monied. He thinks that's all that matters. Men like him, they never change."

Aryn watched through slitted eyes as Tyriel passed by the man in question. A merchant, Aryn suspected. Rich, too. He had two guards with him and neither of them reacted as the man reached out to stop Tyriel.

She slowed her steps and gave him a polite look.

"Should have just kept walking, elf," Aryn muttered. Some of the pub's customers were already looking toward Aryn, but the merchant took no notice as he settled a hand on Tyriel's hip, smiling as he spoke.

With a firm shake of her head, Tyriel stepped away.

The merchant fisted his hand in her skirts and yanked. Aryn winced, wondering if that move would end with a knife in the man's bollocks.

But Tyriel stayed in character and wobbled, as if thrown off balance and when the merchant caught her arm, she tumbled into his lap, her mouth an open, startled *oh*.

"*Stupid man,*" Irian said as Aryn shoved away from the wall. "*Very, very stupid.*"

Aryn ignored him as he strode across the room. The two guards were already on their feet, one moving to his employer, the other coming around to intercept Aryn.

Aryn pulled his sword from the leather sheath at his back without breaking stride and swung, clipping the guard on the temple. He went down hard.

"Stay out of this and you can keep your tongue and your sword arm," he warned the other guard.

The man glanced between the merchant and his fallen partner and backed up, hands raised.

Satisfied, Aryn turned his attention to the merchant who had just now noticed he was the center of attention.

Pressing the tip of his blade to the man's nose, he said, "That's my woman."

"She's got no marriage band." The merchant glanced at his guard.

Aryn lowered the blade and pressed it to the merchant's throat.

"Do you want to leave this town with bloody stumps at the end of your wrists, and a bloody hole where your cock once hung? If not, I suggest you let her go."

The man's answer came out more a squawk than anything else and Tyriel slid smoothly from his lap. Aryn thought he glimpsed laughter in her eyes, imagined she could have dealt with the pig in fifty different bloody ways, but it would have shown her hand.

"Now," Aryn said, letting some of his savage temper bleed through in his voice as he hauled the merchant up. Kicking the man's feet out from under him, he let the bastard drop to the floor, side by side with the fallen guard. "Perhaps we should establish rules of etiquette."

"Don't hurt him, love," Tyriel said as she rushed to his side. Once there, she pressed her face to his chest.

Aryn pressed his free hand to her back, groaning inwardly at the soft, sleek feel of her against him.

And damn the wench. She was *laughing*.

Aryn stroked a hand down her arm, aware that the people in the pub saw her trembling form and suspected tears.

He had to get them out of here.

"You've upset her, you bastard pig."

"I did not know she had a man!" the merchant bellowed. He went to rise but Aryn pressed his blade to the man's throat. "Bloody hell, she's been up there half the night twitching her ass and swaying her hips, looking like a bitch in heat—"

A serving girl walked by at that particular moment.

Aryn watched as she stopped, then deliberately upended a large goblet, filled to the top with a foamy brew, onto the man.

"Oh, beg your pardon," she said when he screeched and flopped around like a landed fish.

"You fuckin' bitch!"

"'ey, that's my—"

"Easy now." The pub's owner, Gordie, appeared just as a solidly built man went to grab the merchant from the ground. "I think Master Aryn has it all well in hand, Jeo. And your girl, Lenna, has already defended her honor rather well, hasn't she?"

Gordie gave Aryn a sidelong look before turning his attention to the one guard who had escaped unscathed. "I'll have you haul your employer out of my pub. His kind isn't welcome here. I won't have my girls mauled and manhandled in one moment, and insulted in the next. One of my boys can bring your companion out."

"We...uh...we had us a room here, sirrah," the man said, darting another look at Aryn.

"And if you can pay for it out of your own pocket, you're welcome to stay but your employer goes. He won't be welcome at the *Bee & Crook* by the North Wall, either. Only other place is somewhere down near the East Wall, close to the Alley. A bit loud there, but he might find an open bench if not a room."

As Gordie dealt with that mess, Aryn sheathed his blade and focused on the woman in his arms.

She was still 'crying'. Voice low, he murmured, "Don't you think you're carrying on a bit much?"

She snickered, forcing it into a fake sob as she wrapped her arms around him.

"*Perhaps we should establish rules of etiquette...*" she said, feigning his deeper voice. At his look, she started giggling all over again, barely keeping up the pretense of sobbing.

Sighing, he swept her up into his arms and started for the stairs.

"Oh, now I'm about to swoon," one barmaid murmured as he walked by.

Tyriel's body shook even harder.

"You're a bloody witch," Aryn said with a sigh.

Aryn lay on his belly on the bed late that night.

In the bed above his, Tyriel on her side, her breaths soft and steady. Occasionally, she sighed or hummed as she dreamed whatever a magical thing such as she dreamed.

He could still smell the scent of her skin. It seemed embedded on his own and he ached to touch her. *Really* touch her.

How in the hell was he supposed to do this—sleep so close to this beautiful woman he craved, yet never touch her?

Except he had to. She was a star, beyond his

reach. He'd glimpsed that the very first night he'd seen her.

She would live centuries—was already nearing her first. She had the power of divine beings in her veins, and she called the two most mystical, most feared races in all of Ithyrimir her blood kin. The elves and the Wildlings.

Aryn of Olsted was not going to insult her by asking if she'd fancy a quick fuck, just so he could sate his need for a woman.

"It is not just a hunger for any woman, you daft fool. you ache and hunger for her."

Aryn tried to ignore the whisper in his mind, but it was like ignoring the pressure in his loins, or the feel of her against him, near impossible.

No matter how much he may wish to at the moment.

"It is no insult if she wants it," Irian groused.

"Go to sleep."

"*I'm dead, remember? Little good sleep does me. I'll rest when you do, lad. And a good fuck would help us both,*" he suggested slyly. As Aryn stared at the wall, Irian flickered into view, a little more in focus this time than he had been earlier. Aryn closed his eyes, but a sharp afterimage remained.

"Why in the name of the Gods am I seeing you now?" he demanded irritably.

Irian tossed him a wolfish grin that seemed to glow in the dim room. "*Wouldna you like t' know?"*

"If I didn't want to know, I wouldn't have asked," Aryn muttered irritably.

"Be quiet, both of you, so I can sleep." Tyriel's voice was husky. "I don't know what you are carrying on about but I hear your voices in the back of my head and it's quite bothersome."

Aryn thanked the Gods she hadn't been able to pick out the words of the conversation.

Irian chuckled before fading into silence.

Chapter 9

Aryn developed a reputation for being a very possessive lover, but one who strayed.

Tyriel was thankful there was no true bond between them because as the days turned into weeks, he developed a habit of leaving their room at night, and in such a small village, his comings and goings could not go unnoticed.

Since his first visit was with the sister of one barmaid, Tyriel had the pleasure of learning about it. Not directly...the people in this inn were actually very kind. But with her kind's sharp hearing, she heard it well enough as she passed down the hall.

Tyriel had known there had been women—hearing names only added salt to the wound. She had smelled the woman and the sex on his skin as he came into the room, though he had bathed well.

Tyriel was displeased with the hurt she couldn't brush aside.

After more than a month of the same treatment, it was only getting more painful. She was fighting an attraction to the sexy swordsman that would not fade away and if he would just turn his midnight eyes her way—

"Bloody hell," she hissed. In a fit of rage, she spun a dancing ball of fire in her hands, a harmless illusion, and then she lobbed it at the wall, watching it break and shatter into nothingness. "Bloody hell."

Shaking and sucking in air, she covered her face with her hands as the dying remnants of her magical temper tantrum faded.

It was as she was turning toward the door it happened—an attack from nowhere that sent her reeling back in surprise.

She tasted blood.

She heard the screams of the damned.

Blood magic wrapped around her and tried to take hold, while a slow, painful death yawned before her.

*Stupid, stupid, stupid…*Her little flare of temper had captured somebody's attention and this was the result.

Cutting off her self-castigation, she steadied herself and formed her own magic into a blade that cut through the binding magic seeking to trap her. More magic swelled but she deflected it.

Her assailant raged—she sensed him then. A flicker of his presence. Close. He was so close. And…hungry. Desperately so.

She launched her magic after him, a belated attempt to trap him.

But she'd waited too long and he was already fleeing.

* * * * *

Tyriel was polishing Irian when Aryn came

through the door in the early morning on their day off. He spotted her and frowned.

"That isn't necessary," he said.

Sliding him a neutral glance, she responded, "It is if I want to speak with the enchanter and you aren't available. Any luck finding a bed mate? This is too small a village for the Whore's Guild to have a hall, but there's no shortage of available women, I'd imagine."

"Ah..."

"Too personal a question?"

"A bit, yes," he snapped. "Maybe you're used to celibacy, but I'm not."

"That wasn't why I asked. Although why you'd pay for sex when you could find a willing partner..." She shrugged. "But...again, that's not why I ask."

"Then why *are* you asking about my bedmates?"

Turning her head, she watched Irian flicker into view now that his bearer was there.

This...being wanted her, had used Aryn's body to take her. Misery almost overwhelmed her. An enchanter long gone from the world desired her desperately. And he could only exist by forcing his will on the man Tyriel wanted with equal desperation.

The temper clouding Aryn's eyes faded as he saw Irian. "What is amiss?"

"The enchanter and I have been...discussing the situation. I had a problem of sorts when I did a bit of magic. Small, very small, but something seemed to have been waiting for it and tried to grab me. He failed, miserably, and I got an idea of what and where he was."

"And what, pray tell, what do I have to do with anything this?" Aryn asked, confused, looking from Tyriel to Irian. "Or my bedmates?"

"*How do you feel about bloodsport and pain in your sex, brother?*" And the enchanter proceeded to fill Aryn in on what Tyriel had learned.

* * * * *

Aryn's stomach was roiling.

His entire body shook with rage, yet he felt slightly ill.

Staring at Tyriel, Aryn thanked the Gods Irian had finally gone silent.

After what Irian had relayed, he wanted little more than to race down the streets and find the house she spoke of. And kill. Murder. Maim. Mutilate. The last thing he needed was the bloodthirsty rumblings of an ancient warrior murmuring in his ear.

"When the night lies heavily, Aryn. Only then," Tyriel said quietly. "The mage was looking for a new offering."

"An offering." Aryn shook his head. "Is this mage the one who has been grabbing children? It's not yet the Solstice, so it should be a while before there is another attempt."

"He's growing more impatient." Tyriel shifted on the bed, swinging around so her back pressed to the wall. Her pretty face set in hard lines, she looked at him fire alight in her golden eyes. "I can't truly *see* everything within him, but he seeks worship. He has...followers, like a god. Their offerings fuel his magic but only for a time. Blood, pain, fear...sex, all of these can boost a blood mage's power. Spells that feed off a lifeforce are strongest on the Solstices, but there are certain spells a blood mage can do...like on a dark moon...that will give another boost. He's becoming addicted to it and he needs that power surge more and more."

"You think that's why he took a girl just a few weeks past," Aryn said, eyes narrowing. "He's losing control."

"Yes. And for him to be looking for another offering so soon...this doesn't bode well, Aryn." Eyes troubled, she drew one knee to her chest and looped her arms around it. "I can't explain what it felt like when he sensed me. But he was so...*hungry*. Ravenous. He's been looking since the new moon. His followers brought him a slave child, hiding her as they came through the village gates. He meant to make her last but he was careless."

"Careless." Aryn kept the rage from his voice, but only barely. "Is the girl dead?"

"I believe so, yes." Eyes flat, she looked out the window. "I picked up little beyond regret she hadn't lasted long enough—and his...impatience. He feels safe in taking another from the streets here again. He prefers the street kids here, older youths prone to disappear as they head off to larger towns in hopes of changing their fortune. They're rarely missed, even in a town so small. People like that, well, they are easy marks. But he's been known to…cast a broader net from time to time, especially if he senses a tasty morsel, as he considers it. And apparently, I'm quite tasty."

"So he thinks to take you. He must not know what you are."

Tyriel laughed.

The cold edge to that laugh set the hair on Aryn's neck and arms on end.

The sharp-edged smile was even more chilling.

But most unsettling of all was how Tyriel started to *glow*—as if a luminescent light lived just under her skin.

Even Irian took note. Aryn could feel the enchanter's sudden watchfulness as he took in the magical being before him.

"Tyriel?"

Her lashes swept down and the glow dimmed. Aryn watched as the glow slowly sank back inside her skin until it was gone.

"I apologize, Aryn." She sighed and shivered.

Something about it made Aryn think of a great bird settling its swings. A bird of prey.

Her lashes swept up and Aryn realized she hadn't pulled in all her…power, magic, whatever it was that had caused the glow.

It still burned in her eyes. Miniature suns

burned behind golden-brown of her irises, turning them to blazing, fire-drenched jewels.

"It's nothing, my friend." She flexed her hands and wisps of colorful light dripped from her fingers. "Magic lives and breathes in me. It's in my every breath. And when I get frustrated or angry..." Her gaze fell away and she shrugged. "Strong emotions bring it out. I can control it, but I only do it when I feel it's necessary." She arched a brow. "If it makes you uncomfortable, I'll hide myself."

"No." Aryn would not tell her that he'd found the ethereal light rather...lovely. Disconcerting, yes, but lovely. The air was still heavy with the pulse of her magic, a silence weighed down with tension as the whole world seem to...wait. Just wait, to see if the fae woman acted. "I still intend to have you as a partner after we see this done. I'd say I best accustom myself to the ways of a Wildling fae."

"You might yet regret that, Aryn." Tyriel's lips bowed, but the smile faded as she looked back to the window. "I can still feel his magic, pushing and probing, trying to get past my shields. It was like a *nhui*, shoving its fingers into my brain, trying to suck my life away."

Aryn grimaced, the memory of his one and only encounter with a *nhui* rising up from the recesses of his mind. "And yet you sit here calmly instead of shuddering and cringing like a babe. You're a stronger soul than me, Tyriel. I've only dealt with a *nhui* once and it was one time too many. Sometimes, I still have nightmares."

"You've dealt with *nhui*? On your own?" Her brows winged up.

He gave a short nod, rising to pace over the window. He'd stripped down to his trousers to wash when he'd returned and had yet to pull on a fresh shirt, his boots, or the weapons he wore as if they were clothing. "It's been some years. It was shortly after my foster father died. He was my mentor as well as my father, his only home the only one I'd ever really known. His death was...unexpected. He'd planned to see the town clerk and have his home and property deeded to me, as he and his wife had no children of their own. It never came to pass. After he died, his step-brother came to claim the home. I could have tried to fight it should I want to see it argued before one of the justices when they next traveled through, but without Ransu there, it was just a house, a building, not a home. So I left with nothing but my clothes and my sword. I hadn't even the money for a horse at the time so I made my way on foot. I had no destination in mind, but found myself on the road to Thanisbridge."

Tyriel groaned. "Please tell me you weren't traveling in by the southern roads."

"Very well." Aryn shot her a grin over his shoulder. "I will not tell you that I came via the southern roads. I'll simply say my village lay south of Thanisbridge and at the time, I was a green youth of nineteen summers. I had never ventured more than a few days travel from my home of Brita."

"So you were unaware of the swamps."

"Yes." He turned and leaned his hips back against the solid shelf jutting out from the window. Tyriel left a decorative hair comb there and he picked it up, absently running his thumb over the teeth of it. He knew little about women's fripperies, but he did have an eye for things with a resale value, since more than once, as a hired sword, he'd collected bonuses in 'spoils' when bandits would attempt to raid the caravan or traveling traders he guarded. The piece in his hand had no jewels, but it would feed a small family for a month. Elvin work, it had been carved from carnelian. Dragging his thumb along the finely carved teeth, he thought back to that terrifying time. "I had nightmares about that time for years. Sometimes, I wondered if they'd ever stop. But that was a long time ago."

Putting the hair comb down, he met her gaze. "This mage, whoever he is, how do you plan to take him?"

It was an inelegant way to change the subject. But the sympathetic light in Tyriel's eyes told him she understood.

"Ah, the plan. It figures you would want to know about the *plan*."

Aryn lifted a brow. "I'm hardly about to sit by while you traipse off without knowing what you are going to do and how I can help. I'm the reason you're here."

"Yes, yes." She huffed out a breath and fell

Of Mischief & Magic

flat onto the bed, lifting one hand to sketch through the air. "The problem is...I'm still working on said plan. I know his scent now, his blood, his feel. He cannot hide from me. But as to how we can contain him..."

Her words trailed off as she let her hand drop, falling to lay carelessly over her belly.

A silence, heavy and cold, stretched out. Or perhaps it only felt cold to Aryn. Give him a foe of blood and bone, one he could strike down with his sword or a knife across the throat. But magic-users, they never sat easy with him. Although he'd survived more than a few magical attacks since he'd started selling his sword to earn coin, he knew it was just as likely the next one could kill him.

Now he thought of a magic-user targeting Tyriel, and all because she'd come along to aid him.

"He will know you as well."

Tyriel pushed up onto her elbows and gave him a narrow look. "Please. The fool was too busy seeing me as prey. He had no idea I was the hunter. Had he any sense, he wouldn't have blindly sought to attack someone with fae blood without making sure he or she was alone. We rarely travel alone outside the kingdom and anybody with sense knows that—so, he's either senseless or he's never tasted fae magic before. Either way, he has no idea what he faces."

She lapsed into a silence and her lashes drooped, a look of distaste on her face. "His magic is fouled. So unclean."

Thinking of it made Tyriel long for a long, hot bath, or a long hard swim through the icy waters of the river behind her father's ancestral home back in Eivisa. Part of her wanted to leave for home *now*, to get distance between herself and a monstrous mage who had befouled the very land around him.

It was a sickness, his magic, something sinking into the very land around him. Tyriel had been fighting a low-level headache for several hours and had brushed it off as stress. She wasn't completely fae and had taken ill a few times in her long life, most of the time with an illness that had a magical cause.

But that was rare, so rare it had taken her hours to realize her headache had a magical root as well.

The land around her was tainted—the land, the source of energy for her elven magic.

The mage she would soon hunt had committed acts so unnatural, it was fouling the natural energies around him, energies that came from the earth. It was little wonder she longed for her father's lands.

And maybe she'd travel there for a visit, soon.

But first—there was a battle to win, an enemy to fight.

"There's no need for complicated plans, I suspect. He will come looking for me, and soon. His greed demands it. Already, he's searching."

Of Mischief & Magic

She saw the hard glint in Aryn's gaze and wasn't surprised when he said, "Then you'll stay shielded."

"Oh, is that so?" She sat again and brought her legs up, crossing them in front of her as she studied the blond swordsman. "It will make it hard for us to trap our prey if we don't offer bait. And if I don't offer a tempting morsel for him, he'll look for another elsewhere. His blood lust demands it."

"You know all of this from one chance encounter when you were doing..." Aryn scowled and sketched a hand through the air, fingers wiggling in an imitation of what some street mages used when they used bits of their magic for entertainment to earn coin. "Whatever it is you fae do when...you do whatever it is you do?"

"Do you realize how little sense you make?" Cocking a brow at him, she decided against being insulted, because while Aryn carried an enchanted blade, he understood little about true magic. "And for the record, I don't need..." She wiggled her own fingers in a mockery of what he'd done. "To do *that* to use my magic."

Aryn stared at her, hard-eyed. "You understand my meaning, Tyriel. You've not even laid eyes on this mage you say we must hunt."

"He gathers power, harvests it from the young ones he kills. And when he can't find a youth with power, he settles for reaping the power he wants through fear and blood. We can't let this continue."

"And there is also the brothel he runs—the ones he doesn't kill, he breaks and they serve there it would seem," Irian added softly, his voice gruff with sympathy for the lost.

"So why are we standing here talking about it instead of killing him?" Aryn asked, his voice rough and deep with rage. He held out his hand for his blade and Tyriel offered it with a lifted brow and a bow of her head. He closed his hand around the pommel, feeling his fingers settle familiarly around the curves and grooves, like an extension of himself. As he touched the blade, he felt Irian's own rage. It felt like coming home, oddly, or like the other half of his own soul as he donned the sheath and settled the blade in position down his back.

Tyriel continued to sit on the bed with her legs folded, her long narrow feet bare, a slim gold ring around her second toe winking at him in the dim light as she studied him with calm, appraising eyes.

"Aryn, if we go in there and kill him, be it with steel or with magery, you and I will be risking our necks. Now, it may just be, literally, a pain in the neck for me. But it would good and well kill you. And if my Da hears of a bunch of humans laying hands on me for trying to help them, tsk, tsk, tsk, do we really need an elvish army raining down on mortals if I miscalculate and end up getting us both killed?" she asked, unfolding her legs and shifting to lie on her side, stretching her long legs out and crossing them at the ankle. "Da would be well and truly pissed, and I wouldn't be very happy myself. Not to mention the reaction from my mum's clan."

"Oh, then we ignore it?" he asked sarcastically.

"No," she drawled, lifting her gaze skyward as if praying for patience. She took a deep breath that strained the laces of her chemise and Aryn wished she had bothered to don a little more than that and her breeches as her nipples pressed against the cloth, the peaks taunting him to madness. "We gather proof. And we let...reinforcements arrive. This snake we hunt, he's not alone. He has at least two other mages. I am good, quite good. But I am not stupid. And Irian, beg your pardon, there is only so much you can do without a body to call your own."

"If the stubborn swordsman would let me use—"

"It's the stubborn swordsman's body," Aryn said stubbornly.

"And he has a right to it," Tyriel agreed. "And I think we should establish that now. Can you offer your bond to no longer try to take over his body simply at your own behest?"

"I took a vow at my death, lady of the Jiupsu. Do you no longer honor vows?" Irian growled.

"We honor them. But you do not honor your wielder when you force your will on him," she said coolly. "I understand your vow, better than you would think. While you seek to fulfill an honorable vow, forcing your will on another is *not* an act of honor."

Irian was silent. And then grudgingly, "No more forcing my will at my own...behest," he grunted. "But when the need arises...?"

"Your version of need had better have been revised very recently," Tyriel said softly, an edge to her voice.

Aryn stared at her, hard. And then he turned his head, searching for the flickering form of Irian, but the man had not reformed again. In the back of his mind, he heard Irian's voice, but not his words, and watched as Tyriel lowered her lashes in acknowledgment, but no words were spoken out loud.

"I think there's something going on that I need to know about," he said to Irian.

"No. It's not your concern," Irian said. "My bond has been given. I'll not be forcing my will on you. But y' must be understanding. My vow, I cannot break, not now, not until I am no more."

"Bloody hell, you stupid piece of tin, I'm here, aren't I?" Aryn snapped, resisting the urge to take the blade off and fling it against the wall. It wouldn't hurt the enchanter any and worse, he knew better than to treat a weapon like that.

"Exactly what sort of proof do we need?" he asked slowly, lowering himself to the floor, shifting Irian to an angle and staring at Tyriel with hard eyes. "And why do I get the feeling you're going to send me to this house?"

"Have you any idea how many times I've

heard 'poor Tyriel', or worse—'she must not be very good in bed if he has to wander so much'. Look at it this way, darling. You owe me." She gave him a sly smile. "Otherwise we could have waited until Jaren arrived."

"Jaren?"

"Back up," she answered. Her amber eyes gleamed. "One of my father's men. An elvish...you would probably call him an assassin. He was one of my teachers. He will be here come morning. But you will sort of wander into one of the pubs tonight—I've sensed some of his...*flock*, you could call them and I know where at least a few like to gather after the day is done. You'll go there, have a drink or day, mingle, then leave."

Skeptical, Aryn eyed her. "That's it?"

"You'll be on the look out for whatever information you can glean." Her mouth went tight. "They have dark tastes there. Pain lingers like a bloody stain on the night."

Chapter 10

Aryn stood at the bar, unimaginatively painted black, and drank his ale.

A slim courtesan, barely old enough to be called a woman, stood at his elbow, trying to coax him upstairs with an offer to let him 'discipline' her as he chose.

She wore only heavy gold rings pierced through her nipples.

And her eyes were frightened.

Frightened. Most of the girls here were frightened, frightened and broken.

Aryn's gut churned and rage painted a red wash across his mind until it was a miracle he even see straight.

This poor girl, he wanted to take her away and find her a safe place, some clothes to wrap around her slender body, wash away the paint they had applied to her face.

She didn't want to be here.

So far, he hadn't seen a single woman who actually looked pleased about where she was.

He had a healthy respect for the sex trade when the whores enjoyed their work and were treated well, such as those affiliated with the Whore's Guild.

But this place...it was no guildhouse. It was as far from one as a brothel could be.

He wanted badly to take the young woman at his side out of there, wrap her in his cloak, take her someplace warm and safe.

Yet he hesitated.

Tyriel's words lingered in his thoughts. It wasn't just her words that kept him here. The very place made his skin crawl. The iron-rich scent of blood. Bitter smoke that came from no wood-burning fire. The cloying taste of fear that lay on the back of his tongue.

There was something else going on here besides a whorehouse where the women, and a few men, were treated like chattel by clientele.

If he took this sad little waif out of here, it would destroy his chance of helping the others he sensed were trapped. So he told her no, trying to act as though he was just curious about the place as he offered her a flirtatious smile. "Maybe next time...?"

"Eira," she said with a sad smile before she left to go find somebody else. Only problem was, he had been the only one who didn't look at her like he'd enjoy hurting her.

Aryn blanked his face as he watched one patron bend his whore over his lap and administer a spanking. He didn't have a problem with spankings—but then the man stood and had her unfasten his breeches right there as the young woman's face flamed with humiliation.

Now that, he had a problem with.

She shook and fumbled as she realized how many people were watching her.

"Bloody hell," he muttered.

"Anybody can cut in," a silken voice offered. "And if you pay...oh, twenty-five silvers, she's all yours. Of course, Eira would be disciplined since she offered for you first."

Aryn turned his head and met a pair of boldly painted blue eyes and a slicked red mouth. The woman staring at him had to be none other than the madam. Dressed in a rather elegant evening gown that was a buffer against the cool night, while her whores wore nothing.

Aryn set his ale down and started to decline, but then he saw the whip being pulled out across the room, Eira trembling as she cringed away from one of the uniformed guards.

Grimly, Aryn reached for his money belt instead.

"How much for both?" he asked, sending the madam a smile.

"I think I'd rather have you for myself." He watched her eyes settle on his mouth and she hummed slightly. "Too bad I have a policy of never taking a customer to bed."

"But I didn't offer for you, did I?" Aryn bared his teeth at the viper before him, ignoring the flash of insult in her eyes. "The ladies? How much?"

Shortly thereafter, with his coin purse much lighter, Aryn found himself staring into the eyes of two women who had more familiarity with rough usage than gentle, and he didn't know what the fuck he was supposed to do.

But he sure as hell couldn't touch them with the smell and sweat of other men all over them.

So he was shown to a rather opulent room and fed while the ladies were taken to bathe. One of the women moved to shove Eira and Aryn rolled out of his chair and caught her hand, smiling silkily. "I realize this is a house of pain and pleasure, but I've paid well for these ladies. Any marks on them tonight will come from me, and only me. Otherwise, I mark you," he warned.

By the time they returned, he had decided to just leave. Slip them what little money he had left, and leave.

Eira took one look at his face and knew.

So did the other. Her name was Shaelin and she was bolder than Eira. She moved like a spring storm, fast and light, sliding her arms around his neck and plastering herself to his front, cuddling her curvy little body against him. Under the guise of kissing his neck, she whispered, "Please. Don't leave. They watch us, if you leave they'll know. And we'll be punished."

Aryn froze. He lowered his head and caught her face as if to kiss her, nuzzling his way around and down to her ear where he asked, "What?"

She giggled flirtatiously, ran her hands over his shoulders to keep up her act. In that same nervous tone, she continued, "You don't belong in here. We both know that. But if you leave without us...performing our duty, we get punished. We're being watched. It's one of the house entertainments."

Well, hell.

Threading his fingers through her hair, he licked and nuzzled his way down to her ear, then her neck as Eira moved behind him and started tugging at his clothes. He ushered them to bed, his mind racing.

"And just what...duty must you perform?"

Shaelin smoothed her hands down his chest as she answered. "We must obey your commands. Please you."

Aryn couldn't touch them. Couldn't do this, not here in this house of forced carnality.

But he wouldn't have them punished, either. Stroking a hand down Keely's cheek, he murmured, "I see."

The woman behind him was still tugging as his clothes, his leather vest unlaced all the way down the front and the heavy buckle of his trousers now hanging loose. If he didn't do something soon, she'd have him utterly naked.

Taking Eira's hand, he tugged her around from behind him and nudged her down until she sat beside Shaelin. Eira, her form delicate and softly curved, shivered, goosebumps roughening her flesh. Although Aryn was warm enough, he doubted the women were so he moved over to the fire to toss on another log.

"I can do that—"

Aryn finished the task even as Shaelin

moved to intercept him. Slanting a smile in her direction, he said, "And I can do it as well. You've both bathed and smell so sweet. I don't want you dirtying your hands over a log when it's just as easy for me. Besides, I'm still trying to decide how to spend the time."

He nudged her back to the bed and noticed that when she sat this time, she sat closer to Eira.

Wondering, he settled in the luxuriously soft chair and leaned back. "If I took pleasure in watching, Shaelin, would you please me that way?"

Neither pretended not to understand and while Eira's gaze fell away, her cheeks a soft pink, she didn't pull away when Shaelin took her hand. Keely's smile was downright luscious, even if her eyes remained wary. "I think Eira and I would be *most* delighted, sir."

"Lovely." Aryn glanced around, keeping it casual. "Let's lose some of the light in here. Shaelin, the candles. Eira, pull back the bedclothes. You're a bit chilled. That's a lass."

As he'd thought, once the candles were doused, the light from the fire barely reached the high bed. Aryn thought he'd located most of the peepholes and knew anybody watching would need excellent night vision to see much of anything...save for the one almost directly behind him, and the one above the bed.

A plan already forming in his mind, he gestured at the girls. "As you will, loves."

*****

Tyriel waited until nearly midnight.

He hadn't yet returned from the house.

Clenching her jaw, she slid into bed.

"If y'would not be so stubborn, little elf, I could help—"

"I'm not touching you. There is no reason that you should be able to speak to me," she said coolly.

"I can speak t' you at any time I choose, so long as you are near," Irian murmured huskily as his body shimmered into view. He moved to lie beside her, studying her with dark, fathomless eyes. *"I can bring him t' you, whenever you want him."*

"Hardly. Because I only want him if he wants me in return," she said. "Leave me be."

Then she rolled onto her side, giving the enchanter her back as she wondered if maybe she shouldn't just pack up and head back to the Kingdoms with Jaren when he arrived.

*****

She smelled it on him as he walked in, early the next morning. Sex and sweat, rich, pungent. But something was different.

She smelled *two* women.

Holding back the screams of pain and rage, she threw her legs over the side of the bed and rose. He glanced at her but she ignored him as she gathered her clothes. She didn't bother pulling anything on other than the large shirt she'd worn and as she strode out, she could feel Aryn's eyes on her.

But she didn't look at him. It hurt too much.

By the time she reached the small communal chamber set aside for washing, her eyes were hot with tears she refused to shed.

* * * * *

Jaren arrived later that morning.

Tyriel was wiping down a table when she felt his presence, then a moment later, his rage.

"*A princess of the People acting the menial?*" He stood rigid in the doorway, face expressionless.

The words came into her mind, chilly and remote. But the hot anger she saw in his eyes was a burning fire.

If he hadn't had years and years of deference to her father bred into him, he probably would have crossed the space between them, jerked the cleaning rag from her and paddled her ass.

She turned her head slowly and winked at him.

It only made the rage in his eyes burn hotter.

Jaren Everess, Lord of Remme, one of the legendary De Asir, vengeance killers, narrowed his dark, glittering green eyes at her audacity. His skin was pale, almost translucent ivory that glowed against the emerald of his eyes. His high, arched brows, his carved cheekbones and pointed chin, all were the defining features of the beautiful elvish race.

But Jaren was...more. He was beauty with a hint of danger, a poisoned rose, an arrow carved from black diamonds, fascinating, sensual...utterly compelling.

He moved in a way that made women sigh and wonder if he could fulfill all the sensual promises he seemed to offer.

Tyriel knew, for a fact, he could.

She had sighed dreamily over him a time or two in her youth, and while he had trained her in the halls of De Asir.

Until she had met Aryn she had always thought Jaren was the most sensual, desirable man-creature she had ever met in her life.

He was certainly the most arrogant.

A muscle in his jaw ticked as he continued to stare at her, enraged that a Royal dared to clean a table.

And for humans.

"Jaren." She sighed dramatically and turned to him, crooking her finger. He came toward her with the slow, sensual prowl of a predator barely contained.

He stopped an arm's length away and she closed the remaining distance, standing close enough that their boots touched at the toes. His eyes widened slightly at the intimacy the gesture implied—while elves were a people known to be sensual, it was never assumed that a previous...escapade meant the door would open for future repeats.

Tyriel had just made it very clear she

wouldn't mind a repeat.

In fact, she was all but dying to have his hands on her. She needed to feel...*desired.*

Jaren brushed her hair back, the taut lines of his face relaxing minutely, but his anger still burned hot.

Tyriel didn't mind. Perhaps a bout of rough, angry sex was just what she needed to clear her head.

"Don't be such an arrogant bore," she murmured, pitching her voice so low only he could hear. "I'm not doing anything *I* find bothersome, so you best not take any offense. It will annoy me."

"Yes, pet." The words came out a rough, sensual purr. "I'd hate to *annoy* you, darling Tyriel."

"You beast. And stop acting so dangerous. You aren't supposed to attract too much attention."

The rigidity slowly left his shoulders. After a couple of deep breaths, he banked his anger.

Banked it, though. It wasn't gone; she could still feel the rage pumping off of him in waves.

"Let's find you a table, *min brun,*" she said. Turning away, she tossed the cleaning rag into a bucket and glanced around the mostly empty tavern.

She hadn't expected him until later in the day, or perhaps the following dawn. She'd cast the call for aid, uncertain if any of her kin would be close enough to help and had been both surprised and curious when she learned

Jaren had been the one to feel the spell's ripple.

"Can you tell me why you sent for me?" he asked as he settled on the wide, hard bench at the table.

"Aye. But I need to let the publican know I'm going to sit." Before he could respond, she lifted a hand. "I'm playing a part, Jaren. Don't ruin it. You'll understand soon enough."

* * * * *

Tired and with a headache from drinking too much ale the night before, Aryn left his bed far later than normal.

He thought perhaps some hot *cava* and a meal, then a few minutes with Tyriel to explain all he'd seen might ease the sourness in his gut.

Instead, he walked into the public room of the tavern and found her in deep conversation with a man so utterly beautiful, it made Aryn want to rearrange his face.

It did not help that Tyriel sat across from him, smiling bright as she spoke with him, her features animated and open in a way he'd never seen.

Another fae, Aryn noted, then reevaluated not even a moment later as he took in more about the man's appearance.

An elvish warrior, and one with whom Tyriel clearly knew rather well.

The intimate smile on her lips as she leaned in closer, and the warmth reflected on the man's face said it all too well.

"Master Aryn! A good morning to you."

Gordie, the publican, came striding toward him, his voice too loud, eyes too wide, and Aryn saw the greeting for what it was easily enough. The pub owner, concerned Aryn might take jealous offense at the flirtation between 'his' woman and the stranger at the table so he was giving Tyriel time to set things straight.

Although gods knew, had this been a real relationship between them, he'd have given her plenty of reason to not only stray, but to boot him out on his ass. But if she *had* been his...

"She could be."

"Bloody fuck," Aryn snapped, forgetting to keep the words silent as he cut Irian off.

Gordie froze, as did every other soul in the pub, save for Tyriel and her...friend. Her bright laughter rang through the room and Aryn felt all eyes turn toward him.

Except for Tyriel.

And her friend.

The fucking elf.

"Master Aryn," Gordie tried again. "Your lady tells me that a friend of yours is here, Lord Jaren of Averne, a noble from the High Kingdoms."

Not just an elf. A fucking *noble*.

Aryn wanted to run him through and he hadn't even met the man.

But he looked at Gordie—the poor tavern keeper looked like he might expire from a heart storm.

Aryn had never wanted so much to commit utter, bloody violence and mayhem. And he couldn't do a damn thing.

"Yes." Forcing a smile, he relaxed the tense muscles in his body one by one. "It's been an age but we made plans to meet up in these parts. Thank you for welcoming him."

Aware people were perplexed, he lowered his voice. "He saved her once, the poor girl. She's always been dazzled by the Kin. I put up with it. We all have our weaknesses and if that's her only flaw...well. We don't see him that often and it's not like he'll run over with her and steal her from me, is it?"

He had no idea if that trite bit of idiocy would work, but he could barely think through the red swath of rage coating his mind. Cutting around Gordie, he made for the table where Tyriel sat with her friend—*his* table.

That was where he sat, and where she sat with him on rare occasion. Now she sat with one of her own.

I'm a bloody fool.

He took the seat next to Tyriel and saw cool, bright green eyes cut into him even as Tyriel said in a voice too low to carry, "Say nothing, Jaren. We're playing a part and you will *not* interfere."

The air was so cold, ice could have formed as the two men stared at each other.

Finally, the elvish warrior looked at Tyriel. "As you will, my lady."

Of Mischief & Magic

"Really, Aryn. My *only* flaw?"

Aryn looked over at his partner as she touched his arm.

He gazed into her wicked, laughing eyes and forced a smile. "Well, I could have mentioned that you snore, too. But what would be the point of that?"

"Ugh." She rolled her eyes. "As if anybody would hear *my* snoring over yours."

* * * * *

Gordie, once no longer terrified his pub might suffer wrack and ruin at the hands of a jealous mate, became enamored with having a fae lord in his pub. He'd gone out of his way to welcome Jaren, calling for a servant to run to the market in search of better fare and what had been a rather tame meal turned into one fit for a king—or as close as the small-townsfolk could remember experiencing.

Jaren, arrogant bastard he was, had set aside his normally aloof ways and enjoyed the revelries, spinning tales of battles he'd fought, side by side fae lords who were all but lost to legend outside the fae lands.

When benches were pushed aside and one barmaid entreated Tyriel to play, Jaren surprised even her by pulling out an instrument of his own, a piece made of wood and string he used to bring forth melodies so beautiful, it seemed a sin to play such music for anybody but divine beings.

When someone asked how to thank him for

such music, he'd winked and nodded at Tyriel. "Ask her to dance for the next one."

"Are we here to parade about like popinjays or is there some task before us?" Aryn muttered.

Tyriel heard him, but opted to ignore him as she watched the barmaids approaching her, heir faces flushed from Jaren's attention, eyes wide and hopefully. They were out of luck, although she wouldn't tell them.

She'd already spent too many nights alone and while she could do nothing about how a certain blond swordsman had no interest in her, she wasn't sacrificing a bit of fun with a man she'd taken to her bed more than once, just because a couple of dewy-eyed girls were spinning daydreams about his lovely eyes and wide shoulders.

"Mistress Tyriel..." The brunette was the first to speak.

Aryn made a rude sound under his breath.

She kicked him, hard, under the table. Tyriel had no idea what grievance he'd brought with him to the table, but he had no business being so surly. He gave her a dark look, but she ignored him, smiling at the girl. "Hello, Izette."

Izette glanced from her to Aryn, then back, clearly more adept at reading the atmosphere than some of those in the room. But the lovely young barmaid was more interested in pleasing the fae lord than appeasing a grouchy blond swordsman.

"M'lord Jaren says you dance, Mistress Tyriel."

"Does he now?" Tyriel shot her former weapons and tactics teacher a sidelong look. He'd likely had a different idea in mind but this...well, it rather suited her purposes.

Aryn had to get out of the pub before he lost his fucking mind.

Tyriel had pulled off the leather corselet and outer blouse she'd worn, now clad only in her skirts and a chemise that laced up tightly over her lithe form, the sunkissed gold of her skin glowing in the firelight as she spun around, skirts flying high to reveal elegant ankles and bare calves, her body swaying to the music Jaren pulled from his lute with careless ease.

Her arms lifted, palms up as if seeking. Hips swaying enticingly before snapping in a move so sharply, it should have hurt but she made it all look so easy, graceful and fluid like water.

Several men reached out to touch her as she spun by. She easily evaded them, the teasing smile on her lips both a promise and reproof.

The music swelled, rising in volume and intensity.

She passed by him and he caught a hint of her scent, curled his fingers into a fist to keep from grabbing her.

For a moment, her eyes locked with his.

Her lips parted.

But then the music changed and with it, her

rhythm.

And she spun away, this time toward the fae lord.

She spun faster and faster. Jaren had risen to his feet, fingers skipping adroitly over the strings as he stood before her.

Abruptly he stopped.

Tyriel stopped dancing.

Applause broke out as Jaren caught her hand and bent forward, his hair falling in a curtain to shield them as he pressed a courtly kiss to her skin.

Aryn turned on his heel, storming away.

"I don't have much time," Tyriel said as she led Jaren up the staircase to the room she shared with Aryn. "You fine fae lords can sit on your laurels while human servants fetch you food and drink, but some of us work for a living."

"Yes," Jaren said, voice a velvet stroke in the dim hall. "I spend so much time sitting on my...laurels. Are you going to wait on me, Mistress Tyriel?"

The rest of the words were spoken almost directly against her ear as she came to a stop outside the room she shared with Aryn, fingers suddenly clumsy as she dealt with the simple lock. The solid iron was uncomfortable against her skin, but nothing she couldn't tolerate, thanks to the Wildling blood in her veins and once she had it open, she pocketed the key, ready to push inside, pull Jaren in with her and jump him.

Her breaths came raggedly, heart still pounding hard from the Wildling dance she'd performed, and from needs too long suppressed.

Jaren recognized the dance for what it was, an invitation and now, alone in the narrow hall with her, he crowded her against the door and bit her earlobe. "Open the door, my lady."

Door. Yes. They should *really* go inside.

The latch sounded impossibly loud as she opened the door, only to replaced by the roaring in her ears as Jaren came in behind her and kicked the door shut and fell back against it, hauling her in close with his hands on her hips.

"Say yes," Jaren murmured against her neck as he brought their bodies into alignment.

"Yes." Tyriel shuddered as his hands moved up from her waist, cupping her breasts, plumping them together, plucking her nipples until they throbbed as he lowered his mouth to her neck and raked it with his teeth.

She moaned as he cupped her between her thighs, rubbing her through her skirts as he whispered, "You're already wet. Needy. Good. I'm in no mood to be gentle tonight."

He half-carried, half-hauled her to the nearest bed and bent her over, shoving her skirts to her waist. Weak in the knees already, Tyriel had to bite her lip as he pushed his hand inside the loose, short garment she wore under her skirts over her most intimate places. Body already tight with anticipation, she bucked against him as he plunged two fingers inside her.

"Jaren—" her cry broke as he screwed his wrist, pushing deeper before slowly pulling out.

"Beautiful, princess...come for me..."

She shivered in reaction, her muscles going limp. She might have slipped down his body in a puddle to the floor if strong hands hadn't held her steady.

"My turn." Jaren bit her earlobe.

Her heart stuttered at the harsh need in his voice and she gasped at the speed in which he bared himself, then filled her, hard, with no hesitation. Tyriel bounced up onto her toes in reaction to the thick, hard invasion of Jaren's cock, a sob tearing free.

Magic pricked over her skin, stirring her awareness but her instincts settled as she recognized Jaren's magic, wrapping around the room in a muffling veil.

He drove into her again, the head of his cock passing over one of the sensitive, nerve-filled bundles in her core and she instinctively tightened around him. His cock jerked and it only had the effect of her inner muscles squeezing him again, and again.

Jaren snarled and he shoved a fist into her hair, pulling. Her spine arched, her scalp tingling from the sensation.

Of Mischief & Magic

"So hot," he muttered. "You burn me. Let me burn you, my lady."

Tyriel moaned as Jaren breathed a whisper of magic down her body, sending hot little flicks of illusory flames to lick at her skin, teasing her nipples before arrowing down the wet heat between her thighs to pleasure them both.

"Beast," she whispered.

Then there was no time left for words as he drove them to the edge and over, his natural shields containing the small magics that erupted from them as they lost control.

Tyriel lay against him, judging the time by the angle of the sun.

She felt loose and languid, her mind sharp despite her body's relaxed state.

"I so needed that," she murmured as he stroked a hand over her hip.

"Why didn't you turn your lovely eyes to your human companion?"

Tyriel didn't control the flinch in time. Embarrassed, she sat up, dragging the bed linens up to cover her body in a rare display of self-conscious modesty.

"You noticed that."

Jaren arched one brow. "Hard not to, the way you made it a point to *not* stare at him. You could bring any man to your bed if you chose, Tyriel."

"I'm not resorting to fae tricks for bed

mates," she snapped.

He sat up, the muscles in his finely carved torso tightening with the movement as he leaned in until they were nose to nose. "I speak not of fae wiles, old friend, but of female ones." To punctuate his meaning, he cupped one breast. "He's a man. You're a woman. And while I might be reading him wrong, I don't believe he's attracted to other men."

"No." Tyriel flopped onto her back and flung an arm over her eyes. "Leave it alone, Jaren. I beg you."

Instead, her former instructor, sometimes lover and always friend continued. "As I thought. So that's not why you're hesitant."

"He's a bloody hound," she said when he lifted her arm and bent over to peer into her eyes. "He'll fuck anything in skirts—or I should say anything with tits. But he doesn't so much as *look* my way."

Trying to hide the hurt would be much harder if Jaren could see her eyes so she sat up and gave him her back.

"Is it your pride that's wounded or something else?"

She sniffed. "Please."

"You've a damnable lot of pride, even for us, my lady. But methinks there is more to this tale, something you don't want me knowing."

Eyes closing, she sank back against him. Why hide it? He already knew. "I—"

She stopped, feeling a vibration in the floorboards. Unless Gordie had rented out a room in the hour they'd been away from the public room, Aryn was back. And the sun had slid down to kiss the horizon, so they had plans to make.

"He's back," she said quietly, rising from the bed and moving to the washbasin. She needed a real bath after tussling on the sheets with Jaren, but there wasn't time for that just yet. She barely had time to freshen up and pull on a fresh chemise and tunic before the door swung open.

Jaren was still lounging on her tumbled bad, black hair a silken tangle over one shoulder and unrepentantly naked.

Aryn barely glanced at him, but he paused in the doorway. "I thought you might want to start making plans." He waited a beat. "Should I come back later?"

"No." She tossed him a look over her shoulder. "If you're not modest, you might as well come in. Jaren has no shame, so you won't bother him. Jaren, clothing."

"Of course, my lady."

She stiffened and shot him a narrow look at the silken, suggestive tone but he had a look of pure innocence on his face when their eyes locked.

After pulling breeches on, she crossed to him while Aryn went to his bed.

"Behave," she warned, using her father's tongue.

"Of course, my lady." Wicked humor lit Jaren's eyes.

Tyriel bit back a sigh. Whatever mischief had taken hold of him, she didn't know. But if she tried to rein him in now, it would only make it worse.

Chapter 11

Jealousy, red and ugly, raced through Aryn at the easy interplay between them.

Although he didn't speak a word of elvish, he had come to know Tyriel's moods and he saw the amusement and irritation as they both dashed across her pretty face. The other fae? Well, smug male arrogance sounded and looked the same regardless of the language being spoken.

That they had a history was obvious.

Now, the room smelling of woman and sex, he had an even *more* obvious picture in his mind and the enchanter's heightened senses only added to the picture forming in Aryn's mind.

"Why do you tolerate this?" Irian demanded. "Just give me permission, brother of my soul, and I'll kill the long-ear before the sun rises."

Yes, Tyriel would appreciate that. Aryn didn't bother pointing it out to the enchanter.

"There is trouble in the streets," he said, wrenching his focus to the problem at hand.

Tyriel was instantly alert.

She spun to him, slim fingers still on the lacings of her breeches while an eerie glow lit her eyes. "Is it him?"

"How would I fucking know?" he bit off,

temper edging into his words, courtesy of the jealousy he couldn't control.

The nude elf had been gathering his clothing but now he dropped them, the movement somehow absurdly elegant, as if he practiced letting his clothing fall to the floor for hours daily over a period of years.

Aryn decided maybe the arrogant ass did just that. What else did fae lords have to do with their time when they lived so fucking long?

Jaren had been looking down, but now, he angled his head up slightly, gazing at Aryn through the veil of thick, spiky lashes with eyes that glowed a vivid green, as if a fire burned within.

"You will watch how you speak to her," he said, his lightly accented words carrying a command.

Aryn felt that down to his very bones.

Irian stirred inside him, the enchanter's anger flaring. "*He uses fae magic.*"

Aryn put a hand on Irian's hilt, felt the clouds in his head clear.

Curling his lip at the elf, he began to draw the blade.

And Tyriel stepped between them, slapping her palm against Jaren's bare chest with enough force that Jaren should have fallen on his arse.

But the bloody fucker wasn't human so all he did was go still, body humming with alert readiness, as his eyes burned into Aryn's.

"Enough," she warned.

Of Mischief & Magic

Cursing himself and this weakness, Aryn let go of the blade's hilt.

"Work your fae magic on me again, elf, and you might be regret it."

"Oh, might I?" Jaren's bland smile was almost as insulting as the magic itself had been.

"Aryn, on my people's behalf, please, I apologize," Tyriel said, her voice carrying a formality he'd never heard.

"You *apologize* for me?" Jaren said, breaking the eye contact with Aryn to look at her.

"*You* used magic on a friend of mine," Tyriel snapped, each word coated in ice. "I shouldn't *have* to apologize for you, you big oaf."

At that, Jaren rocked back on his heels. Then, with a heavy sigh, he bowed his head, long black hair hanging like a veil around him. "Well, damn me."

He stooped and rooted through his clothes, closing his hand around something before rising—not bothering to pick *up* the clothes, either.

Aryn had never considered himself particularly modest but he wished the bastard would clothe himself. Standing here with Tyriel's lover still naked and smelling of her was...awkward.

"I already offered to kill him for you. You said no."

Jaren cocked his head, eyes narrowed. "What's...that?"

Aryn felt Irian withdrawn from him and

knew without a doubt the elf had sensed the same thing Tyriel had—the enchanter's presence.

"What's what?" Aryn asked politely.

Jaren's gaze sharpened, but instead of asking questions, he stepped forward, hand outstretched. In it, he held an unsheathed blade, presented hilt first. "For the insult given."

Puzzled, Aryn eyed the dagger. "Do I get to stab you?"

Jaren's lips twitched.

Tyriel cleared her throat. "It's an old custom among the People, Aryn. Jaren's use of magic against you was an insult—you're a friend of...mine."

He caught the faint hesitation and wondered at it, but knew she wouldn't answer questions.

"Normally, he wouldn't care about insulting anybody," Tyriel continued, giving the other man a dry look. "But he does value certain bonds. I just reminded him of one. He seeks to make amends."

"By letting me stab him?" Aryn wasn't put off by the idea.

"No..." Tyriel cleared her throat. "In ancient times, such an insult would strain bonds like the one between Jaren and my family. Such bonds, if broken, could lead to betrayal, death, war. The People take bonds seriously, and insults against them just as seriously. An iron blade, such as that one, used to pierce the skin for a blood offering, was once used to forge an alliance between two warring factions within Eivisia just moments before the sun would have risen on the day of a battle that likely would have annihilated easily half the race. He's offering you the blade as a symbol."

Aryn liked his own idea, but he got the point. Giving Jaren a short nod, he said, "There's no harm done. Apology accepted. Why don't you put some clothes on so we can talk about the...situation?"

* * * * *

The situation was simple to explain, more complicated to deal with, and the plan...well, if it didn't end with several people dead and more than a few townspeople calling for blood, then Aryn would consider them all lucky.

And if the bloody townsfolk *did* try to call for blood—or their heads—he'd wring their fool necks. They'd invited the murdering sot behind this into their *homes*—and none had realized it.

Tyriel had sent him back to the street after they'd put together a quick plan and told him to watch for any changes while she and Jaren gathered up *supplies*. Whatever they needed, he had no idea, but he was no magic-worker.

Impatient, he fought the urge to pace while Irian groused in the back of his mind, as edgy and restless as he.

Jaren appeared first, moving out of the shadows like he was one of them, coming from a different direction than the pub, his dark clothes and hair all but lost to the night while the pale oval of his remained set in those hard, impassive lines. Cat-bright, gleaming eyes assessed Aryn without a blink and he settled next to him on the wall as they both waited for Tyriel to join them.

"It's an unusual blade you carry," Jaren said softly.

"Is it? I never noticed."

He could feel the fae watching him and trying to decipher the meaning behind his words. Turning his head, he met the man's gaze. "That is called sarcasm."

"Is it? I never noticed." Jaren's lips curved faintly and he went back to the leaning lazily against the rough wood of the pub's outer wall. "Hope the magic in it is good enough to protect your thick, fool head."

Aryn scowled and looked away. He was tempted to just leave the arrogant prick and head to the blood house on his own.

"No, Aryn, brother of my soul. You'll wait," Irian said, his mental voice sour with irritation. "Y' would hate for that one t' have t' take you down if y' took off before it was time. And he'd enjoy it, too."

"*Fuck off, old man.*" Aryn wished, and not for the first time, the bloody enchanter could take form so he could knock him down. At least once.

Irian chuckled. "Until the scales are balanced, the sword is the form I have, unless I take yours."

The question, "What scales..." faded from his mind as Tyriel landed between them on the balls of her feet, clad not in her serving girl's skirt, but in black leather like the other elf wore, her hair woven into a tight braid, her own blade lying snug in its sheath down her back, her amber eyes glinting.

"Are you still feeling it?" she asked, her eyes on Aryn.

"Something pulls us," Aryn said, unable to explain beyond that.

It was enough. She waited for Aryn to take the lead and she followed along behind.

Jaren fell in behind her, his steps soundless.

Aryn's hearing was sharp, especially for a human's, but while occasionally he could hear Tyriel's light footfalls, if he hadn't looked back from time to time and seen him, he would not have known Jaren was there.

A deadly one, that, Irian murmured as they took the final corner before the street opened up to the Alley—the town's small collection of impoverished families and the lone, non-disciplinary temple set aside for those who might worship there.

Religious sects came and went among humans although in small towns such as this, they usually followed the old ways. Just inside the town on the main road a larger, newer temple dedicated to the twin goddesses Evine and Evinore, protectors of flocks and farming, stood ready to accept those willing to pay the requisite offering to the priest.

But here in the Alley, a handful of the impoverished had no access to the house of worship except on two feasting days.

The undedicated temple had been built by a wandering priest decades earlier but mostly went unused.

Yet tonight, golden light burned behind draperies drawn against the damp and cold. The few people out in the street rushed by the small structure, heads bent as if they feared to look up.

Fouled magic, blood, old and freshly spilled, and fear filled the air, the reek of it a noxious perfume.

"They use enchantment to make those around this place walk on by, as if it there's nothing here." Irian's mental voice was hot with rage. "It bleeds fear and their natural instincts have them taking care to avoid this place, leaving those in the temple free to wreak have."

They'd end all of that tonight. Aryn said nothing out loud, but he felt Irian's savage agreement.

The shadows gave cover to the three prowling the night, allowing them to draw close to the temple, until Aryn could have drawn his blade and pressed the tip to the old, scarred wood of the eastern wall.

Magic prickled against his skin, standing so close.

It made him itch.

"Men come," Jaren murmured.

The warning was needless. The drunkards made enough noise to wake the dead buried outside the town walls, but as they drew nearer, the three warriors retreated back into the shadows to listen and wait.

"...a nice, plump bitch meself," one said. "Tired of that skinny cow at home. Grinding into her's like fuckin' a board. Nothin' soft."

They passed by, allowing a look at their profiles as they climbed the steps.

After spending some time in the town, Tyriel and Aryn knew some of the people here by face, if not name.

And the man who'd just spoken was familiar to them both.

Tyriel's blood burned.

"I hear there's an auction comin' soon. He's bringin' new girls from Nenu. Some, I heard, are from rich families...not servants or farm girls, but *ladies*, with soft hands. I'd sell my left nut to get a soft, sweet virgin."

The moonlight fell on the second man's face.

Aryn found his hand closing on the hilt of his sword, Irian's growl a thunder in his head.

"We wait," Jaren warned in a near soundless whisper, gripping Aryn's upper arm in an unbreakable grip.

Aryn dropped his gaze to the man's hand, stared.

It was Irian who cut through the red haze of fury. *"He's right, brother,"* the enchanter said. *"We wait. So we can destroy all of them."*

"I'm fine, elf," he said in a rough voice.

Jaren searched his eyes, then nodded before looking back toward the front of the building from their place in the shadows. "For this, my lady, you have left the Fair Kingdoms. Where men talk so casually of buying a girl likely stolen from her own family to be bartered and sold."

"No. Not for this," she said, shaking her head. "For freedom...but...being the one to put a blade to the balls of the monsters behind this? Well, I call that a life worth living."

They entered through the sewage tunnels, the way lit by mage light Tyriel called forth.

Aryn had grown used to her small magics and appreciate the gentle glow as they descended into the earth through one of the access points. Once they were within, the mage light split into thirds, one settling at each person's shoulder and never flickering.

The light also gave off enough to light the way but illuminated little else.

Aryn didn't want to see anything else.

A sewer tunnel wasn't his preferred route to...anywhere, even if this one had been out of use for years.

Small though the town was, it wasn't so small the inhabitants hadn't learned how to take advantage of their position on a hill, using the area's natural terrain to develop a rather advanced sewer system, considering most families there had little personal wealth. Nearly every home and business in the town limits had access to the system, provided they paid their yearly allotment to maintain the system, dumping human waste and soiled liquids through a carefully covered hole that drained to those tunnels.

Those tunnels hadn't been used on the eastern side of the city in some years because the families there didn't have the resources to pay those allotments. When the money missed one season, perhaps there would be leniency. But two or three? Well, eventually, those charged with maintaining the tunnels would come in and seal up the grates.

Nobody in the Alley had made use of the tunnels in decades.

At least not proper use.

The air inside the narrow space was still fetid, although the heavy seasonal fall and winter rains had long since washed away most of the foulness.

As they drew closer, Tyriel's senses whispered a warning and she found one of the narrow spots that were tall enough for a man to stand upright. For some distance, they'd all walked bent over and her back whispered thank you as she straightened. Jaren and Aryn met her eyes but said nothing as they waited.

"Can Irian protect you against most magic?" she asked. "He protected you against sorcery once before, but what about attacks from elemental mages? Enchantment?"

Aryn felt the soft rustle in his mind as Irian moved out of his 'resting place' and then the enchanter shimmered into view. "I am an enchanter, lady of the Jiupsu. A sorry one I would be if I could not protect him against the very magic I practice. But I would have to borrow his body and blood for a time."

"A time?" Tyriel and Aryn asked in unison, doubtfully.

Jaren studied Irian with curious eyes, but said nothing.

Irian laughed, a deep, husky laugh that filled the tunnel and made both Aryn and Tyriel shiver. Jaren just continued to stare at the enchanter.

"A time, a few moments. Long enough to draw blood and raise wards," he said, smiling slowly at Aryn's obvious discomfort. "'Tis a sad day when I must beg permission to protect my ward, Aryn."

Aryn asked grudgingly, "What must I do?"

Irian moved closer and Aryn felt the enchanter settle inside him, but not taking him over, more like he was sliding inside his skin with Aryn.

"Watch...learn...remember," Irian said, his mental voice quiet inside his head. "First, we draw the blade. His name was Asrel. Once. Long ago. Much magic had to be forged into him for him to withstand the ages. He belonged to my father—"

Images swirled inside Aryn's head as he

drew the blade—no, not him. Somebody else, in a land much more primitive, wilder, newer, a man, similar to Irian forging a blade, breathing magic and life and blood into the weapon as he shaped the enchanted iron. A wide-eyed youth looked on from the safety of the yard.

Blood, death, mayhem, a young girl's scream, the father's sightless eyes, a woman, Irian's mother, somehow Aryn knew, who lay dead, her body raped and battered and mutilated before they granted death. And the youth, not even fifteen, taking up the sword.

"*Asrel.*" Irian whispered the blade's name as Aryn whirled the blade in front of him, almost hypnotized, remembering. No, reliving Irian's memories. *"We must place our palm along the blade's edge, my brother, but we cannot cut too deep. Don't be worrying, though, Asrel will heal the wound. He always has before."*

And Aryn remembered other times had done this, Irian controlling the movements and then stealing the memories. Why he remembered now, he didn't know.

Aryn barely felt the sharp metal slice through the toughened flesh of his palm and he stared at the welling blood for a long moment before Irian guided him into sheathing the blade with his uninjured hand and smearing his index finger through the blood. *"If we were protecting the ground we watched, it would be a circle we paced. But we ward ourselves. Gather earth, spit, and salt."*

"I don't carry salt," Aryn said. His voice sounded loud. Too loud.

Irian laughed. "Aye, but you do. Look in your belt, my brother. What kind of—"

"...Enchanter would you be if you let your ward go out without salt," Aryn finished in a mumble as he reached into his belt and rifled through it. And lo and behold, a small vial of salt. Fine-grained, and worth a small fortune. Cupping his bleeding fist to keep the blood from spilling the precious grains, he added the salt, the earth and then spat into his hand, listening to Irian's voice and making the paste with a curl of his lip.

He dimly heard Tyriel laugh.

"Never thought I'd see the day. Aryn makes a fastidious enchanter," she murmured to Jaren. "Oh, wouldn't he hate earth witchery?"

He was also distantly aware of Irian's amused chuckle but he was too focused on the heat in his soul, something he hadn't ever felt before.

"That's the magic, boy. It's becoming a part of you...the more we do together, the more it becomes a part of you," Irian said softly. Aryn felt Irian settle more firmly inside his body and realized he was just a watcher now as Irian's magic took over. *"Not mine...ours...and soon...it will be yours."*

Symbols etched onto Aryn's face, wrists and hands. One on his chest. Irian's deep, guttural voice echoed out of Aryn's mouth and foreign words filled the tunnel as the runes on Aryn's skin seeped into his body. The heat spread outward and took on color and form, a silvery blue in the corner of Aryn's eyes that disappeared every time he tried to focus on it.

"The ward. And you can see it. Enchantment takes its hold on you, more and more," Irian mused as he left Aryn's body with a sigh and shimmered back into view. He bowed to Tyriel and said, "He is protected against any magic that may be thrown at him—save for mind magic. The protection from mind magic has always come from the blade. Asrel's magic still holds, after all these years. A fine blade, like none other in the world. Only the Jiupsu could have forged such a blade of steel and magic and have it hold after all this time."

Jaren turned to look at them, his dark-green eyes gleaming against his pale skin.

"We must go—something calls to me," he murmured. "One of them...I sense someone with fae blood. She's suffering and screaming."

He took off, moving at an impossible pace, considering the low ceiling and how it demanded they all scuttle half-bent over. Soon, though, the ceiling opened up, catching Aryn off guard.

He went still, uneasiness flooding him as he looked around.

"This isn't part of the town sewer," he muttered, more to himself than his companions.

"No, but I imagine pieces of shit spend a great deal of time here." Tyriel wasn't smiling as she made the cutting remark, her eyes shifting around as she took in the rough-hewn walls, carved into earth and stone by no natural means.

Dark sigils marked the space every few hand spans and Aryn suspected he knew it was no simple ink or paint used to make them.

Jaren stood in the direct center, staring upward. His breath came in hard, staccato bursts and a faint green glow burned from his eyes as he turned to glare at Tyriel.

"We need to *move*."

The next few seconds happened too quickly for Aryn's mind to process. Jaren *leaped*—it was more like he *flew*, but even the fae couldn't do that.

Halfway to his goal, Tyriel lunged and caught him, twisting as she did so, bringing him back down to the hard-packed earth with a solid *thud*.

The fae male jerked back, snarling soundlessly.

"*No*," Tyriel ordered.

Jaren went to shove past her and she shoved back.

Aryn knew the fae were strong. But this was the first time he'd seen such clear evidence. Jaren went flying back, striking the wall behind him with such force, dust flew out from the wall and small bits of gravel rained down.

"I hope nobody up there heard that," Aryn muttered.

"No. Nobody will have heard. The air up

there's thick with magic. It's why you're itching under the skin," Irian told him.

Aryn looked down at the wrist he'd been scratching. Closing his hand into a fist, he lowered it to his side.

Jaren pushed away from the wall, his green gaze glittering with anger.

"Get out of my way," he said coldly.

Tyriel advanced on him instead and when she was close enough, she caught his arms and shoved him back until he was pinned between her and the cavern wall. "Stand *down*, Jaren. On the oath you gave to my father and family, I command it."

"Then I renounce my—"

"*Mecaro! Esiyencio!*" she rasped, gesturing with one hand toward him and the taller elf's eyes narrowed as he opened his mouth but no sound came out. He started to lift a hand but froze.

"Ceano mora fovan."

"High Elvish hasn't changed much—silence, still your tongue. Do not move," Irian translated with a smile. "An odd package, this Wildling-elf. Not just an elemental mage, like she tried to tell me. She bespelled him well and truly."

But Aryn heard little the enchanter said. His attention was locked on Tyriel, the anger in her eyes and voice, the desperation.

"You think I don't hear her?" Tyriel said, voice thick with emotion. "Yes, there's a girl with fae blood in there—that's what draws you. But you only sense *her.* I can feel *all* of them. Not just the girl with fae blood. There are others, scared and desperate. all of them on the verge of adulthood and all of them terrified. If you rush in focused on just *one*, you risk *all* of them. I won't have it."

She made a sharp motion with her hand and Jaren could move again. He swore, reaching out.

Aryn lunged, sword drawn. He had no thought of even moving, but he had his blade, Asrel, the tip pressed to Jaren's throat.

"Be at ease, Aryn," Tyriel said, smiling slightly. "Jaren might want to wring my neck at times, but he means me no harm."

Without even glancing at Aryn, Jaren whispered savagely, "Sometimes, Tyriel...you push even me. If you weren't right..." Then he released her and stepped back, his eyes never leaving Tyriel's face. "Every second we wait takes her closer to things worse than death."

"Then shouldn't we stop wasting time?" Turning from him, she drew a small blade and pierced her flesh. "*Viastra...*"

Dust drifted up from the earth while the mage light at Tyriel's circle moved to the center of the artificial cavern. The dust seemed to fuse with the mage light before they both burst into flame. Tyriel called the ball of flames to her hand and fed it her blood.

Aryn's ears popped at the rise of pressure hitting the room.

The flame-infused mage light went blood-

Of Mischief & Magic

red before arcing away from Tyriel, back to the cavern's core and up, spinning, spinning, spinning...then it exploded outward and the cavern disappeared—or so it seemed.

A veil of misty white hung before them and across it, as if painted by the muses of the gods, there was an image. Then the girl in that image blinked and Aryn realized this was no *image*.

"This is the main room," Tyriel murmured. "Just above us. Count the men. Guards..."

"I count four," Jaren said, voice coolly logical now.

The misty white image because more focused and Aryn could clearly see the young woman now, trembling as she stood there, waiting with her head bowed, arms crossed over her mostly bared breasts. She stood in profile, and men around her leered. One even circled her.

What kind of magic was this?

Irian's attention focused. "Fae sight...she's worked a spell so you can see what she and the other long-ear see, brother. Quite some feat."

Aryn gripped Asrel's hilt as the tension in the cavern continued to mount, the image in the whirling while the dust on the ground rose to swirl around them in a lazy whirlwind.

The image reformed.

"Aryn, Jaren. Deal with the guards. The men from the village will scatter once they see us, hopefully most of the guards will, too. They likely don't expect trouble on a magical front." Tyriel's voice was cold, the promise of bloody violence on those who didn't flee.

The image spun and swirled, reforming to show another room, this one darker. It held only a moment, then faded. But Aryn saw another young woman. She was restrained, her body bent into an unnatural position while thin slices marred soft golden skin.

Jaren vibrated with rage.

"We'll save her," Tyriel whispered to him. "But we have to deal with the sorcerer first. It's time. We must move—fast. Aryn, it will get very dark in a moment. If you can't see, let Irian guide you. We can't wait any longer."

Aryn heard her urgency and was about to ask for the cause.

But she was moving and following instinct, he moved with her, seeking out the narrow staircase built into the hacked-out stone wall.

"Don't touch the sigils, brother," Irian warned as they drew close. "Nasty work there."

Aryn didn't need that warning. His skin crawled just looking at the foul marks.

He could barely make out a deeper shadow when Tyriel stopped.

"The door," she murmured, reaching out to grip Aryn's upper arm. "Hold steady, Aryn. Jaren. Now."

An explosion shook the ground. Aryn clenched his teeth against the curses that wanted to tear out of him, pressed his head back against the stone and told himself he wasn't going to be buried alive with a couple of

Of Mischief & Magic

insane fae for all eternity.

The shaking went on and on.

"That..." Jaren said, raising his voice to be heard above the earth's protestations. Abruptly, everything stilled. "Should do it. The sorcerer's circle is broken. We can enter."

Aryn's ears popped, the pressure changing yet again, and although muffled, he could hear beyond the door just in front of Tyriel now.

Voices. Men shouting and curses, a few quiet cries.

"We go now," Tyriel said.

They rushed in. In the flickering light of the fire, Aryn saw Tyriel fling one hand to the fire—the flames rose as if reaching for her—then died, gone in a blink, not even embers glowing in the hearth of the massive fireplace dominating the north wall.

Candles guttered and lanterns went dark.

In just a few heartbeats, the small temple was as dark as a tomb, only a few beams of moonlight falling through the gaps in window coverings offering any illumination. People went still. Others crashed into tables or benches or companions while cries of alarm and cursing rent the air.

"*My turn...our turn,*" Irian said, reminding Aryn of the plan they'd put together in the inn's room earlier.

Aryn let Irian guide him, yielding to the experienced enchanter as the scent of blood, swear and fear painted the air.

Irian had laid the groundwork for the

enchantment before they left the inn and now, pulling a small strip of paper from its place inside Aryn's vest, he lifted it upward and Irian—he—they blew on it.

It caught flame.

Again, Aryn saw sigils. These had been written by his own hand and as the flames touched them, they burned bright, then disappeared.

Before the first was gone, a man had started to scream.

Fear spread out from them, a magical illusion set to affect anybody and everybody who'd come to this place seeking the worst of foul vices.

"Lets show these monsters what it is like to be the prey, my brother."

Irian settled behind Aryn's eyes, almost like Aryn was drawing on a set of protective gloves—a useful tool, not a blindfold. Somebody fell into him and through the enchantment, he knew it was one of the abusers.

"Yes," Aryn said simply, replying to Irian's comment. Then he drove his sword into the man's gut, sight unseen.

Someone—a man—began to chant.

Jaren shouted out in high elvish.

"*He's found the girl...no, several girls...one is wounded.*" Irian translated, speaking in a practical tone as Aryn drove his blade into another stomach, turned, hacked, sliced, turned, sliced. More high elvish, this time in a husky feminine voice. "*She wants the other long-ear to find –*" Jaren again. "*Never mind, he's a fast fucker, even if he is a bloody ass.*"

The chanting continued.

"Irian? Hear that?"

He felt Irian's focus sharpen and they both moved toward the unfamiliar masculine voice.

Tyriel spoke again, answering something from Jaren. A door flew open. Fresh air rushed in as some of the men fled, seeking to escape before being identified.

Aryn went still as a small form crashed into him. Before the youth could dart away, he reached out, snagged the arm. With Irian's spectral eyesight, he could see the young woman, and the other two she tried to hide behind her slim form. "It's alright," Aryn said. "We're here to help."

But the girl jerked against his hold, likely too scared to believe in anything.

He didn't blame her. But he didn't let go, either. Some of the men had started fighting back and while they were no threat to Tyriel or her fae friend, these scared lasses here were a different matter.

Once they were within arm's length of the door, he let them go. "Just wait—"

The rest of the words died as the girls disappeared out the door, fleeing.

With a sigh, he turned.

His gaze locked on a collection of swirling dark clouds and the man who hid behind them.

The chanting rose again to fill Aryn's head

and Irian's presence rose with it.

"*We'll kill him*," Irian said, the thirst for blood so hot and thick, Aryn could all but taste the hot, rich iron.

But Tyriel blocked him, just a few feet before Aryn could have run the bastard through with his sword.

"This one is mine, enchanter." She stared at Aryn and he knew she meant those words for both him and Irian. "Guard my back."

The scrape of a booted foot over the floor had Aryn turning, blade up to catch the downward stroke of a guard's sword. Metal clanged against metal.

Magic flooded the room.

One of the guards pulled something from his belt, opened it and tossed what looked like sand at Aryn—it scattered, the air going dense and black.

But then the spell touched Aryn's sword and the blade all but drank the hex up, swallowing the darkness into itself until it no longer existed.

"I don't think that worked," Aryn said with a taunting smile as the guard stared in stunned disbelief.

The other guard rushed him, one hand drawn back, a sickly yellow orange glow swirling in his palm.

Mist rose up from the ground, separating them, completely wrapping around Aryn's would-be attacker for a span of heartbeats.

When it fell, the man was on his knees,

hands at his throat as his tails tore bloody gouges into his skin. He choked and gasped for air.

In seconds, he fell over.

Tyriel knew her two companions had everything under control, so she smiled as she closed on the dark enchanter. He stank of blood power, dark sorcery and evil and as she came closer, he sneered at her, flinging one hand in her direction.

She batted the magic aside with a laugh.

"*Mecaro*, you sick monster." *Be still.* His eyes widened as the command locked him into place. "*Esiyencio*, before I cut your tongue out myself."

Stalking closer, she pulled a blade from her belt. She released the fire she'd called to her, letting it returned to the hearth and candles and lamps, lighting the room and the beautiful destruction the three of them had wrought in just moments.

The loveliest thing of all, though, was the flicker of fear in the eyes of the man she now knew to be one of the wandering priests who visited this town, a revered one who had been given the trust of nearly everybody in town, invited to spend a night in many a home, share a meal.

And he repaid that kindness by stealing the town's sons and daughters.

Pressing the tip of her blade to his chin, she

murmured, "Now...what am I going to do with you?"

"Mind, I wasn't asking *you*," she said, giving him a sweet smile when he went to speak. "I'm just thinking out loud. Not that you could answer anyway...I think the elf caught your tongue."

Rage burned in his eyes and he fought to take control of his mouth.

Curious, she eased her hold.

He snarled something in a language she didn't know. A wind whipped through the temple, blowing his hood back and revealing a pale face and long hair of a deep dark red, almost skin to a ruby.

He spat at her feet and hissed something else.

The wind sharpened and Tyriel felt its punch, then incredibly, a sharp, thin pain sliced her cheek.

"Is that the best you can do?" she asked, touching the bloody spot with the back of her hand. "How boring. And since you didn't do anything interesting with those few seconds...I won't waste any more on you. *Ceano mora fovan.*"

As Jaren had done, the man went stock-still, frozen in place a second time as Tyriel paced a long, slow circle around him.

"Now, what to do with you? Death is too good for you, but it's the most sensible solution. Perhaps we could let the—"

Something knocked her down, unseen,

Of Mischief & Magic

unfelt, but there all the same. A black, stinking evil filled the room, and Tyriel's eyes narrowed as she climbed to her feet. Drawing in a careful breath, she tested the air. Then with a disgusted mutter, she looked at the human once more.

"Bad, bad little human...calling up a demon, don't you know what they can do to you if they don't catch their prey? You become the prey." Turning, she tried to track the new creature that had let itself into the chamber.

"I don't fear you, darkness," she whispered, waiting for it to manifest. She reached up, closing her hand around the moonstone and crucifix she wore. As her mind cleared, she slowed her breathing and willed her heart to calm.

A conjured demon could only take what you yielded to it, whether through fear or bargaining. Tyriel would give nothing.

Something cold twined around her ankle. She held still. "Really? This is boring, creature. Show yourself."

Her captive sorcerer sneered, his amusement sharp and cutting. But it quickly turned to dismay as the shadows gathered in on themselves and began to take form.

She shot him an annoyed look. "You called this thing from a hell plane and have no idea how to care for it, control it? Such a stupid creature you are. Demons feed on fear. Their power comes from it. Their illusions stem from it—he is not truly invisible, on this plane, or any other. Not since you summoned him here. I don't fear him—I didn't call him and he can't take anything I don't yield to him—that destroys any power he might have over me."

The shape forming in front of her was a frightening one, yet...lovely, a gleaming white spear of ivory beauty, carved into a sensual temptation of perfect man flesh. Until she looked into its eyes and saw the very fires of hell gleaming there.

"Leave me to the master, long-ear." His blood-red eyes slanted toward the sorcerer, still silent, and a cold smile creased the demon's face. "I will not harm you. Just let me have...*him*."

"Not going to happen."

The demon's head whipped to her and ice flooded her veins in response. "He's *mine*."

"If he survives long enough for you to claim him in your hell, fine." She shrugged. "As much as we'd like to wash our hands of him, it's not going to happen. He deserves the death you would mete him, but then you would not be bound to him or any place or thing. And what creature, mortal or fae, deserves that, other than him and his ilk?"

"It is not your fight, go now." The gleaming demon turned away.

She studied his horned head, the spiked shoulders, his long, oddly slender form so stretched and out of proportion. Her eyes closed and she remembered. "*Mevitecar.*"

The demon froze.

"Mevitecar."

He whirled to face her with a roar and lunged for her. Throwing up her hands, she braced herself just as the ward formed and he struck it.

"The Kin hold the Book of Demons. We learn it, each page, before we ever learn our first spellwork. I know who you are and why you were banished from the Fifth Plane. Shall I send you to an even lower level?"

The strangely beautiful demon shrieked.

Aryn moved to rush forward but Jaren said softly, "No. Just watch."

Chapter 12

It was hours after dawn and Aryn had still not slept.
Tyriel lay on the bed, so pale and still.

Before disappearing earlier, Jaren had told him she was only drained, her magic bottomed out.

That didn't sound good to Aryn, but the fae male told him she would be fine.

Fine.

She'd battled a demon—a fucking *demon* and now she was stretched out and taking a *nap?*

He needed a drink but couldn't leave this room until he spoke to her himself and knew she would be well.

Irian, too, was restless.

Tyriel had banished the captive demon, and according to Jaren, sent it to the lowest level of hell just as she'd promised.

All Aryn knew was that the thing had fought hard and long, and when it all over, Tyriel had been on the ground and bleeding.

She'd bear a mark from this night—a mark from the demon—a long silvery slash that had torn across her breast, slicing through her clothing to brand her. There was bruising around it, but the mark itself was silver and felt hot to the touch. Aryn had touched it while cleaning it and it had left a burn on his hand that had blistered and even now pained him.

Her mark crossed from her right shoulder down her breast, just below the nipple and on down her torso, stop in a slight curve around her hip. How much worse must her pain be? He couldn't imagine and he'd take it all if he could.

"It will heal, but scar." Jaren stood at the foot of the bed.

"How did you get in here?" Aryn asked wearily. The door bloody well did not open.

Jaren simply shrugged.

"Tyriel is strong. This weakened her, but she will be fit and whole within a few weeks," Jaren said, his gaze on her face, not the damp cloths Aryn used to cover the wound, changing them out as soon as her body leeched away the cooling comfort and replacing them with fresher ones. "But how much of the night she remembers, I do not know. The heat of a demon battle sometimes takes on a strange quality. We oft times forget them, in pieces, or in whole. But the mark may remind her. The one who summoned the demon escaped, but the others are dead. I would hunt him but I must get the child to Averne."

"Tyriel—"

"She needs you at her side," Jaren said coolly, lifting a black brow. "She will not go back to Averne. If I send back warriors to bring her, she will level them with a blink. But she cannot be alone. If by chance I encounter her mother's people, I will send them."

"I wasn't about to leave her alone, but we can't allow him to just flee and hide himself, can we?"

Jaren's eyes gleamed red around the edges. "Neither man nor beast can hide from De Asir. I have his scent, his name, his magic. I will hunt him, I will find him. But not now," Jaren said softly. His eyes, his thoughts drifted down the hall to the sleeping young woman on his bed.

There were others he'd need to care for as well. Some of those they'd rescued had families here, but most didn't.

The town constable had offered—*insisted*—on handling the task, but Jaren would trust no humans with this task. Perhaps Tyriel's swordman, he could have trusted, but that man needed to be at Tyriel's side as she healed, so Jaren would handle this ask well. "I must help those with families return to their homes, find places for the others and...."

When he didn't elaborate, Aryn pushed. "And...? The woman with fae blood? What of her?"

"That one, I'll take to my people. She's a wounded soul, part of her shattered from how the sorcerer let the demon feed on her power," Jaren said, looking away. His fury still burned inside him, so hot it was a wildfire

"A wounded soul?" Aryn snorted. "You think I buy that rot? Your people threw Tyriel out because her mother was Wildling. And you want me to believe you're will they care for this girl who has hardly any fae blood at all?"

"Tyriel wasn't broken," Jaren said, tired down to his very bones. He knew his people, knew all the flaws. Aryn said nothing but the truth. "There is nothing the Kin like more than to feel needed. But I am not taking her there for them to fix. I am taking her there for my lord and lady. If my sister cannot heal her body, and Averne cannot heal her soul, nothing can."

Aryn lowered his head to study Tyriel's face. "No, Tyriel is definitely not broken—"

But he was talking to himself.

The room was empty.

* * * * *

After making sure everybody was comfortable in the traveling wagon he'd procured for the trip, Jaren went to his rooms and paid the innkeeper for watching over the young woman who lay in his bed, drugged into sleep because otherwise, she screamed or tried to hurt herself.

Fury burned in his veins as he carefully lifted her, avoiding the numerous injuries on her slim form.

Your days are numbered, blood mage. Know that...and think of me while you sleep.

He sent the thought out on the night winds, pushing them on with magic and his thoughts focused on the sorcerer with blood-red hair and a demon's taint under his skin.

The words would find their mark.

Eventually.

With his precious in his arms, Jaren made his way outside to where the groomsman waited with the wagon. Hopefully within a few days, he'd cross paths with some of Tyriel's Wildling kin and they could take charge of the wagon and those who traveled with them, so he could take the fae-blooded woman onto Averne.

"Here," Lesele said, a pretty girl with warm brown skin and black hair shot through with gold, patting the nest of blankets they'd helped build for her. "We'll watch over her."

He gave her a gentle smile as he put the unconscious woman down. Despite the potion he'd dosed her with, she moaned weakly. Touching his hand to her brow, he whispered, "It is well. You are safe."

He would remember whimper, every soft cry.

Chapter 13

Five years later

Irian was pulling at him.

Tyriel could see the strain in his eyes, almost hear the internal fight.

Their voices were also a soft murmur in the back of her mind, so it wasn't a surprise when Irian's presence welled up, pressing against the barrier she'd erected between them.

She blew out a tired sigh. "What do you want now, blasted enchanter?"

"*You.*" He flooded her mind with images of them, nude on brightly colored silk sheets, in the tents favored by her Wildling blood.

She blushed to the roots of her hair and turned her head away so that Aryn didn't catch sight of her reddened face and wonder why.

Irian would have shielded his thoughts from his bearer, the way he always did when thinking of Tyriel in an earthier sense.

"*The man is a bloody fool, he is,*" Irian murmured into her mind. An unseen hand seemed to stroke down the back of her head, along her thick braid and down her back to rest above the curve of her ass.

"I thought when you took up arms together as partners he would take your bed as well, but 'tis pure madness. And he torments me w' his talk of not bedding a swordmate. Bah! Five long years has he resisted...how much longer must we wait?"

She suppressed a shiver as those final words seemed to be whispered right into her ear. *"Would you leave me be?"*

"But you are so much easier t' torment," Irian purred. "Warm, female, sweet. I'd rather be sinking into your sweet cunt, but your mind is almost as sweet."

"And is this why you torment your bearer? You insist on fucking me?"

"No." Irian's voice grew strained. "You know me better, wild elf, pretty Jiupsu. I cannot stand the thought of goin' to Ifteril. Something is there. Something evil, something dark, something that threatens us. But Aryn says we winter there. Contracts. Fucking contracts."

"We've signed no contracts to fuck," Tyriel answered absently. She didn't like it. Never had the enchanter balked at the thought of going anywhere.

Something evil...something dark. A shiver took her body and she absently touched her fingers to the chains that hung between her breasts.

"I fear for you, elf." Irian's voice came to her on a gruff whisper and his presence folded around her like a cloak, safe, protective.

And Aryn rode on, oblivious.

The blasted enchanter was talking to Tyriel again. Irian had been railing at him, then abruptly broke off, but Aryn couldn't pretend it was because Irian had given up.

He'd just shifted his focus to Tyriel.

Aryn could hear the throaty rumble in the back of his mind but the words were unclear.

Whatever Irian had said unsettled Tyriel. And it disturbed her clear into the night.

Her smooth dusky skin had gone pale, and her face was tight with strain. Her naturally fluid grace was gone, leaving her to move about the camp in erratic stops and starts as they prepared for the coming night.

She'd washed up and changed into a fresh shirt, loosened the tight braid that had bound her hair after they ate.

It wasn't yet late enough to sleep and he wondered if she'd talk to him as she lowered herself to sit by the fire, her dark eyes haunted and sightless.

Her glossy black hair fell in chaotic ringlets, veiling her features as he settled beside her.

She'd said nothing to him and he knew if he didn't push, she would continue to be silence.

"What bothers you?" he asked quietly.

She tucked her hair back behind her ears, the elongated point holding the wild curls away when a human's ears would have done nothing. The left one had a golden ring pierced through, halfway through the top, and a cuff that hugged her lobe, the gold reflecting the firelight as she sat staring somberly into space.

She lifted her gaze to his, but for several long seconds, said nothing.

Finally, with a heavy sigh, she said, "Irian doesn't want to go into to Ifteril." She hesitated, licking her lips.

It distracted him, seeing her pretty mouth gleaming, and he had to bite back a groan as he resisted the urge to taste her. It was second nature by now, but that didn't mean it was *easy.*

Fuck, we've got to get to Ifteril, into a city, before I lose it. For five years, he had managed to keep a hold on his craving for her, but long treks like this, between cities, when there were no women around to ride and pretend it was her underneath him—it drove him mad.

"We signed a contract, Tyriel." His words were strained but she seemed not to notice.

"I know that. But...I don't want to go, either. The enchanter's words bothered me. Greatly. Something dark...something evil," she whispered, her lashes lifting slowly. When she looked at it, it was with glowing amber eyes, jewel-like in their luminosity. Her power welled up inside her and she held his gaze. "Contract be damned, something deadly waits for us in Ifteril."

She was hiding something. It was there in her eyes.

"What aren't you telling me?" he asked quietly.

Her lashes lowered. "Nothing. I just do not

wish to go. We can winter elsewhere. Anywhere. With the caravans again, or even in Averne. I dare say my cousins could drum up a dozen good substitutes for us, and a dozen good reasons why we cannot go."

"Does our word mean nothing, then?" he asked softly.

"Don't try that bit with me. I've money enough to pay the fee for breaking the contract five times over *and* I can send word out, likely finding a replacement within a week or two." She gave him a narrow look. "All we've been asked to do is act the muscle at the inn there. It's a simple job and anybody can do it. It doesn't need to be us."

"Not all of us have a fae prince for a father, Tyriel." He wanted to kick himself when she flinched. "Fuck...I'm sorry. I...look, just tell me why. You know more than you are saying, elf. What waits in Ifteril?"

"I don't know the answer to that." Tyriel's shoulders slumped. She shifted and rose, moving to her bedroll before speaking. As she settled on it, her back to him, she spoke. "Very well. We go to Ifteril."

"Danger and darkness wait, and all for her."

Aryn rose from his bedroll, unable to sleep. He was pacing far away from camp to avoid disturbing his partner, and of course, the blasted enchanter couldn't leave him be.

Turning, he met the eyes of the long-dead

enchanter as he wavered into view.

"*Tyriel* is in danger?" he asked doubtfully. "She can handle any blasted thing that comes her way."

"Not this time. Turn back, before she is lost to you."

"Why do you insist on talking like the woman belongs to me?" Aryn growled, advancing on Irian. "She is not mine. Not *ours*. You're nothing but a ghost and I'm..." He sighed and stopped, still several feet away.

"You're what? A fool? Yes, you're a fool for not seeing what's right in front of you. I might be dead and unable to take her for my own, but you are not!" Irian's form blazed even brighter in his frustration. "You stupid fool. It's no wonder you're the one I finally forged a bond with after so many centuries. You, like me, will let honor and pride prevent you from being with the one you desire about all else, and you'll let honor and pride block you from seeing reason. You're a daft fool."

"Irian, it's late. I'm tired. I'm in no mood for your theatrics."

"I speak of a deadly danger to her and you call it theatrics." Irian's face tightened in a thunderous scowl. "You're not just a prideful fool. You're a halfwit. Otherwise, you'd never risk that treasure. You'd take her, keep her for you own, love her for all time."

"Love her? Take Her? Keep her?" Aryn sputtered, unaware that Tyriel had risen from her bedroll and stood in the distance, listening.

His words, solid and real, drifted to her easily on the night air. Irian's voice, though she could see his spectral form, had less substance and she heard nothing he said.

"Aye. The girl loves you madly. The need is an ache in her belly to be with you, to love you and be loved...to stay at your side as more than just comrades in arms. You feel the same for her."

"You'd tell me any damn thing you thought might get me to climb atop her and fuck her. You're a damn perverted voyeur and damn me for not knowing how to block you out of my mind," Aryn growled, his hands closing into fists as he fought the urge to do *exactly* what the enchanter suggested. "She is not for me. I am not for her. We are partners, nothing more. We will *never* be more."

"You deny that she is in your heart. You will admit you want her, because wanting a woman is easy," Irian said softly. His long curling hair shifted around his shoulders as he moved closer to Aryn, his golden skin gleaming in the black night. His widely spaced dark eyes narrowed. *"You want to touch her, taste her, fuck her...love her, and* yes, *keep her, for always. You want her to be yours."*

"No. If I need a woman, want a woman, I'll find a fucking whore in Ifteril," Aryn snapped, glaring at Irian with furious eyes, his body rigid and aching with hunger. His cock throbbed and all he wanted, *all*, was lying in her bedroll, not far away.

Yes! All I want lies there. All. But he kept the words locked behind his teeth. "But I am not fucking Tyriel just to please a dead enchanter."

"And what about to please her? Yourself?"

"I can please myself with my fist."

Her eyes stinging with tears, Tyriel backed away in silence, her belly hot and tight with grief. She made sure to muffle her presence, physically, magically.

Aryn and Irian couldn't know she had been there. She doubted her pride could handle it. She knew her crumbling heart couldn't.

She just had to hold it together long enough to get some rest, then slip away from camp in the dawn hours.

She'd had enough, wished for enough, been rejected enough. She was done.

This...this impossible dream was over.

She was leaving.

She could avoid whatever danger lurked in Ifteril long enough to gather supplies. And then she'd go home.

To Averne.

* * * * *

Aryn awoke the next morning to a cold, silent camp.

That alone told him something was terribly wrong.

Tyriel never slept longer than he did. An elvish warrior needed so little sleep. She was always awake before him, always had the fire built back up, breakfast ready, the camp broken down as she walked around humming under her breath.

"The elf isn't here."

Aryn looked up to see Irian's form striding into camp. "I can see that, you blasted hunk of tin."

"She heard you last night, saw us talking."

Aryn's mouth dropped open.

"And you didn't say anything?" he rasped, rising off his bedroll, chest bare, hands clenched. *If, by some slim chance, the enchanter was right, and she had heard him...* "What in the blasted hells were you thinking?"

"I did not know she was there. I knew only after I worked enchantment. Watch, see." Aryn felt his hand lifted even though he wasn't the one lifting it. He drew his blade without realizing it and pierced his flesh—and saw the ball of smoke rising from the ground. He knew it, easily, and could do it of his own free will now. Irian's gift for enchantment had taken root in Aryn, just as Irian had predicted, several years earlier.

Now, that magic had settled in Aryn's bones and blood. He could easily do small enchantments, with no help or guidance.

But Irian's displeasure had him taking Aryn over, a sure and certain sign of just how fucking mad the enchanter was. Aryn saw why as the smoke cleared, revealing Tyriel as her sleepy eyes opened. She slid from her bedroll, stretching, the camisole riding up, her breeches low on her hips. Her slim, toned belly was revealed as she lifted her arms high and arched her back, her lithe form sleek and strong. Her hands slid unconsciously up her torso before she slid them through her tumbled curls and absently rubbed her eyes before looking around for something.

Someone.

Aryn knew when she spotted them. A soft, sad little smile appeared on her face.

The smile gutted him. Naked and unhidden now as she thought she was clearly unobserved, Tyriel's face showed him what he'd spent years pretending not to see.

Now he couldn't look away. The love that burned in her eyes was so naked and real, even in the ephemeral mist of the enchantment Irian had created.

As he watched, Tyriel moved closer, in total silence, and he couldn't sense her magic, realized she'd quieted her own magic as she left the protective circle of the camp, which is why Irian hadn't sensed her.

Aryn had to watch as tears filled her eyes, as she heard his words and staggered from them.

"Bloody blasted, cruel bastard."

Aryn couldn't disagree, his gut souring as guilt twisted through him.

"Where is she?"

"I know not. I am not omnipotent. And Tyriel is not my bearer. I know not her heart and mind, other than what she tells me and what I can see for myself. But I suspect she has gone on into Ifteril. It's the nearest city and she's low on supplies. Ifteril. Damn it all. The last place I want her to be. Aryn, she's in danger there. And she's alone."

* * * * *

Her supplies would have to wait until she had money. She left Kilidare untethered outside the town walls since Bel wasn't there to keep him company and the elvish stallion took off at a wild gallop. With a stern thought, she told him, *Be ready. We are not staying long.*

Ready. Ready. Promise.

Painting a bold as brass smile on her face, she made her way through the gate and into crowded streets, unaware that she had caught the eye of somebody who knew her face, her magic. If she hadn't been shielding so tightly against Irian, she would have sensed her watcher.

His dark eyes roamed over her face, his blood-red braid pulled back into a queue, hidden under his shirt. His hood kept him in shadow. He made note of the inn where she stopped, and waited.

She didn't come out.

Tainan Delre smiled slowly, coldly. She had walked right to him. The little bitch who had taken his power circle five years ago had walked right to him. And without the two powerful warrior men at her side. Oh, aye, she had battled the demon and won. But it was the dark-haired male that had truly frightened Tainan.

A snarl spread across his face—frightened. That she had brought *fear* into his life still sickened him, that still caused him sleepless nights...oh, she would pay for that. That she had led somebody into his world who had caused him fear—that anything had caused him fear—was something unforgivable.

She would pay. With her blood, her body, her own fear...and death.

And she would pay *slowly*.

All it would take was her blood, her magic, and he would be restored to what he had once been.

What he had been before that battle five years ago.

Then he could start again, anew, but he would be more careful. No cities this time. Only his homeland, and he would pluck stragglers, or lone women traveling. Even couples, and kill the man before he took his time with the woman—that fear and anger would be a bonus.

Soon... he could have it all again soon.

And all because she had wandered into this town. The blood of an elvish warrior was a fine pure rush, and such a sacrifice she would be, once broken.

The scar marring the right side of his face twisted as he smiled. Walking away from the inn, he felt lighter, filled with purpose. He would return, tonight. And he would take her.

* * * * *

Irian homed in on Tyriel like a beacon, finding the inn where she had lit within an hour of entering the crowded, dark city of Ifteril. Aryn could have searched for hours, days, or weeks, and perhaps never have seen her.

The enchanter found her easily, quickly.

And furiously.

"The lass bloody well knows she is in danger...I warned her foolish hide—she doesn't listen t' reason."

Aryn stood in the shadow, listening to her play. She had donned one of her few Wildling garbs, a brightly colored, low-cut red blouse, with a corselet laced over it, a full skirt, her hair flowing wild and free down her back.

Taking one look at the wild beauty of her, he knew exactly what she was up to—looking for money, and fast. "I don't think she is much in the way of reasoning right now, but Tyriel isn't helpless."

"Tyriel isn't thinking at all right now, you fucking fool," Irian snarled at him. He shimmered into view. It no longer worried Aryn that others would see him. Irian could allow others to see him, if he chose, but only by his choosing was he seen. *"There is something black, something hideous after her and she needs t' be thinking but she isn't thinking at*

all."

She was so lovely, so ethereal, and so earthy at the same time. With the blood of the elves and the Wildlings in her, how could she be otherwise?

"Go to her." Irian's urging was bone-deep, blood boiling urgent. That Aryn wanted to so badly was all the more reason to resist. *"She is safe, so long as she is by your side."*

"So now I fuck her to keep her safe?"

The lively music of the flute skipped a beat, and Aryn swore, his eyes flying across the room, meeting hers, those dark, deep eyes. She had heard him. Again. Over the music, the laughter, the shouts, those damnable exotic, elvin ears had heard the one thing he had said out loud, the one thing that sounded so damn cruel.

Her lids lowered and the music played on.

Tyriel had known the minute they came through the door. Irian's presence, his overwhelming rage and relief crashed into her mind, and she couldn't help but feel relieved herself. Darkness had eaten at her almost all day, but she wasn't sure if it was her own pain, or something more.

Aryn's eyes had roamed over her, like a hand, firm and strong, almost palpable in its intensity. Her nipples were still peaked, pressed hard against her silk blouse, the gay colors of her clan garb bringing false color to her skin. Under the long skirt, she shifted her legs, crossed them, the leather of her thigh-high boots hugging her legs. She was wet with want for him and yet her heart felt bruised.

His words rang once more in her ears.

So now I fuck her to keep her safe?

She hardened her heart and willed magic into her playing, uncaring that she crossed a line she'd once set for herself. She wanted, *needed* that money.

She would leave in the morning, and return home to Averne.

"Stop playing."

She ignored his low voice. And played.

Aryn had paid the pub owner for a table near where she played when she hadn't listened—paid him well enough that the man had evicted the patron sitting there and now he watched her, eyes brooding and intent.

She didn't look at him as she played on, the music pouring from her flute as magic danced in the air.

A dark shadow came through the door and she looked up instinctively, the hair on her neck standing on end.

A cloaked man took a table in the corner and although a hood shadowed his face, she could feel his eyes on her.

Fear slid through her belly.

There lies death. The man, tall, obscured and hidden in his robes, settled in a corner watching her.

Tearing her eyes from him, and her concentration from Aryn, she played.

Time had passed. Aryn paid the innkeeper more coins, securing himself a room, a large comfortable, clean one, the best the inn had to offer, and after that he had accepted some ale and food from the passing barmaid.

She had offered him a bit more as well, and Tyriel wondered sourly why in hell Aryn had told this one no.

Shoving it out of her mind, she let her eyes wander back to the man in black, whose eyes and face she couldn't see.

"Tyriel."

Aryn had left his table again, moving to stand next to her. Her skin felt alternately hot and cold, goosebumps breaking out only disappear as shivers threatened. She didn't dare look at Aryn, infusing her will into the song in hopes that nobody would take notice of either of them.

The cloaked man, however, wasn't affected.

Aryn wasn't swayed, either. He placed a hand on her neck, hard, firm, oddly possessive and warm. As his skin touched hers, the black, terrified feeling in her belly lightened and faded.

Something inside her whispered, Forget your pride, your heart. Stay with him.

If only...

Aryn lowered his head and whispered into her ear, "Stop playing, now, or I'll carry your fine little ass out of here." He squeezed her neck in warning.

He let go and she gave him a withering look.

But she drew her song to a close and finished with a flourish, then stooped to gather her money.

With a quick, expert eye, she figured the money would buy the basic supplies she needed and then some. And she could always do some busking along the way if the need arose.

Scooping it into her pouch, she stowed her flute, but before she could toss her second, larger pack over her shoulder, Aryn had taken it and moved through the small door to the side that led to the rooms upstairs.

Damn him. Knowing she had little choice now, she followed him out of the inn's public room and up the stairs to the sleeping chambers.

"What?" she demanded coldly after following him into one of those rooms, several doors down from the one she'd secured for herself.

He didn't speak.

Heart racing and stomach in knots, she folded her arms over her chest and glared. Her smaller travel pack still hung over her right shoulder, flute in the outer pocket but when he held out a hand for the pack, as he had a hundred times in the past, she refused, eyes narrowed in challenge.

She heard Irian...not his words...just a murmuring, in the back of her mind. With a snarl, she said, "Stay out of this, you bloody, blasted enchanter."

Aryn lifted his eyes to her face, those dark, dreamy blue eyes that had totally captured her heart almost from the first.

Irian shimmered into view and stared at Tyriel as well, his intense, hungry gaze rapt on her face. *"You cannot understand, Tyriel, love. You did not hear all—"*

"I heard *enough*, thanks, so fuck that, Irian. And fuck you both."

"Damn it." Aryn turned away and paced to the window. "Tyriel, would you just..."

He trailed off, hands braced on either side of the window as he looked out into the night.

"Oh, that's fascinating. So glad I followed you up here for this chat," she said snidely. "Now, if you'll be so kind as to give me my pack, I'm going to my room."

She moved forward, putting her elvish speed to use and grabbing the strap before he could even reach her.

But Aryn was rather fast himself, especially for a human and he caught her before she reached the door, his hands shockingly warm on her upper arms, burning her through the fine silk of her bright red blouse.

"You don't understand, Tyriel."

She tensed, hands closing into fists while humiliation and rage vied for control inside her.

"I don't *understand*? Oh, I'm afraid I do. You don't want me, Aryn. That's simple enough. I'm no fool."

She wrenched away, but he didn't release her. When she tried a second time, he hauled her closer and twisted, jerking back to avoid the fist she swung at his head, then capturing both of her arms and pinning them at her sides by simply wrapping his arms around her entire body.

Tyriel went stock still, all but frozen by his action, because Aryn's nearness made one thing painfully clear.

This...whatever it was...had nothing to do with Aryn not *wanting* her.

She sucked in a breath, face going hot...and her body even hotter.

Aryn turned her around and backed her up to the door, leaning fully into her.

"Tell me again how I don't want you, Tyriel," he whispered, his lips to her ear. He pushed his thigh between hers, the thin material of her skirts hardly any barrier at all. "Tell me again."

She shivered, unable to speak.

"*Wanting* you is the problem. We both *want*, Tyriel." He stared at her with an expression she'd never seen—at least not when it came to her. Eyes hotly focused, a faint flush to his skin, he rocked against her, slowly, positioning her so he could drag her sensitive, vulnerable mound against his hard, muscled thigh. "Maybe that blasted enchanter is fine with the idea."

"Fuck that—he's obsessed." Aryn's tone changed, hardened. He rocked against her harder and she tried to silence her needy cry, but couldn't.

Aryn shuddered. Then, with a savage curse, he yanked himself away.

Tyriel had to slam her hands against the door to stay upright.

"But he's a fucking fool. I'm a realist and when I see the two of us...?" He barely glanced at her before turning away. "I see what is. A human and a fae woman. I am not going to condemn myself to pining after a Wildling-elf who will be forever young and lovely while I'll soon fade away. I am human, just a man. You are...you. You have the blood of divine beings in your veins."

Tyriel's heart cracked, the pain inside spilling out, thick and bitter.

Aryn looked at her over his shoulder and she met his eyes, for once seeing the lust he'd kept hidden. But that was all she saw. Heat. Desire.

Not *need*. Not love.

Aryn was wrong.

Irian wasn't the fool here.

She was.

"You have never been just a man, Aryn of Olsted," she said softly. Her voice was so level, she almost sounded unaffected. "You won't believe that but that's the truth of it."

She grabbed the packs she'd unwittingly dropped and threw them over her shoulder.

"Take care of yourself, Aryn. Irian, watch over him." She turned away, desperate for escape now, desperate to mount Kilidare and race the wind, race until maybe she left this pain far, far behind.

Staring at her back, angry and frustrated and hurt, he opened his mouth to say her name.

Irian took control.

"She cannot go...I am sorry for breaking my word."

Aryn shoved against the enchanter's hold, furious now and in a panic—he wasn't letting her walk out that door.

She looked back then, jewel bright eyes, meeting his one last time, lips curved in a bittersweet smile.

"*No,*" he said. Or he tried.

Then...he...Aryn...simply ceased as Irian swarmed up and overwhelmed.

Tyriel glimpsed Aryn in those eyes, grim, determined. But then his eyes went blank and it was another man staring out at her.

The hair on the back of her neck stood on end as he walked toward her. The body, the face, the hair and eyes, they might all look like Aryn's, but this wasn't Aryn she faced now.

"Irian. You said you wouldn't do this to him anymore," she said, bracing herself. "Does your word mean so little?"

"There was a time when my word, when my honor was everything. Yet, now, I've discovered how paltry such things can be when lives hang in the balance."

"Don't be dramatic." She pressed her back to the wall, one hand sliding out to seek out the door latch.

"It's not drama. You simply mean more than any promise I've made in..." He paused, clearly thinking hard. "Millenia. I won't let you risk yourself. Not just to preserve my *honor* and not because my bearer is a thick-headed fool. You, your life. You're everything, Tyriel and you cannot leave us, him. You are safe with him. You will stay."

His voice was deeper, slower, gruffer than Aryn's, his eyes hotter, heavier. "

"Irian, *nebaste*..." she whispered half-heartedly as he took her packs, tugging them away from her hands and dropping them to the floor. "Please...this solves nothing. You are not Aryn. I am not in love with you."

"No. Yet part of you wants me almost as much as you want him." Irian aligned Aryn's long, rangy powerful body against hers, his thick, throbbing cock fitting into the notch between her thighs. "You cannot deny me that, girl...can you?"

Tyriel's words died in a moan as his hands fisted in her hair and arched her face up. He took her mouth hungrily, tongue sweeping past parted lips to bring her Aryn's taste, his scent, but something darker, and different, something more primitive, wilder.

Irian.

He rasped, "You will scream my name this night...before this night ends, I will hear it, I swear you that."

Tyriel wasn't so certain that he was wrong.

His hands, hard and callused, grasped the sleeves of her silken blouse and she gasped into his mouth as she felt him tear it away. Then from under the form-fitting leather corselet, until the silken blouse was lying in shreds at her feet. She stood there with leather lifting her breasts, while her skirts and boots remained almost primly in place.

Irian moved a few steps back, keeping one hand on her neck in a hotly possessive grip as he gazed at her, lust burning in his eyes as he looked at her, gaze lingering on her tight nipples, on the breasts lifted and displayed by the corselet.

"*Jiupsu...aakin su rrieul Jiupsu...*" he crooned, staring at her.

Disconcerting, it was, hearing ancient, archaic Wildling flowing from Aryn's mouth, especially as her vision started to waver and Irian's image kept trying to superimpose itself over Aryn's body.

"Lovely lady of the Jiupsu." His hands gripped her skirt. Watching her, he pushed it down over her hips until she stood naked in front of him, save for her boots and the corselet, her cheeks flushing pink. His dark eyes heating with an inner flame that turned Tyriel's blood into lava. "Be wild for me."

She was already wet and now, under his gaze, heat pulsed between her thighs, an emptiness she'd never known centering there until she ached to be filled. Her breaths came in ragged pants while her heartbeat settled into a slow, almost rhythmic drumbeat, the music of lust that was a prelude to good, hard sex.

Irian's nostrils flared and he scented her, his lips parting. His eyes focused on her body, clad in the corselet that rose to just under her breasts, pushing them up, two thin straps trailing up over her shoulders, and down her back. In front, the laces were pulled tight, revealing an inch of tanned toned flesh and Irian lifted his eyes to study her breasts so prominently displayed, nipples drawn tight and puckered, waist cinched down by the gleaming black leather. The corselet ended in a *vee*, the pointed ends bringing attention to her mound.

Almost as devastatingly erotic were the black boots that came up over her knees, elvish made, form-fitting, tight, thin and tooled, the supple leather soft against the gold of her skin.

"Lovely." His voice was guttural and deep. Kneeling, he whispered it again as he leaned forward and nuzzled her belly, licking her navel as he reached around her and cupped her ass.

"Irian..." Tyriel gasped out his name as he caught her in his arms before she could slide to the floor, and he spread the lips of her sex and licked her.

She swayed and he rose, swinging her up into his arms. "No swooning. Tonight, I'll have you screaming and sighing, but no swooning."

She clung to his shoulders as he carried her to the bed.

He spread her out, pushing her thighs wide, running his hands over the gleaming black leather of her boots before traveling back up to the apex.

"I'm going to bury my face in your cunt, Tyriel, and lick you, suck you, taste you, until you lose yourself."

Tyriel shivered. He touched her then and she jerked in response, moaning as he spread her open her with his thumbs and stared with bald, naked need.

"Your pussy is so wet," he whispered before looking up to stare at her. "You're all wet and ready for me, aren't you?"

She flushed under that burning stare, the afterimage of Irian's true self trying to merge with Aryn's to her fae sight while the pulse of his magic filled her like a drug.

She was going crazy—maybe it had already happened, because this was the last thing she should be doing. But was she pushing him away? Demanding he step back and yield control to Aryn?

No. She lifted her hips, a needy moan escaping her. "Please..."

Irian clenched his jaw. "So stubborn."

Then he bent over her and bit her lower lip. "I'm just as stubborn. You should already know this."

He touched her then and she jolted at the shocking, almost painful pleasure. "Irian!"

"That's it," he purred. "That's it...say *my* name..."

She whimpered, unable to say *anything* as he worked two thick fingers inside her slippery, tight channel, then began to thrust, ruthlessly driving her straight to climax. He bent his head, taking one tight nipple, then the other into his mouth and sucking on them until they were tight and red as berries.

She thrashed under him, tearing at the sheets and at his shoulders, begging for completion.

And when she was *almost* there, he moved, shifting to sprawl between her thighs, even pausing a moment to rub his cheek against the leather of her booted knee, giving her a sinfully seductive smirk before pressing his mouth to her and dragging his tongue through her swollen, wet folds.

She shoved her hands into his hair and arched up with a cry,

"That's it," he murmured again. "Lose yourself, wild love."

He pushed his fingers back inside her, pumping harder, faster, tongue stabbing and swirling around her clitoris. But…again…when she was close, he backed off.

"Irian…" she all but growled his name. "If you don't…"

"Tell me," he ordered after one sensual, suckling bite on her inner thigh. "Tell me what you want of me."

"Make me come, damn you."

"Yes, my lady, my wild love…" Then, as he'd promised, he buried his face against her cunt and licked, sucked, and finger-fucked her until she lost herself, completely and utterly.

She was still shuddering and whimpering from the multiple climaxes when he rose, some untold time later and began to methodically strip naked.

"I can't," she said with a moan.

But the sight of that long, pale body rippling with muscles and marked with scars from battle made her quiver.

"No?" Her lover looked at her with gleaming eyes as he casually unlaced his breeches, freeing his cock. Moving to the side of the bed, he closed his fist over it and stroked. "Perhaps I'll handle this myself then."

Tyriel licked her lips as she stared at his erection, thick and hard, rising from a thatch of golden hair, a gleaming drop seeping from it. Her eyes blurred again, fae sight pushing in on her and Irian's true form wavered in her vision. Her heart twisted in her chest, reminding her which man had come to her, which one had reached for her.

The pain nearly tore her in two.

"No," Irian said roughly, kneeling on the bed between her thighs.

She shook her head mutely. It wasn't a denial of touch—that she craved, and it hurt to the very core of her that she was so needy, she'd settle even for this.

But that Irian could see that pain...

"No," he said again, but softer and magic pulsed from him, until it wasn't fae sight causing her vision to blur and alter him. Enchantment wrapped around them both and when he touched her this time, she felt broader hands. When his hair fell over his shoulder to tangle with hers, it was longer, waving locks of black, similar to her own.

The heavy body mounting hers was broader and more scarred and when she dared looked into his eyes, it was the dark brown gaze of a Wildling man she saw.

"It is Irian who takes you," he said as he grasped her hands and jerked them over her head, pinning her down. He wedged a muscled thigh between her legs, spreading her thighs wide to take him. Eyes locked on her face, he rocked against her wet heat.

"Tell me, wild love...who touches you?" he murmured as he lowered his head to take a reddened nipple into his mouth.

Straining against his grasp, a sob fell past her lips. He pushed her nipple against the roof of his mouth and suckled deep, rolling his eyes upward to stare at her. Hot and wicked, his tongue and teeth worked the nipple into one aching point of pleasure until she was whimpering and squirming from just the lightest touch of his tongue on her flesh.

She stared down into his eyes, then let her gaze roam over him as she took in minute details she'd never noticed when he was in his spectral form.

A hair-thin scar bisected his left eyebrow, and another sliced down his right shoulder...scars she had never noticed before.

"Who touches you?" he demanded as he kissed a blazing line of kisses between her breasts and locked his teeth around the other nipple drawing it tight and listening to her gasp.

"Irian..."

With a ragged groan, he tore his mouth from her breast and positioned himself at the wet, swollen entrance to her pussy, staring down into her eyes. "Years, I have waited. Years without end." Then he said nothing else as he slowly forged his way into her body, his thick, hard length slicing through her as she stared helplessly, fascinated, into his eyes, arms stretched overhead, ragged gasps falling from her lips.

She was begging by the time he was buried inside her, pleading and rocking against him, whipping her head back and forth. His cock jerked within her sheath and she whimpered, the muscles in her pussy tightening around him hungrily as she rocked against him.

Slowing, Irian lowered his body down atop her.

If she'd been capable of thought, she might have wondered at the heaviness of him—it was only a glamour enchantment, wasn't it? Truly, it was still Aryn's body, under Irian's control.

But everything felt different.

His weight, the feel of his body, the texture

of his hair, even his taste and she was too tangled up in the spell of his lust and her own to think past anything but the glory of him filling her.

"Harder," she begged, needing to chase away even the memory of the empty ache she'd lived with for so long.

Her mind spun out of control and she sobbed as his mouth covered hers, feeling his cock jerk within her sheath. His hand released her wrists, trailed down the length of her arms, over the side of her breast, her ribcage and waist as he shifted his weight. She felt the phantom brush of his fingers on her clit and she screamed into his mouth as he rode her harder, filling her with deep thrusts of his cock, a groan vibrating from his chest.

He shifted his angle, moving higher on her body so each time he slammed into her, he rubbed against that bed of nerves buried by the mouth of her womb. Tyriel's pussy convulsed around him rhythmically and Irian growled against her mouth, rising up to his knees, grabbing her legs, spreading them wide, holding her open with one hand behind each knee as he stared down at her, watching as he pushed his thick, dark cock between the plump wet lips of her sex, his lids low and hooded over his dark eyes.

With short deep digs of his hips, he filled her, staring down into her eyes hungrily, greedily.

"Y' cannot know how long I've waited," he

muttered. Her eyes locked with his, captivated, as he released one of her legs and trailed his hand down her body. "Days, months, years without end."

Thumb and forefinger closed around one dark rose-red nipple and he plucked it, smiling as she arched with a weak scream.

"Such a pretty, pretty thing...wild, wild Wildling-elf. So tight, so wet, soft as silk, sweet..."

Tyriel's head was spinning. Her heart pounded in her chest, heavy and hard, echoing the slow, pounding thrusts of his cock inside her vagina as he pushed into her. The tight wet clasp of her sex hugged his cock, clung to him as he pulled out and surged back inside. His hand slid further down her body and pinched her clit, then rotated over it in sure steady strokes until her pussy started to convulse around him.

He growled, bending low and wrapping his arms tightly around her, bracing her weight for his thrusts with a steely, corded embrace and banding her against his heavy length as he shuddered. Against her hair, he started to groan. "My name...who am I?"

But Tyriel barely heard him as she fisted her hands in the silky skeins of his raven-black hair, the climax inside her womb exploding outward and arching her up until she was breathless and blind from the pleasure, bucking against him, liquid pleasure sliding from her, coating his cock, the muscles in her pussy locking down rhythmically around his sex and stroking him into climax.

And in a low, broken moan, she whimpered, "Irian."

Moments later, she sighed as he stroked her hair and soothed her into sleep. His name slid from her lips one final time as she slid into slumber. "Irian..."

The guilt in his gut faded away to a dull ache as he wrapped his arms around her and rested.

He didn't really sleep, not even in this body. He hovered in a semiconscious state that charged his mind and magic, and allowed his soul to wander, his mind to remember. So much to remember, and so very little that was pleasant. When Irian dragged himself back to the present, he was aware of Tyriel's firm little ass, snug against his cock, the sweet scent of her hair, those wild Jiupsu curls spilling all over his arms and chest, tickling his chin. His cock throbbed against her ass, a sweet ache, one he hadn't had the luxury of feeling in years.

Ahhh...what was he to do? He could not allow the lass to leave. Such danger lurked for her. The blackness crowded at the very edges of Irian's mind, his soul. Such a powerful thing she was...how could he force her into staying? If she wasn't elvin, he could make her—not through physical force or violence. The idea sickened him. Had she been weaker willed, he could have intimidated her into bending to his will.

But not Tyriel.

And of course, if he tried to bar her from leaving, well, she could throw his bearer against a fucking wall. Elf-kind were strong, stronger than mortal men.

She must stay safe...they needed her. And whether the fool admitted it or not, *Aryn* needed her. She already owned his heart. Irian lived inside the man's head—he should know.

She murmured and sighed in her sleep.

The swordsman's name.

She fled for fear the swordsman did not love her.

Aryn loved her well and truly, and even he knew it. It was his own mortality he feared.

If the daft fool would simply open his blind eyes.

But he didn't and Irian had to resort to taking over simply to ensure their Wildling elf stayed safe.

Their Wildling elf.

Irian ached, brutally jealous of the foolish mercenary who bore him. He'd given anything to be real and here and whole—*alive*. He'd claim what Aryn was so willing to walk away from, steal away with her to whatever part of the world she wanted to go.

But he was chained to a hunk of metal until he fulfilled a vow, and then he'd...go on to whatever existed beyond this.

For now, I have this.

And if neither of them will do it, I'll be the one who makes sure she stays safe.

He lowered his mouth to Tyriel's naked shoulder, the black curls tangling with and mingling with hers until he couldn't tell where her hair ended and his began. Gripping one naked hip in his big, scarred hand, he pressed a hot, opened-mouthed kiss to her shoulder and started to pump his cock against the curve of her ass, using the heat and touch of his body to distract her as magic whispered through the air, dispelling the illusion he'd worked earlier that had let Tyriel see through time and age to the man he'd once been.

Now it was the form he was forced to wear she would see when she opened her eyes.

Blond hair spilled across Tyriel's body, straight, thick, golden as the sun. A firm strong hand caught her face and guided her head around so he could kiss her as he continued to rock against her, the channel between her tight ass growing slick with sweat and the clear fluid seeping from his cock as the need to climax edged closer.

"I want to push inside your snug ass and fuck you there," he murmured, reaching down and gripping one cheek to spread her before rocking against her again. "Can I, love?"

Tyriel shivered, but didn't respond, her sleek body tight with tension and he lapsed into silence, playing her body with the same expertise she used with her flute.

Again and again, he moved against her, until she was rocking back against him, her movements timed to echo his own while broken cries escaped her.

Irian used his body and their combined lust to keep her distracted as he reached out with his magic-honed senses and rifled through Aryn's pack, easily finding a small vial of oil the swordsman kept on hand for body aches.

Once it floated to his hand, he tucked the bottle into hers and brought it closer so he could easily reach it, but still yielding the control to her.

She shivered and rolled her head to meet his eyes as he whispered what he wanted again, and what he'd like her to do, if she was willing.

When she spilled the oil onto his fingers, he could have howled in victory, an animalistic instinct to let all know that he'd won her.

Instead, he brought his lubricated fingers down between their bodies and worked them against the tight, clenched opening of her ass. She gasped as he pushed inside, but she didn't pull away. Instead, she drew in a ragged breath and bore down on him.

"Yes, love...yield to me," he murmured, taking slow possession and delighting in every second of it.

He added more oil, then as she squirmed and whimpered in his arms, all but begging for him to mount her, he closed his oil-slicked fingers around his cock for the final preparation.

Still bent over her, most of his weight on one elbow, he took her free hand and guided to her bottom. "Hold yourself open for me...like that...spread your cheeks so I can watch as you take me."

"Hardly fair," she whispered, staring at him with a gaze gone glassy with desire.

"You've driven me all but mad since the day you flashed that beautiful smile, love. I think it's perfectly fair that I can get to watch as I sink this prick inside your snug bottom."

Her mouth parted and again, Irian condemned his owner to be a fool.

Not now, he told himself. Now he was going to enjoy every hot, wicked second of the night.

She gasped as he pushed into her, the flared head of his cock breaching the tight ring of muscle. He held there, not surging deeper as he wanted to. Instead, he rocked, slow and lazy possession in each move as he slid his free hand down between her thighs.

"You're wet as rain, love. So, so wet..."

She whimpered as he circled his finger over her clit, jerking when he stopped, then going rigid as the movement deepened his penetration of her ass.

"Am I hurting you?" he whispered, pressing his mouth to her shoulder.

"Yes...no...Irian...move...*please*...it's too much."

Her broken pleas and the hungry demands of her body told him what she needed and he rolled more completely on top of her before dragging both of them onto their knees.

She quivered, bent on her hands and knees before him, her graceful spine undulating as she rocked and fought to acclimate to this intimate intrusion.

"Irian..."

"Tell me what you want, love."

She arched her spine. "*Move*...fuck me. Please."

Her words left him shuddering, his paper-thin control falling to shreds around him.

"Aye, that. I'll fuck you, love." He gripped her hips and hauled her back roughly on his cock, lunging forward at the same time so that he filled her completely on that first, deep thrust.

Her sharp, broken cry was followed by a desperate whisper. "*Again...*"

So he gave it to her, fucking her deep and hard, hands gripping her hips and holding her still as he pummeled her ass.

She sank face down into the mattress and his eyes almost crossed when his felt her fingers brush over his sac. The thought of her stroking herself, how swollen and tight her clit must feel under her touch, how close to the edge she must be, it all but drove him mad, and he growled her name.

The orgasm slammed into him only seconds after she started coming, her body clenching down tight around him and milking him until he yielded to her demands.

* * * * *

He called down to the innkeeper for a bath.

In the back of his mind, Aryn prowled, restless and angry as he battered the walls of the prison Irian had used to temporarily cage him away.

It was an act of desperation and one he'd regret, of that, Irian had no doubt.

But he could think of no other way to bring Tyriel back to their side, to convince her that she couldn't walk away.

After a long, lingering soak in the tub where she silently let him bathe her, he took her to bed and settled behind her a second time.

His mind raced.

Tyriel slid into an exhausted sleep and his panic grew stronger with every passing second.

She'd leave because she thought Aryn didn't want her, didn't need her.

So, he'd show her what Aryn truly felt.

* * * * *

"...Aryn?"

He kissed her, his body, lean, powerful, and pale as he covered her. He pushed his thigh between hers and wedged himself against her core, murmuring her name as he stroked her, kissing her each time she tried to speak.

His hands raced over her body, cupped her breasts, pinched her nipples, plucked them. His hot, wet mouth closed over them and Tyriel sobbed out his name, reaching up, fisting her hands in his thick golden hair.

His teeth bit down on one nipple and she screamed, arching up. One hand cupped her, and one thick finger worked its way into the tight, slippery channel of her sex and she shuddered. His groan reverberated against her breast, sending another shudder through her body.

The fog clouding her brain was slowly, reluctantly lifting and she couldn't keep herself from thinking.

She pushed at his shoulders. "Aryn?"

"Shh..."

His mouth covered hers again and he moved back up her body and gripped her thighs with his hands, pushing deep inside her body with one driving thrust. She moaned, closing over him in welcome as he surged forward, deeper and deeper until he was buried inside her to the hilt, the head of his cock resting against the mouth of her womb. She felt his fingers threading through her hair, his hands cupping the back of her head, magic whispering through the room, wild, and untamed.

"Aryn...ahh...all I've ever yearned..." She moaned against his mouth as he ate at hers hungrily, his tongue sweeping and tangling with hers, withdrawing so that he could nibble at her lower lip. Pushing his tongue back inside, past her lips and teeth, he greedily took in as much of her taste as he could and all around them, wild magic lit up the room in chaotic bursts.

Wild magic...

Tyriel moaned as he moved higher on her body, rubbing against the sensitized bud of her clit with each thrust of his hips. She reached down, dug her nails into the taut curve of his ass and pulled him more tightly against her, rocking her hips up, taking him as deeply as she could.

She felt the rasp of his cock inside her, raking her swollen, wet tissues, the rounded blunt head passing over the sweetly hidden area inside, and she whimpered, her head falling limply back.

Through the veil of her lashes, she stared up at him as he pushed up onto his hands, planting them beside her head, staring down at her with dark, hooded eyes of midnight-blue, golden hair falling like silk around his strong, broad shoulders, raining down his back. Her eyes trailed down his body, lingered over his chest, the sculpted form of his pectorals, gleaming with a fine sheen of sweat before moving down to the bunching and flexing of his belly as he thrust inside her.

Her breath caught inside her throat, staring down at it as he drove that long ruddy column of flesh back inside the wet well of her sex. A hungry, helpless whimper fell from her lips.

She reached up, clutching at his shoulders, her eyes staring raptly at their joined bodies, his cock gleaming with the liquid evidence of her desire as he pulled out, then slowly pushed back inside.

On the third slow thrust in, she climaxed with a strangled cry, the muscles in her vagina clamping down around his cock rhythmically, her hips jerking, her heart racing.

Magic broke open inside and flooded the room.

His cock jerked within the tight grasp of her pussy.

She felt the hot jet of his seed fill her as she started to drift back down.

It wasn't until she was sliding back into sleep that something started to niggle at her mind.

Something wasn't right.

There had been free magic before she climaxed.

Tyriel may lose control when she climaxed, but rarely. Now if she willingly dropped her control, that was another thing altogether.

And while the enchanter's magic was slowly filling Aryn, it had not yet taken hold of him completely.

The magic had not been Aryn's.

Irian...

You bloody bastard.

That was her waking thought as well.

She knew he was trying to protect her.

If the darkness looming at her mind didn't frighten her so, she might have been angry. But even with that blackness looming around, Tyriel could not stay. Slowly, she sat up, wincing as muscles rarely used so vigorously went on vicious protest.

Behind her, Aryn slept on, deeply. Irian

forcing his control over Aryn's was no longer such an easy task and had drained both of them.

That, at least, would work in Tyriel's favor.

She reached up and stroked the amber moonstone between her breasts. Her nipples grew tight in the cool morning air as she rose gingerly, still stroking the pendant.

It was time to go home.

She'd visit the cousins in Bentyl first, pay her respects there.

But then...home.

To Averne, where she belonged.

Dawn wasn't even a thought when she slipped out of the room, looking over her shoulder at Aryn's nude body sprawled across the sheets. He was inhumanly beautiful, more than even the elvin kin to her eyes. The muscled curve of his ass, the sleek lines of his back, his long golden hair hanging in a glorious tangle down his back and across his shoulder, one strand lying across the sharp edge of his cheek.

Damn you, Irian...what a memory to leave me with.

A hot, bitter wash of pain filled her chest and throat.

She turned away, closing the door in silence. The heels of her hard-soled elvish boots were soundless on the wooden floors as she moved down the hall and the stairs.

Tears burned her eyes and a lingering ache throbbed between her thighs, inside her cleft. Riding wasn't going to be such a pleasant act today.

"Kilidare, you had best behave yourself," she said aloud as she headed down the already busy streets. In her mind's eyes, she could feel the mount's interest, almost see his ears perk up.

And she never noticed the shadow moving up behind her.

Kilidare was worried.

His breed wasn't horse.

His kind was far more intelligent than a mere horse. And even among his own kind, he was unique.

He could run like the wind, track like a hound, puzzle and reason like a primate, but he needed a focus.

He needed his mistress.

And when his mistress didn't appear right away, he forgot his worry after a time and he started to wander yet again.

Elvish steeds were originally wild.

What separated the elvish steeds from their wild forebears were their masters. And his mistress had yet to return to him.

So he started to roam. But he remained near the city where she had told him to wait and he remembered.

Time passed, though. Their bond stretched

ever thinner as he roamed the woods and plains of the area around the town of Ifteril.

She could still come. She would. She always did.

Chapter 14

Her eyes were swollen, battered.

Nearly impossible to open from the beating she had taken only hours before. An elf's healing abilities made a human's look laughable. Within three days, the marks from the beating would be all but gone. But it was draining.

The iron at her wrists, at her ankles, wrapped around her belly was sickening her. And the collar around her neck, a slave's collar.

On a Princess.

The blood of a Royal, which she so rarely acknowledged, was so very, very enraged—the death of this man would be...painful. Painful. Slow. Bloody.

He had put a slave's collar on an elvish Princess, the daughter of Wildling chieftains.

She stared blankly at the man in front of her. Tainan.

Her mouth twisted in a snarl when he came through the door.

"Are you ready to yield?" he purred.

"*Haik ilo biloi nu takimi,*" she spat. *I'd rather fuck a goat.* Since she hissed the words into his mind as well as through her busted and bruised mouth, her meaning was quite clear.

"Will you yield?" He turned and lifted a

whip, topped with little metal balls. "I've broken better mages than you. You were foolish, wandering around unshielded, alone. I could smell the stink of that man on you. Perhaps I should have waited before taking you, shouldn't have beaten you so cruelly. Ahh, but that's in the past. Will you yield?"

"Will you die a thousand and three painfully slow deaths?" she rasped, her throat achingly dry.

The whip lifted and flew, and her shrieks filled the room.

Tainan purred, "And now you are trapped."

"*Va takimi*," she muttered. She turned her head aside and withdrew into herself. She barely managed to close the door inside her mind by the time the second blow fell.

She took the first month of abuse with almost good humor. She wasn't De Asir, but she had trained with them. And the legendary assassins knew how to take abuse and torture, for years and months on end.

But Tainan was after something.

He'd guarded that intent well, so well, she almost didn't see it in time.

Time passed, time that left her weakened and malnourished, her reserves not just drained but completely emptied.

Then he made a casual mention of his true goal, when she was almost too weak to fight at all.

As she stared in stunned, sickened amazement, Tyriel realized just how utterly fucked she was.

It wasn't her body, or even her blood he wanted.

It wasn't her suffering or pain.

She could have taken the abuse, the rapes, and the starvation. She had the ability to retreat so far into herself, nothing he did to her body would even affect her.

But it wasn't just her own suffering he was after, though he reveled in her pain, drinking it and feeding from it, the way a demon could feed from blood.

It was her magic, her knowledge, her soul.

He was a soul-eater and he called up magics only those versed in such dark practices could call.

Tyriel fell back away from the black shadows that came to her, reaching for her, touching her, grabbing her. A scream fell from her lips, terrified and broken, and she slashed out with magic even though she had sworn not to. The iron on her body burned her with every bit of magic she used, and it blinded her, deafened her, sickened her, weakened her even more.

He would get her.

Eventually. Her fear would break her.

She fled inside herself and wrapped herself in the lights of the magic that made her what she was, the sorcery, the mage gift, letting the bright, burning lights warm her. She felt safe here—which was laughable. As long as these lights burned, he would torture her, pursue her, try to take her soul.

As long as they burned.
If the lights went out—
It was forbidden.

"Da..." she called out to him, but the stone around her neck that bound her to him had been taken and smashed. And some power blocked her from him. She was alone. Well, and truly, for the first time in her life, completely alone.

She knew what she must do. But was so terribly afraid of it.

Some of the Kin could not even manage what she was thinking. It was dangerous. It was deadly. It was beyond foolish.

But if the magic was not there...

She could not let him take her soul. She could not. He would have too much, too many secrets, knowledge of the elvin kin, the haunts and hiding places of the clans. No, he could not have those. And Irian. Ahh, the damage he could do with a blade like Asrel, with Irian bound to him?

To have Irian, Aryn must die.

No.

It was with a shuddering, frightened spirit that she reached out to the first light, and put it out.

Chapter 15

Aryn stood outside the gates of Ifteril and closed his eyes.

The last place to look. There was little else left to do after this.

"As though you intend to stop lookin'," Irian murmured. The enchanter stood at his side, his long hair in a thick braid that hung over his shoulder. He seemed so solid at times, it often surprised Aryn that no other seemed to notice him. *"We will find her. Something here will be leadin' us t' the elf, I know."*

Aryn's hands closed into tight fists.

"I never should have let her leave. You knew this would happen. Why didn't I listen?"

"We did not know she would drop off the face o' the earth, or that she would slip away in the wee hours. I tried, truly, to convince her t' stay."

"I bet," Aryn muttered sourly, sliding the long-dead warrior a bitter glance. The question was how?

The third in their group—or, second, as far as the wide world was concerned, was a Wildling named Kellen, from the clan of Tyriel's mother.

Kellen stood at Aryn's side and barely

blinked when the mercenary started talking seemingly to himself. Kellen had learned that the swordsman had odd ways, to put it mildly.

He had the odd habit of waking at night, riding off in silence to a town miles and miles away, where he'd find a young child cowering in fear from a monster, human or otherwise.

Several times Tyriel had come to the clan with an 'orphan' she'd come across. Now that Kellen had seen the swordsman return with an 'orphan' himself, and he knew the story behind the child, he had to wonder.

It had happened more than a dozen times since his cousin Tyriel had taken up with the swordsman.

It was the blade. Others in the clan speculated, but Kellen knew. His own da had been a mage. Kellen was not gifted, but he knew how the craft worked, had the sight of it, if not the powers. And his eyes itched every bloody time he looked at the sword.

When he looked toward Aryn, sometimes he thought he was damn well going insane. He would catch a sight, just behind his eyelids, like nothing he had ever seen, a towering, powerful Wildling with yards of wildly curling hair and a savage smile, and eyes so achingly sad it made Kellen's heart hurt.

And then it was gone.

Kellen glanced at Aryn now and asked, "To the inn?"

Passing a hand over his eyes, Aryn nodded. "The inn is really all we have to work with.

Tyriel was here but a few days. Irian had ways of keeping up with her. He knew when she had left us."

Kellen knew when the man's attention had left him again. Irian. Over the weeks since they'd started trying to track Tyriel, Aryn had finally spoken of Irian, the Soul trapped inside the sword Aryn carried.

With a sigh, Kellen brushed aside the itchy feeling it gave him and followed the tall swordsman to the town gates, boldly meeting the guard's eyes with a smirk as the guard studied the Wildling appraisingly.

Soon, they were off into the city.

And Aryn, Kellen could see, was arguing again, seemingly with himself. Again.

"Like a hole in our souls, she left. Do you admit it yet, swordsman? That she is yours?"

"I always cared, always wanted her." Aryn tossed the enchanter a snarl. "But why pledge my heart and soul to a woman who will still be young when I am no more than dust in the ground? Why wish that grief upon her? Do you think I didn't realize she cared? And could do more?"

"Your foolishness has cost you and her much. And my silence hasn't helped." Irian retreated back into himself, gone in less than a blink, a cold wind of grief blowing across Aryn's body as they came to the inn where they had last seen Tyriel all of twelve months past. A night he didn't remember, when Irian had swarmed up and taken over—what had happened?

Ah...his body remembered. His cock thickened and swelled, pressing against the lacings of his leather breeches, blood pulsing thick in his veins, the whispering echo of her scent flooding his nostrils.

An image assaulted him.

Her beaten starving body, mauled and scarred, her eyes so dim and lackluster.

No power on earth—his hands closed into fists and the blade at his back felt heavy.

No power on earth would stop him from finding the one who had done this.

Who are you? Where have you taken her?

Without his intent, the magic that had begun to seep into his very bones lashed out, stamping its mark into the words and when the thoughts left Aryn, his ever-growing magic followed.

An image slammed into his mind.

Blood-red hair, blood-red mouth, pale, pale skin, blood magic.

And...he had a *name*.

Tainan...

"Aryn?"

"Wait," Aryn whispered, his voice low and harsh. His lids lowered until only bare slits of his eyes showed and his breath came in harsh gasps as he remembered that night six years earlier.

Jaren, Tyriel and he, in the bowels of the city as they sought the man who wanted to sacrifice innocents to the Darkness Below.

Tainan.

His prey had a face.

* * * * *

Aryn woke in the silence of the night with a blade pressed to his throat.

Magic choked the room, the kind that sought to peel flesh from bone and boil the blood in your veins.

"I trusted you, human. Into your hands, I gave my princess, to love, and keep and protect. And my Lord Prince tells me she is gone, away from his power, his touch, even beyond his reach—*his* reach—one of the most powerful fae in all the land. For six long months I have searched for her." The low, almost silent whisper brought a dread fear into Aryn's belly but he threw it off and opened his eyes, staring into Jaren's face, all but lost to the shadows.

The elf moved away and threw a mage light into the air, staring at Aryn with glittering, angry eyes. "Six long months. Six months is nothing to the kin. Nothing unless you seek what is dear to your heart, as Tyriel is to me. I trusted her to you. And you did not keep her safe. For that I should kill you where you lay."

Aryn sat up slowly, staring at the elf as Irian came out of the darkness, wavering into view, solidifying and staring at the elf with cool eyes.

"And these past three months, I have searched for *you*, swordsman. I was led here and I have waited. Now you arrive," Jaren murmured as he drew his blade and ran one finger down the deadly edge, ignoring the enchanter.

Aryn felt the cold fear sliding through his belly as the assassin continued to stare at him with gleaming green eyes that glowed and shifted with a morass of colors and magic that swelled from within. There was a power there, like what he had sensed inside the half-elf, but it was more deadly, finer, focused—all of it focused on him.

"I know who has her. Are you here to fight it out with me, or here to help me save her, you long-eared son-of-a-bitch?" he asked in a low, harsh voice.

A flashing smile lit the elf's poetically beautiful face and Jaren threw back his head, his long, razor-straight hair falling down his back as his musical laughter filled the air.

"'Tis no wonder the Princess was so drawn. Not a bit of fear in you, though you're stupid to not have *some* fear. And so very unmortal do you act." Then he moved like a streak of lightning across the room.

Aryn fell back on the bed, rolled backward and landed on the balls of his feet, barely managing to draw his blade and lift it before Jaren was at his back. In such close quarters, a sword did little good. Unless it was enchanted. A long knife at his throat, Aryn breathed shallowly as Jaren whispered silkily, "Where is my lady Princess?"

"Go fuck yourself and the bloody steed that

brought you here, you magicked son-of-a-whore." Aryn didn't bother to reach for the hands that held him. Jaren was centuries old. He slashed his roughened palm down the blade as Irian stood watching it all with what looked like very amused eyes.

"So nice of you to help me here."

"Oh, it's not your death he wants. He's just bloody pissed. If he tries t' kill you, I'll stop him." Irian leaned back against the wall and crossed his arms over his broad chest, lifting a curious brow as Jaren continued to ignore what Aryn did with the blade. Was the elf truly so ignorant of what Aryn did?

Aryn mouthed the words silently and too late, Jaren felt the magic rustle through the air just before the air above Aryn's body grew fire hot. Aryn whirled away just as Jaren fell back silently, the front of his body scorched and smoking. Most men would have been screaming in pain, but the elf just stared appraisingly at the swordsman before lifting his reddened hands and studying the blackened, blistered flesh as it formed.

"What an interesting change," he mused.

"Tyriel is not your lady."

Jaren's eyes narrowed and a feline smile, predatory and sharp, settled on his face. "And pray tell, why not?"

Irian perked up with interest as Aryn lifted the blade and pointed it at the elf. "She is *mine.*"

Shiloh Walker

* * * * *

The firelight flickered across Aryn's face, casting half of it in shadow as he sat staring into the night. Irian had swarmed up from the recesses of his mind and forced his damnable will upon Aryn's body until Aryn sullenly agreed to stop for the night.

Tyriel's cousin Kellen had erupted into fury when Aryn said he wouldn't be traveling with them to rescue her, but he'd finally acquiesced after seeing the elvish steed. Aryn's mount Bel couldn't keep even half the pace, although the gelding was fast.

However, Kellen rode a plains pony when he rode anything at all and no plains pony could keep pace either warrior's beast.

He'd given both of them a scathing send-off, but promised to send word through the Wildling clans that they believed they'd found a line on Tyriel.

Bring her back to us or you'll face all the fury of the clans, Kellen had promised.

It hadn't been an empty threat.

They'd already encountered four Wildlings out on a 'roam' as they called it, each of them asking after Tyriel. Aryn knew only one of them.

Word had already spread. They'd been gone from Ifteril just three days.

Three days of solid, hard riding, Aryn brooded, and the blasted elf looked as rested, and as out for blood, when they stopped as when they started.

He lay on his bedroll, smoking a long, oddly scented pipe, stroking a crescent-shaped metallic stone of black at his neck as Aryn stared into the night.

The swordsman had no idea how closely the elf was watching him. And likely wouldn't care either.

He had sat for the longest time alone, undisturbed, aware of nothing but a sense of her...somewhere in the east. Closer and closer.

Now Irian was at his side, lowering himself to his haunches, his rough-hewn features puzzled, curious, almost too afraid to hope. His voice, when rarely he spoke in a voice for somebody other than Aryn alone to hear, had a deep, rippling quality, like a stone cast into a well.

"I sense something...Tyriel...but not her. I know not what." Irian glanced over as the elf rose to his feet in one smooth graceful movement, his muscled body gleaming in the firelight. "It sensed me. Doesn't know me. Mayhap you, brother mine. Come."

Aryn was already mounting Bel bareback.

Irian disappeared into the night, inside Aryn, guiding him to the source of what he had sensed.

When Aryn slid from his mount sometime later, what he saw pacing in the moonlight was the last thing he had ever expected.

The elvish stallion was taller, broader than Bel, with larger eyes that had the uncanny, unsettling ability of glowing. It resembled a horse, the way a tame house cat resembled a wild mountain lion some faerie minx had tamed.

But this elvish steed looked very unlike the mount Aryn had seen just months earlier. His neatly groomed coat had grown long and shabby, his eyes no longer had that 'settled' look in them. He looked vaguely lost as he turned considering eyes Aryn's way.

He looked...wild.

But he kept cocking his head at Aryn as the swordsman slid one leg over Bel's head and circled the clearing, his intelligent eyes trained on the swordsman's face, rapt and fascinated. Curious. Hungry.

And then Jaren charged in, lips peeled back from his teeth in a snarl as he launched himself in a low tumble at the elvish stallion that ended with him underneath the beast, a long wicked blade drawn and ready.

His own mount went nearly wild, pawing at the air, her screams filling the night.

Aryn kicked Jaren's wrist, hard enough, he hoped, to numb it and grabbed the elf's ankle, hauling him out from under the stallion.

"He betrayed his mistress," Jaren snarled, flipping to his feet, snarling at Aryn and whirling back to the stallion.

"He looks rather lost to me." Aryn turned back to the stallion, rubbing the beast's black face, his cheeks and neck with gentle hands, staring into the dazed, helpless eyes.

"Pretty mistress...good hands...she never came..."

The voice filled the air, echoing in their minds...*and* around them, clear as day.

Even Jaren stumbled back in shock from it.

Aryn recovered first, and brought the stallion's attention back to him. "Tyriel. She was coming to you that morning. She never came, did she?"

"The elvish mounts are fantastic creatures, but none can comprehend that well." Jaren moved again in Kilidare's direction. "'Tis like a guard dog. And he sorely failed at his job."

"Neverneverneverever."

Aryn ran his hand again down Kilidare's cheek and slid Jaren a look. "We go to find her. The lady. The pretty lady with the good hands, your mistress."

"Evil man, evil dark take...I scent...not see...bad taste. Bad taste—we know."

"Evil man?" Jaren asked, stopping in his tracks. "How do you know his scent?"

"Town, demon mark...all over her. His scent, all over. He take, I feel, then pretty mistress gone."

Jaren's face was blank, simply stunned.

Aryn smothered a smile as he continued to stroke Kilidare, soothing the bewildered stallion.

"We will find her," Aryn murmured soothingly as the great beast rested his head over the human's shoulder, a huge shudder wracking him.

Shiloh Walker
* * * * *

Tyriel knew the end was finally nearing.

Her heart was failing her and the thought brought her peace.

She lay wearily on the cold floor. It was cold in the dungeon, but she'd long grown used to that. If she were to feel warmth again...well, that might shock her weakening heart into stopping altogether. Not that she'd mind dying warm.

Not that she'd mind dying. At all.

"It won't be long now," she said to herself, her voice raspy from weeks of disuse.

Tainan might have finally forgotten her.

She hoped he had. She was tired of looking at him and remembering what life had been...before.

His guards still remembered her, but their cruelties were nothing like their master's. She could no longer block them out as easily, but her strength was so far gone from her, it took little for her to black out.

While she shuddered to think of what they did to her in those periods of darkness, she was grateful for that escape.

Soon, she wouldn't have to think of any of it.

Not ever again.

Soon, she'd fly free. Perhaps she'd even find her mother waiting for her. Perhaps she'd find peace.

Her heart did another skipping bump and

she smiled at the feel of her own heart dying.

It didn't hurt. She hadn't known if there would be pain or not. With her mixed blood, it was never easy to say which trait she'd inherit.

When it came to heart ailments, it seemed the elvish in her had won out again. Her heart's strength was merely...slipping away. Ever slowing beats and eventually she would drift into a sleep that could linger for days or weeks.

Without the treatments her people knew, she would be dead within a month. And mostly likely even those would not help. Human or elvish will made up for so much.

Tyriel had no will left. No desire left to live and suffer and fight.

There was a brush on the edges of her mind that felt oddly familiar as she drifted closer to sleep. The contact warmed her and almost stirred her to curiosity. But her exhaustion won out. Still, that presence warmed her as she slid into sleep.

For once, she didn't feel alone.

The crashing of doors, the burning smoke didn't faze her at all.

* * * * *

The low, sprawling house, so lavishly built, wasn't at all what Aryn expected.

When the songs were sung of heroes heroically rescuing the Princess, it was from a towering, craggy cliff, or a cave buried deep in a jungle.

But the steed had started to liven, and purpose had returned to his eyes. The wildness had slowly leeched out of the intelligent steed over the day and half since they'd found him but now, he truly resembled the beast Aryn remembered from years past.

And he knew why.

They'd found her.

Somewhere in that stately home, Tyriel lay trapped, beaten, alone, likely thinking she'd been abandoned.

We're coming, he thought, wishing he could send the thought winging to her.

This was where Kilidare had led them, where Aryn's heart and soul had been guiding him. They had stumbled through a thick, obscuring fog that tasted metallic, almost poisonous, burning and stinging Aryn's eyes.

"'Tis illusion," Jaren said quietly from atop his mount. His dark-green eyes shifted to a paler color as power rolled through them. One hand lifted and his fingers spread, flexed, and a mist of light formed, then dissipated. "It feels deadly, but it isn't. It's just a protective shield. It hides something."

The something had been this place, this house. After the light had dissipated from Jaren's hand, the fog surrounding them had started to lift. And as they moved, it lifted ever more until they moved into a circle of free air. By midday, it was all gone. And at nightfall, they came to the edge of a clearing in the woods and that low sprawling structure came into view.

In the light of the full moon, Jaren said, "I feel her, her strength wanes."

And the stallion near went mad, scenting her. Aryn could feel her, too.

The strategist in him would prefer a plan of sorts and he muttered just that out loud.

Jaren slid him a narrow look, his eyes gleaming like a cat's in the dark. "As would I, swordsman. But her time runs short. I did not leave my Princess with good words between us. She is young, too young, too good a woman to die in such a place as this. And I know this scent—'tis my fault she is in there. At the time, I did not believe he would come seeking her so quickly."

Aryn lifted a brow, quizzically.

"Didn't you wonder how I knew you were in the city?" Jaren's humorless laugh came, faded. "You are in the presence of one of the few psychic warriors known among the kin, swordsman."

Irian was oddly quiet.

The blade at Aryn's back was becoming heavier, the way it had in the early years, before Aryn had realized just what he held when he first took up the blade. *"Know you, friend, it grieves me that it led to this. If I had known she would come to any danger, any pain...never would I have risked her, never."*

As they crept closer, their presence muffled by the deft touch of Jaren's magic, Irian spoke somberly into Aryn's mind.

"It's not your fault, Irian. Tyriel has always done what Tyriel wants to do—and her actions shouldn't have put her at risk, but they did. That isn't your fault."

"Ahhh, but my wanting her so desperately clouded my thinking. And my fear, that clouded what little rational thought I had left."

Aryn slid the enchanter a wry glance as Irian walked through a tree without blinking an eye.

"You love her," Aryn said quietly. "Don't think I don't know it. Don't act like I'm not aware. The person who is to blame is Tainan. And Tainan alone. Not you. Not me, though I will kick my ass from now until the day I die. And certainly not Tyriel."

"Do not be so quick to acquit me, brother of my soul. There are things you cannot know about me. Things I haven't told a living soul in more millennia than even I can recall."

Aryn drew the blade at the door. Jaren took the back. Very few servants were here. Very few living souls. But many, many magicked traps and creatures. As Aryn drew the blade, he also called Irian, pulling the enchanter willingly inside himself, so that the two were one inside his skin.

Five humans. Including the most important one. Tainan Delre.

And the ever-weakening soul of a very battered Wildling elf.

Aryn launched himself at the door, words he didn't know he knew pouring from him. And not a drop of blood was spilled, not a grain of salt flung on the ground. The magic was well and firmly inside him, and in his rage, the accouterments so many enchanters needed were forgotten, no more than props to the power Aryn now wielded easily.

Irian smiled bitterly. His task was nearly complete. But at such a high cost.

Fire erupted the moment Aryn's body touched the door. At the same time, the very foundation of the building shook as Jaren's magic breached the barriers that surrounded and protected it. Under the onslaught, it buckled.

A berzerker, Aryn lifted his sword and cut through one guard, severing his torso from the waist up.

Aryn's eyes gleamed red with rage as he scented Tyriel on the body of the huge man who came running at him, blade drawn. Aryn flung one hand up, slicing it along Asrel's edge for blood, smearing his blood on the face of the man who stopped, frozen in abject terror at the sight of the warrior standing before him with death and vengeance in his glowing blue eyes. The images continued to shift—from a tall, leanly-built blond man, with an almost inhuman beauty with eyes that burned bright with fury, sweeping down on them like an avenging angel, to a sinister-looking, towering warrior of a man with wildly curling black hair and rough-hewn features in barbaric garb, a wicked smile on his face, the very devil to prey upon your fears.

The guard screamed and screamed, as the man rubbed a smear of blood down his cheek, then impaled him on the tip of the sword, pushing it in slowly from his belly, downward.

"Why is it I smell her on you? All over you?" Aryn asked hoarsely, his rage tightening his throat. As the blade forged through his internal organs, it burned them, searing them, charring them. "My lady—you beat her, raped her and whipped her. If I could spare the time..." A growl ripped from his throat as he twisted the blade.

The blade scraped over the guard's internal sex organs, and then outward, and his screams locked in his throat.

"Die...slowly," and he jerked the blade forward, ripping bone, tissue, muscle, and the man's cock from his body.

In the hall, Aryn came face to face with Tainan.

Jaren had planned on taking this bastard.

But both Irian and Aryn had other plans.

Of course, Tyriel was more important, but if they happened upon him...

"Bury Asrel deep inside his black heart, my brother. Such a simple blow, and he will not expect a physical attack from an enchanter."

Irian formed. Larger than life, full of vengeance, rage, anger, his black hair whipping around his face, the ancient enchanter's voice rang out in a way it never had as he cursed the sorcerer in a tongue no longer spoken. His hand closed into a fist, then he slapped it against the stone wall behind him, setting the old stone manor house to shaking until even the foundation quivered.

Tainan paled as Irian's focus narrowed on him.

"You die today," Irian said, his voice still ringing with that booming echo. He flung his hand toward the thinner, trembling man and a streak of red sliced down Tainan's face.

Aryn lunged, snarling at Irian. "He's *mine*."

"Then kill him. She doesn't have time."

Aryn wanted to linger, wanted the sorcerer to suffer. But Tyriel's suffering mattered more.

So, he did just as Irian said, lunging full-on, but pausing to deliver an arm-numbing blow to Tainan's face, taking him to the ground and straddling him as the man went down. Aryn dropped his sword, normally a sin he'd never allow himself. But he needed to feel the man's blood on his hands as he died.

Drawing a dagger from the sheath in his boot, he pushed it into Tainan's chest. As the dagger pierced the man's heart, shock and denial pierced Tainan's dying eyes. "May the demon you enslaved find you in the afterlife, pig fucker."

Irian's translucent form appeared at Aryn's side and knelt. Tainan's body jerked as Irian touched his hand to the man's brow—sigils appeared as if branded into his flesh.

"He will now," Irian said. "Tyriel gave us his name. And now you are marked. Enjoy your suffering, worm. You earned it."

Tainan's weak scream ended as Aryn savagely twisted the dagger, shredding his evil heart.

As he rose, thick blood bubbled up through Tainan's mouth.

"Now, we must hurry," Irian said, resting a ghostly hand on Aryn's shoulder. "The magics may fall without him here to maintain them."

Chapter 16

Jaren lifted her broken body in his arms, his throat tightening.

Ah, sweet. I failed you, didn't I?

If he had kept his promise, his bond sooner, but he had thought he had time.

She might yet die with bitterness between them.

Their last words had been in anger and while she battled a demon, Jaren stood by with a woman-child in his arms. He'd just *watched*, too enraged, frustrated with her, with her arrogance, her insight...with the very things she'd been *right* about, the very situation that had brought them to where they'd been.

That she'd not needed his help did not matter.

It mattered that he had not offered. Even now, she bore the demon's silver mark on her breast, the insult of it a line down her torso and her normally strong, limber frame now thin to the point of frailty. That silver brand had gone gray and her thick black hair was brittle and dull.

Her heart was failing her.

If he'd sought out the sorcerer as soon as he'd delivered the mortal-fae to his lord in Averne, would he have found him? Could he have prevented all of this?

The guilt all but choked him and it would haunt him the rest of his very long life, not knowing the answer.

If she died...

"No," he whispered, the word nearly lost to the silent night.

As he carried Tyriel out into the clean-smelling night air, he rested his chin on her hair and clenched his jaw against the grief that rose up in his chest.

He'd think only of saving her, because thoughts in beings as strong as the fae had power.

He'd think of saving and doing the work needed to accomplish that—and that work must start now.

The metal at her waist, her wrists, her ankles weakened her. It would have killed Jaren, or another full-blood. If they could get those off, get her onto clean earth to buy them time...he felt a big warm nose nuzzling his arm.

"*My lady...help her...*" Kilidare's wild, too intelligent voice murmured into his mind, another thread of chaos in the whirlwind of his thoughts.

The house behind him was starting to fall into the earth. Aryn had destroyed Tainan. And much magic had been woven into that house. The entire demesne would fall now that its master was dead. Lifting tired eyes to the elvish stallion he said softly, "I will try. But I am no healer, Kilidare."

The stallion pawed the ground and tossed his great head.

"Kilidare help her. Kilidare heal."

Jaren stared at the elvish steed blankly.

"You."

Kilidare stamped a large, powerful foot. *"Kilidare."*

Within Jaren, understanding and hope began to burn. Without another word, he went to work.

He donned a pair of thin leather gloves and pulled a pair of lock picks from his belt before he went to work on the iron. Within moments, he tossed the damnable stuff to the side, away from Tyriel and himself, then spread out his cloak on the ground, the elvin-spun wool thin enough to let her soak in the earth's energy, but still a warm protection from the chill of the ground.

Carefully, the steed settled down and Jaren helped moved Tyriel into the cradle of Kilidare's warm, still overly shaggy hide.

Immediately, the pulse of healing magic filled the air.

"I'll be stuffed," he muttered, shock rippling through him. "You're an animus."

Kilidare gave Jaren a decidedly smug look. *"Kilidare heal."*

The animus—an animal spirit imbued with powerful protective instincts and select magical abilities...like *healing*—were rare in the world.

Humans often called them familiars and associated them with witches, but truly, an animus could choose anybody to be his or her master.

Kilidare had chosen Tyriel.

Eying the steed with new eyes, he said, "Her wounds go far deeper than what we can see with our eyes."

"Yes." Kilidare rubbed his head against Tyriel in what could only be described as devotion.

The clarity of the steed's speech, his intelligence made so much sense now.

Kneeling by the pair, he pulled a vial of vesna oil out and went to work on the angry red and blackened flesh that had formed under the metal bands.

"Kilidare heals body. Kilidare cannot heal hurts inside."

Jaren made the steed's forlorn eyes. "No. But we can love her."

* * * * *

That was how Aryn found them, Tyriel's battered body cupped in the curve of her protective stallion's body, his head arched impossibly around to nuzzle her belly and arm and face as magic and power crawled through the air.

He knew the feel and scent of it by now, but didn't quite trust his mind. "Irian, am I going mad or is the horse working magic?"

Irian chuckled as he shimmered into view. "Stranger things have happened. Kilidare is no more a mere horse than you are a mere human. You stopped being merely human within three o' four years of wieldin' an enchanted blade. Kilidare is an elvish steed, and may resemble a horse on the outside, but all similarity ends there. Heard tales, I have, of warrior-trained elvish steeds, who had no masters, who were their own master...but this surpasses even those tales."

Aryn moved his eyes back to Kilidare and slowly shook his head. *Healing horses? What is bloody next?*

Kilidare lifted his head and Aryn would swear the bloody creature *winked* at him.

"I've gone mad," he muttered. "Utterly mad."

Then, before the grass could begin to serenade them while the trees played harpsong, he knelt at Tyriel's side and cupped her cheek.

She didn't so much as stir.

There had been a time when he couldn't enter a room without her sensing his presence.

Now people strode around her while she slept like the dead, unaware and still.

Rage unlike anything he had ever known tore through him with jagged claws, side by side with grief, and relief.

She was alive.

She was battered and bruised and beaten and scarred.

She was alive.

A soft sigh escaped her.

Her lids lifted slowly and he saw the dullness there, the lack of realization before her lids drifted down again.

Alive, yes.

But she was also broken inside, so deeply, deeply broken.

* * * * *

As the hours trickled by, the bruised and blackened, burned flesh where the iron had bitten into her flesh faded, almost as if melting into her skin.

The steady pulse of healing magic continued, even as Kilidare fell into a light slumber.

At some point, Jaren's own steed went to lay by the other mount. The pulse of healing magic had grown...*quieter*, but after Lieva settled by Kilidare, it strengthened and steadied into the same rhythm as before.

She'd shared...*something* with the animus, Jaren knew. And now he wondered if he'd have re-evaluate his opinion of just what elvish steeds truly were—something he'd have to consider after talking to Kilidare—at length.

But that was a thought for later, when grief wasn't a cloud in the air and Tyriel didn't lay still and quiet, as motionless as a doll.

"She would be the only soul in all the High Kingdoms to bond with a fucking animus

Of Mischief & Magic

masquerading as an elvish steed," he muttered as they built up a camp for the night.

Aryn barely looked at him but Jaren wasn't talking to him. He wasn't talking to...anybody, really. He was trying to convince himself that the Tyriel *he* knew was still with them. Somewhere.

Kilidare flicked one ear and huffed out an annoyed breath, but otherwise paid him no attention.

The elvish stallion had appeared one day in the meadow where Tyriel rode one of the horses from her father's stables. While many of the fae rode steeds, not all succeeded in taming the equine creatures—once tamed and taken to mount, they were called elvish steeds. Before that, simply steeds. Those who had little reason to little their cities often didn't bother with the work involved because there was no guarantee they'd manage to find a steed, much less tame one to their hand.

Kilidare had sought out Tyriel, something unheard of.

"Did she bewitch you the way she's bewitched so many?" Jaren asked the steed.

Kilidare chuffed and Jaren smiled a bit because it almost sounded like the steed had laughed.

She had taken mortal wounds that would have killed even their kind and was up and riding around with a mischievous smile just days after taking to the sick bed.

Now, the odd, near insane look he had seen

in the stallion's eyes after they'd found him just the past day, even that made sense.

When an animus sought out another magic-welder, be it human or fae, it was because it sensed a bond-mate.

These two had bonded. Tyriel had been the stallion's focus and the two of them together had become something more than anybody realized.

And now, Kilidare sensed the thin, fragile threads that held Tyriel to life.

* * * * *

"I thought you said the bloody horse was going to heal her!"

Jaren narrowed his eyes as the swordsman stepped just a little closer and snarled into his face just a little louder.

"You push your luck, human," he said warningly.

"We are wasting our time. She needs healing—and we've already sat here all of yesterday and all of last night. Will we wait another day and night as well?" Aryn demanded, reaching out and grabbing Jaren's tunic. The soft, molded leather bunched under his hands and Aryn yanked him forward. "Remember your word to her. You swore to kill her if her hesitation cost another her life? If yours has cost Tyriel her life, I'll be holding you accountable."

"You," Jaren said dismissively. "You, a mere

human, will hold me accountable. I quiver with fear."

Aryn bared his teeth in a grim smile before he stepped back.

Jaren tightened his hand around the knife he'd drawn, refusing to show any surprise at the man's speed.

Aryn sensed it, though, and laughed. "No longer quite so human, if you listen to Irian. Even Tyriel mentioned that a time or two. Seems I'll never been wholly anything again. And a *mere human...*? I've never been just that."

"Mere? Perhaps not. But...still human. Very, very human." The assassin's blade flashed in the watery, thin light of late evening, the blade wickedly sharp as Jaren tossed it into the air, caught it without looking and tossed it again, eyes on Aryn in a way that said he was considering burying it in the swordsman's gut. "And if you continue to push me, I'll shove this blade so far up your arse, you'll puke it up with that swill you called a meal last night."

"No, you won't." Aryn's thin smile took on a sharp edge. "And we both know it."

"Do we?" Jaren cocked his head. "And why do we both know that?"

"Because you adore Tyriel—and you know she's in love with me." Aryn held out his hands, spread wide in front of him. "Fuck me if I know why, but you'll never do a thing to bring her more pain."

The simple certainty in Aryn's voice served very well to poke a hole in Jaren's agitated anger. "You're a prick, Aryn."

Then he sighed and looked away. "No. I won't kill you. At least not for annoying me."

He tucked away his blade and lifted his hands to his hair, combing the thick length into sections, then expertly starting to braid it. Eyes staring off into the distance, Jaren started to speak. "We spoke in anger the last time we were together—rather, *I* spoke in anger. Though our last parting was not a pleasant one, my Princess knows me well. Doubtless, she knows how foolish I feel. I would move the stars from the sky to save her, and she knows this. I'm doing what I know is the best option for her—for now—though the mounts move swiftly, it's a rough ride to Averne. I want to know she's strong enough to make that trip."

"You think she grows strong enough by lying in the forest with a *horse*?" Aryn snarled.

Kilidare made an indignant, very unhorselike noise in his throat, but didn't move from where he was, still curled around Tyriel.

Irian chose at that moment to whisper reprovingly to Aryn alone, "The Nameless One chooses odd bearers for His powers. Is it our place to judge those bearers?"

Jaren coolly said, "He has healed her ills before. I will take all chances, any chance to save her. However—"

A heartrending shriek tore through the air. Followed by the sound of weeping, gut-wrenching sobs that filled the air.

Tyriel had woken.

Aryn felt like he'd run for days, although he and Jaren had just been beyond the treeline, Tyriel still in their eyesight as they spoke.

He fell to his knees in front of her, lungs burning and eyes wet, as he stared at her bent and hunched frame, her arms wrapped around her knees as she rocked herself, sobs tearing out of her.

Kilidare stood to the side, shifting on his feet, head low, keening sadly in his throat. Her back—narrow, dirty, scarred—shook with the force of her sobs.

Aryn's nails bit into his skin.

He hadn't made Tainan pay nearly enough.

Can we fetch his dark soul from hell and do it again?

It was an absent mental question, but he'd grown used to the enchanter, a near constant mental companion, providing silent commentary even to those random thoughts.

But there was only silence in his mind.

As Aryn reached out a hand to brush Tyriel's hair back, he realized he was alone. Completely. Irian was not there at all.

"Tyriel."

Chapter 17

That soft, deep voice rolled over her skin like a caress, but it wasn't real.

Simply couldn't be.

"Tyriel, sweet, open your eyes and look at me," he whispered roughly as a callused, warm hand gently stroked the side of her arm before moving away.

She scuttled away from the touch. It was Tainan. Of course it was. It was *always* Tainan. Him or one of his monstrous guards.

"Love, he's gone. Dead. He cannot touch you ever again, I swear."

Gone? Dead?

She shook her head. It was too much. That voice was lying, sounding too much like the one she longed for, telling her things she had hoped and prayed for. It had to be a dream.

"You're not *here*," she whispered, her dry throat turning the words to a bare rasp.

"I am. Sweeting, open your eyes." The voice was firmer now and two large, warm hands worked their way into her hair. They didn't pull or yank, although there was a slow, inexorable force—nothing painful, but he didn't stop up he had her chin lifted.

Stubbornly, she closed her eyes. If she didn't look at this newest torment, it wouldn't hurt as much when it all ended.

Oh, *why* wouldn't death just take her?

"No!" he bit off, voice hardening. "You are *not* going to die and leave me, Tyriel. Do you hear me?"

Now his hands did tighten.

She flinched.

But instead of turning cruel, the man brought her against his chest. "Shhh...I'm sorry. I won't yell. I won't snap at you. I'm sorry. But you can't say things like that. You're breaking me, Tyriel."

Why did he have to sound so like Aryn?

"I *am* Aryn." He nuzzled her cheek. "Please...just look at me."

She didn't want to. But whatever magical compulsion Tainan had concocted this time, it was strong and she couldn't resist the urge any longer.

Lifting her head, she opened her eyes and felt herself pinned by a gaze of such impossible blue.

"No." Shaking her head, she squeezed her eyes closed again. "No. It's not you. It's illusion. You're not real."

"Oh, but I am, my lady," he murmured, his lips soft against her cheek as he pressed a gentle kiss there. "Touch me. You'll see. I'm quite real."

"Illusion."

"Then denounce me. Break the illusion," he said, stroking his hands down her arms, running the tips of his fingers over her lips, the arch of her brows, as though he couldn't stop touching her face. "Call up that wild magic of yours to break anything false that may lie here and we shall see what is real and what is illusion."

Call my magic, she thought.

It was then that the bitter laughter started.

And nothing he said could make her stop. But eventually the bitter laughter turned into tears and she curled against him and wept.

At some point, she realized he might just be real and although relief kissed her like a welcome balm, there was pain, too, because the staggering, faltering rhythm of her heart still haunted her.

How little time left, she thought. Aryn had come, as she'd hoped, and she had next to no time left at all.

She wouldn't tell him though.

Perhaps she'd explain some of it.

But not all.

Why trouble him when there was nothing he could do?

* * * * *

"The magic is gone."

Jaren stared at her sleeping figure and tried to come to grips with what Aryn had told him. Such an act would have surely driven most, if not all, of the Kin truly insane. Or just simply killed them. Magic was part of their makeup, part of what they were inside, like their skin color, their hair, their blood.

Tyriel had cut her magic out, extinguished the fire that fueled the magic that made up the cells of who she was. It had been a sheer act of desperation.

De Asir knew what to do against a soul eater. Tyriel did not. No lone elf did. They were wily and cruel bastards, soul eaters, but rarely seen. They never entered the High Kingdoms and no lone elves ever ventured out into the mortal kingdoms.

Tyriel, though...

Well, she had forged her own path, as she always had.

It was insanity, to carve out a crucial part of yourself, something that would result in pain and possibly madness, haunting you your entire life.

It was also one of the most sincere, truest acts of heroism he had ever stood witness to in all his long years.

Jaren's gut burned and his heart ached.

"If you let her see the pity in your eyes, do you really think that is going to help?" Aryn asked quietly as he moved past the assassin to collect his bedroll and place it by Tyriel's, keeping her next to the fire while he slept between her and the darkness at their backs. He arranged his bedroll and shucked his jerkin before turning to face the elf. "She will not want or need your pity."

"I cannot help that I pity her."

"Pity her all you wish. But she doesn't have

to see it all over your face." Aryn moved his eyes to where she lay sleeping, her sleep fitful, but deep, thanks to a restorative brew Jaren had concocted. Aryn had fed it to her, spoonful by spoonful, and now it was helping her rest and further heal by replacing the stores that had been drained dry during her captivity. It would take more than just one bowl of it—more like a vat, or several of them.

But it was a start.

"We need to do more than this—but is she strong enough to move?" Aryn didn't know enough about an elf's physiology to make this choice. If she was too weak, and they moved her, then she would die.

Jaren moved one broad shoulder absently, then rubbed his temple. "I think we must try. She cannot stay out here. Winter is coming. Normally, such a thing wouldn't be an issue to the fae. But her strength is gone. I say we ask the Healer." He nodded his head to the stallion that never strayed too far from the Wildling-elf's side.

The Healer, eh? With a curve of his lips, Aryn made his way to the stallion in silence, his booted feet making little noise over the grassy terrain. But Kilidare heard him all the same and turned dark, turbulent eyes his way.

"She sleeps. Too much. All the time."

That powerful, intelligent voice that boomed into his mind would never cease to amaze him. Aryn rested a hand on the powerful stallion's neck, stroking absently. Kilidare leaned into him, appreciating it even more when Aryn obligingly scratched as his ears. They both looked at Tyriel, worry heavy in their hearts.

"I know, Kilidare," Aryn said finally and it no longer seemed so strange to him that he spoke to what he still considered a very smart *horse*. "We need to take her back to Averne, to her father's people but we aren't sure if it's safe to move her. With winter coming, we can't linger here much longer but we don't know if she's strong enough to move yet. The elf suggests we ask the Healer." Aryn dipped his head in acknowledgment to Kilidare.

Kilidare's ears flicked forward, then he paced closer to his mistress, lowering his large, equine head until he could rub his velvety nose against Tyriel's cheek. *"Averne. Yes. Needs her people's Healer, her home. And you. Heart hurts for you."*

* * * * *

Morning came and they broke camp, ready to leave for Averne.

Kilidare insisted Aryn ride him, holding onto Tyriel.

He'd watched with some worry just moments earlier as Jaren placed a hand on the neck of Aryn's big gelding and murmured into Bel's ear. Bel had stood there, riveted, and oddly docile under the stranger's touch. Jaren had said he could 'show the horse the way' when Aryn had voiced concerns about what to do with his mount. Bel had been his a long time, and although he'd choose Tyriel over his horse, he didn't want to simply abandon the loyal beast.

Jaren had promised no such thing was necessary. *It will take him a bit longer. No horse can travel at the speeds our mounts can, but without you on his back, he can move faster. He'll find you, swordsman, have no doubt.*

He half-expected Tyriel to argue when she heard of Kilidare's suggestion, but she was apathetic and stood there looking lost in the clothes Jaren had given her to wear, the garments hanging from her too thin frame.

Aryn mounted and Jaren made a few quick adjustments to the saddle and stirrups, grumbling about shoddy human leatherwork before approaching Tyriel. She stiffened at first, then nodded and let him carry her to Aryn, her bare feet exposed to the cool morning air, toes curled in.

The sight struck Aryn as heartbreakingly vulnerable and he wanted to hold her close, swear that she'd never know another moment's harm or pain.

Instead, he forced a smile as he took her up onto the elvish steed and helped her settle into place in front of him.

Jaren fetched a pair of thick woolen socks for her bare feet and tugged them into place, apparently as bothered by the sight of her vulnerable, bare feet as Aryn.

Of Mischief & Magic

She sat still through it all, not relaxing until Jaren turned away and headed for Lieva, his own steed.

As Tyriel relaxed against him the faintest bit, Aryn realized he had a problem, one he hadn't considered.

Her soft, frail form would sway against his the entire journey. Her body was cupped in the cradle of his thighs, the scent of her hair flooding his head. Need twisted inside him and he mentally grasped for anything disgusting and revolting as he willed his body under control.

She didn't need this from his body right now. And even as he was thinking it, she felt his body's reaction, and stiffened.

Resting his hand on her hip, he lowered his mouth to her ear. "Shhh. You're safe—you know I would never hurt you, don't you?"

"Yes," she said weakly.

Jaren mounted his own steed and brought the mare around, coming up even with Tyriel and Aryn. "Are you ready, my Princess?"

She still sat rigidly but gave a short not.

"To Averne, then, where you will heal, become strong and healthy." Jaren bowed his head to his Princess. Then, with a soft command, had his elvish mount turning once more to take the lead. Jaren's steed was a tall, willowy mare, golden, with a white mane, and blue eyes, a sharp contrast to the fae male's dark hair and dark clothes.

Tyriel still sat so stiffly.

Aryn feared she'd break. Forcing himself to relax, he shifted in his saddle then took hold of the reins. "Are you comfortable?"

"I'm fine."

He closed his eyes at the stiff formality of her voice. The bright, laughing woman might be forever lost.

"Thank you."

The words were so soft, he almost didn't hear them.

He leaned closer, vaguely aware that Jaren had called for them to move and Kilidare had settled into a smooth, quick trot with no guidance from Aryn.

"Why are you thanking me?" he asked.

"Onward, Kilidare!" Jaren called out abruptly and whatever answer she might have offered was lost as the mount beneath Aryn lunged, taking off at a ground-eating pace.

Tyriel's hand shot out, clamping down onto Aryn's right thigh.

He clenched his jaw and told himself he'd burn in the fires of hell. Then he dipped his head so he could breathe in the soft scent of her hair.

Long moments passed with neither of them speaking.

But then Tyriel murmured his name, voice so quiet, he barely heard.

"You came for me."

Convulsively tightening the arm he'd wrapped around her waist, he turned his face into her hair. "Of course, I came for you."

There was nothing else said for a very long while.

She relaxed by minute degrees and he thought she might have fallen asleep.

But then she shifted and he had the impression she wanted to look at him. He tugged on the reins and Kilidare obligingly slowed. "Are you getting tired?" he asked.

She didn't answer for what felt like an age but finally, she gave a stiff nod. He lifted her and repositioned her, grabbing the blanket he'd secured for just this purpose, keeping it folded up and using it as an extra cushion. Then he pulled her snugly against him and wrapped his cloak around her.

Now she sat practically in his lap. "Alright, Kilidare. Go."

The steed lunged forward again. Jaren hadn't slowed, but it only took the stallion a handful of moments to catch the other man.

Tyriel was looking at him.

Aryn was acutely aware of it, but didn't react until she said his name.

"Yes?"

"How long?" she whispered, voice rough.

"How long have we searched for you?" he asked. Blowing out a rough breath, he said, "Consciously? For more than a month. But...in truth? I haven't stopped looking for you since you walked away. I retraced the routes we'd take, hoping to see you. I was on the outskirts of Bentyl Faire, more than a week late and told myself it was a job that took me there, but it was you and when I didn't see you, I told myself it didn't matter, but...still I looked."

Her gaze had fallen from his and stared at Kilidare's neck, her fingers tangled in his mane.

"Tyriel, I've gone mad without you. You'll never know just how mad. And when I discovered you were in danger, I was ready to tear the land and all its kingdoms apart to find you."

A fine shudder wracked her. But she didn't respond.

Aryn told himself she needed time, time to heal, time to recover. Just...time.

And when she shifted to cuddle into his chest, he told himself that maybe everything would be well.

As the day bled away into late afternoon, eventually giving way into evening, they slowed.

Jaren had traveled this region and had a spot in mind for camp, so Aryn only had to keep his senses alert for danger.

It left too much of his mind free to focus on Tyriel.

After they'd stopped to rest their mounts and let them feed while they took a quick meal for themselves, Tyriel had chosen to take her former position astride Kilidare, but she relaxed into Aryn's body more easily this time and one hand rested on his thigh, her finger drawing a pattern over and over on the worn leather of his breeches.

What is she thinking about? Aryn's thoughts were more to himself, but Irian's answer didn't really come as a surprise.

"Not one thing. She isn't thinking at all, about anything. She cannot think right now, not much."

Aryn hadn't really asked it with any desire for an answer, but now that he had one, he focused his attention on Irian. "*Is she talking to you?*"

"No. I've...tried, and there's no response from her. I feel her presence, brother, but that's it. Her thoughts move around me like water flowing around a large boulder in a stream." Irian sounded...weary. "And that's fine. You're what she needs. Just you being here, touching and holding her brings her comfort. That's a good thing."

Irian withdrew and didn't say another word the rest of the day.

Because of his words, though, Aryn withstood the torture of her hand on him, ignoring the ache in his cock.

He'd enjoy torments far less sweet than this if it would fill a need she had.

* * * * *

As Jaren moved into the woods to fetch more of the mushrooms and foliage needed for making her brew, Tyriel stood staring up at the star-studded sky with lost, lonesome eyes.

She was so awfully quiet, even for her. She knew they worried. She wished she cared enough to soothe their worries, but she didn't have the energy.

Things were broken inside her, and she wasn't quite certain how to handle it.

Two large warm hands landed on her shoulders from behind.

She jolted even as deep inside, she recognized him.

With a sigh, she leaned back against Aryn's hard, firm body. She felt him stiffen, and then relax, his arms coming around her to tug her close. His warmth seeped into her skin. Sadly, it didn't penetrate the aching knot of cold that lived deep within her.

Aryn nuzzled her neck, the simple sweetness bringing tears to her eyes.

She blinked them away.

"I was a fool, leaving the way I did. I felt a darkness waiting, had heard Irian's warning," she whispered softly. "I damn near died. Worse than that, I endangered my people, my mother's clans."

"Don't. You're not to blame for what that monster did."

"Aren't I?" She laughed and it echoed around them, a hollow brittle sound that made her cringe. "I knew something lurked in the shadows. I'd felt it. I'd been warned. I went anyway."

"*Nobody* made him attack you, Tyriel. He did it on his own."

She pushed at his hands. He resisted at first and panic fluttered in her chest. Before it could take flight, he released her and she moved away, hating how even those few steps exhausted her. Turning, she glared at him. "Nobody makes a lion attack, or a wolf. They do it because they are predators."

"Yes—and they attack to eat, to live, to survive. Tainan might have been a predator, but nobody forced him to summon demons, to call up the darkest of magic, to torture and beat." He hesitated, not saying the other humiliations that had been visited upon her.

But they both knew.

Her face flushed hotly red with the shame of it.

"It's *his* shame," Aryn said.

Maybe so, but she was the one who'd bear it. Her tears blinded her and she looked away.

Because she did, she didn't see him move to her. His hands caught her shoulders.

"Irian told me if I'd spoken true that last night, you'd stay. Had I done so, you wouldn't have left, so perhaps it's *my* fault all of this happened."

She flinched, "I don't want to talk about that, Aryn. You did enough. I'm out of that hell. I won't die there. It's enough."

"It's not." He pressed his lips to her temple, his breath stirring her hair. "Will you not look at me?"

She didn't respond.

"Then perhaps you'll listen." He caught one of her hands and guided it to his chest. "Perhaps you'll feel. Listen, feel...this heart, Tyriel? It beats for you, only you. It's been that way for years, for so long, I can't even remember when it started. I only know that its yours, as I am."

Wrenching away from him, she moved to the log close to the fire, then opted to keep walking until she had the fire between them.

"Why?" she demanded, her voice hoarse. After months of disuse, it was a chore to simply talk, but she forced the words out. "Why are you telling me this? You made it quite clear a year ago that while you might enjoy fucking me, you didn't want to get tangled up with an elf. So what's this you say now? Am I so pitiful and weak that you feel a need to throw me this bone? Well, fuck you, Aryn. You can shove your pity and soulful claims about your heart right up your arse."

"Tyriel—"

Adrenaline burst through her, giving her strength. She grabbed a rock from the ground and threw it at him.

He dodged it, but held himself warily.

"No!" She glared at him through the tears she tried to hard not to shed. "You didn't want me when I was strong and healthy and powerful. Now that I'm broken and weak and dying...well, I don't want *you*!"

Aryn's face drained of blood. "You..."

Guilt wrapped a fist around her heart and squeezed.

He likely hadn't known.

Cruel, maybe, telling him like that. He did care for her; she knew that. He'd only been trying to offer kindness, even if the pity was like acid on the brutalized remains of her heart.

Drained, she looked away.

"Yes," she said hollowly. "I'm dying, Aryn. My heart fails." She stepped over the log and sank down on it, her limbs stiff and weak, alien to her. "We'll soon be in Eivisia. My father's people will care for me. It's possible one of the healers can fix the damage. Kilidare is marvelous, but animus magic can only do so much when once the heart becomes too compromised. But I have little hope they'll be able to undo the damage. I've likely seen my last summer, my last autumn."

Her eyes moved to the fading golds and oranges of the sunset. "Soon, it will be my last sunset."

"No."

She jerked at the viciousness of his voice. She'd only ever heard Aryn sound like that when facing a particularly vile foe, usually right before he cut them down.

He came toward her, leaping over the fire rather than circling it and knelt in front of her, shoving his hands into her hair.

"*No*," he said again, the blue of his eyes turbulent. "I'm not letting you *die*."

"Aryn..." The stark pain in his eyes pierced

her anger and she realized it was possible that he did feel something more for her than friendship. She didn't even have the strength to feel bitterness, though. Just sadness. She touched his cheek, thinking back to the woman she'd been before Tainan destroyed her. "It's not up to you."

"Are you giving *up*?"

"Acceptance isn't giving up." Her lashes fell, as if the weight of them wearied her. "I have no strength left in me, Aryn. And I...don't care enough to change that. I'm too broken. Everything in me...it's riddled with cracks and all the jagged edges jab into me."

"I'll fill the cracks. I'll fix the edges." His voice broke. "Just...you can't leave me."

"Don't." The whisper was ragged. "Don't ask me to fight. I'm just so very tired."

When he said nothing, she forced herself to look at him. Once more, shame and misery pooled in her, for the look in his eyes was awful, as if he was the one dying inside.

Hollowness filled her and she looked away.

Better, she thought, maybe, if I'd died in that hole. Then I wouldn't add this burden to his guilt.

He settled beside her finally, saying nothing, strong thighs straddled the fallen timber. When he pulled her against him, she sank into his heat with abandon, taking the strength and comfort he offered so freely.

"Alright, love. I won't ask. Just...let me hold you while you rest." His voice cracked once and was a husky rasp in her ear.

Yes, she'd like it if he held her.

Sleep came soon after and she embraced it, grateful for the oblivion that awaited.

She was still sleeping when Jaren returned to find them, the camp not even half ready for the night and Aryn staring at the fire with dull eyes.

The fae's irritation fell away fast as he approached the human. Just beyond Aryn, the spectral figure of the enchanter bound to the mercenary paced. Jaren knew of Irian, though what he knew could barely fill a thimble. They were bonded and Irian's powerful magic had left a stamp on the human, making him something far more than he'd once been. Be he didn't truly...*understand* what Irian was. Vengeful spirit, an avatar, something else all together, he didn't know.

There was power in the enchanter though, power that had transcended life, then death, and that power crackled in the air, potent with hot anger and raw anguish.

It was the enchanter who first took notice of Jaren and he turned on the fae with a fury that roused something in the elf he'd rarely felt in all his nine centuries.

Fear.

He schooled his voice not to reveal anything as Irian bore down on him, though, offering a faint smile as he asked, "Hello, enchanter. Here to join us for the evening repast?"

The spectral form blurred and reformed, right in front of Jaren, too fast for even an elf's quick reflexes, and he had no time to deflect the attack before Irian grabbed him around the throat with a very *solid* hand and hefted him into the air.

"*My brother tells me that Tyriel is dying. What madness is this?*" Irian demanded, his voice a booming echo that carried off in the forest around them.

Jaren grabbed the enchanter's wrist—or tried. His hands went right through. Before he could try anything else, his mind processed what Irian had said and shock him going lax.

Irian dropped him, disgust in the darkness of his eyes. "Are we to believe you didn't know? You can tell her mount heals her body, yet you know nothing about her heart failing?"

"I know about her heart." Jaren rubbed his throat, his anger already fading as he shifted his attention to Tyriel and Aryn. Grief flooded him, washing away the anger, his ire, everything, until the urge to weep overwhelmed him. "She went malnourished, bound by iron, for months. The iron poisoned her while the starvation drained her. And..." He stopped and sighed, looking at the leather pouch he still held, stuffed full with foraged roots and mushrooms to brew yet another tonic for her. One that might well be pointless. "And none of that did nowhere near as much damage as what she did to herself when she ripped her magic out."

Now both Irian and Aryn pinned him with diamond-hard glares.

"*Explain*," Irian demanded.

"We *are* magic, enchanter," Jaren said, jabbing a thumb at his chest. "Magic is embedded in our very cells. The only reason Tyriel still lives is because she's half-fae. But even the Wildling blood in her...the Wildling race has more magic-users than any other human race in this world. Tyriel's mother was an earth witch. Her grandfather? A seer. Nearly everyone in her matriarchal line was gifted. We know. We looked. So even the Wildling blood that's keeping her alive? She's missing something crucial there. It's why she's so unique among us. Her magic works in ways the fae have never seen and it's the Wildling blood that makes it so. You take away her magic...in essence, you take away *her*."

Jaren staggered then, under a scream that somehow pierced the psychic plain.

He clamped his hands over his ears in reflex, although it did no good.

Irian gave him a skeptical look before turning to the human he'd bonded with and speaking.

Jaren could hear nothing, his entire body shuddering as that scream echoed on and on.

Then...nothing.

Head ringing from the backlash, he dragged in air. It didn't do much to ease his vicious headache, but that would pass in time.

"Elf?"

Irian's surly growl had him looking away from Aryn's rigid back and he met the enchanter's gaze, saw the plea there.

"I'm sorry," he said quietly and he felt those words in the very pit of his soul. "All we can do is get her to Averne, and to her father. The healers there may yet be able to help."

Irian's visage soured even further, then broad shoulders sagged. "She is weary, she tells Aryn. Too weary and inside she is riddled with cracks and broken edges. And she tells him not to ask her to fight. How do we handle that?"

Jaren looked back at Aryn, understanding how the man's pain had somehow pierced the psychic plain as it had moment ago.

"We find a way to fight for her. Or..." He felt his own heart crack and knew if she died, there would forever be broken edges inside him, for failing her. "We let her go, so she can find peace."

Irian's eyes blazed with denial and yards away, though he shouldn't have been able to hear, Aryn's shoulders jerked.

* * * * *

As the others slept, Irian drifted.

He let memories pull him back, centuries and centuries, until he was once more staring into dark sloe-eyes as he thrust deep within a woman's body, loving the hot, wet clasp of her around his cock, but loving her smile, her laughter, *her* even more.

Her name had been Fael. They'd grown up together. He had loved her with all his heart and soul.

He'd never told her, though. They had both been Jiupsu but while he'd been born to a family whose line had been rich with magic, Fael had been mortal through and through.

Like his stubborn brother-in-soul, Aryn, Irian, too, had refused to bind himself to a woman. But while aryn had refused because he'd sensed how Tyriel's power would keep her alive far after he had left the earth, Irian had refused to give his heart to a woman he'd felt was less than his equal.

She would have died and Irian had been the one who would linger in his prime for decades after she faded, perhaps even for a century or two before his strength started to wane.

She'd live a mortal's normal lifespan and then be gone from the world. The thought of it had stricken him his very soul and he never told her of his love.

When she offered him her heart, he brushed away her love, offering *suerta* instead of a binding. They'd have a year together, he'd told her and then he'd give her a bridal package and help her secure a husband.

She'd smiled but refused.

A season after he turned her away, she'd died while traveling to accept the marriage offer of another warrior who lived on the far side of Jiupsu lands, several weeks travel from their home clan...where he'd likely never seen her again.

He'd been both relieved and enraged when he'd heard the news she'd left.

But only a day after they'd set off, one of the escort guards had sent his hawk back to the clan's heart, clutching a red sash, a signal all recognized.

They were under attack.

The raiders had been cunning and sly, killing the guards from afar, planning to take the four would-be brides outland to barter off. But they'd been ignorant of the Jiupsu as many were, thinking only the men could weld magic. One of the women had been a firestarter and the other caused the earth to shudder and shake.

They held their attackers off for a time.

But they were only four and even trained with weapons as most Jiupsu were, they were young. One of the raiders took Mele, the firestarter, out. Then it was a matter of overwhelming the last three women.

By the time Irian found her, her spirit had been broken, her body bruised, torn and bleeding inside, death slowly laying its hold over her.

He had robbed them of decades together and he hadn't realized it until they were left with mere moments, her spirit was drifting further and further away.

But she'd still smiled up at him as he lifted her gently into his arms.

"My warrior. My Irian. Did you fight well?"

"Fael, I'm sorry."

"Shh, you did not do this to me." A hoarse cough racked her, blood flecking her lips. "The men who did...are they gone?"

"Even now they are being run to the ground." If any escaped the plains, Irian would track them down, one by one, and feed them their own livers before he ended their lives. "None will live long enough to dare harm another woman ever again."

"Then it is good. And I get to see you again. One more time. I love you, my warrior."

It shattered him, all over again. Why couldn't she be bitter, rage at him? But not his sweet, loving Fael.

"I'm so sorry, beloved." Tears fell down his face. "I love you, my lovely lady, beautiful, strong woman."

"My handsome warrior, I love you as well. I have always loved you and always will. We will meet again. Our souls are one, they belong together. I will..." But the final words never came. Her eyes went dark and she was gone.

And then he was on the cliff, as a massive fire raged higher and higher.

A season had passed, one season as he made sure not one raider had survived the attack that had stolen her from him.

He'd shed so much blood, it turned the earth into a viscous clay.

And not all of the blood he'd shed had come from those guilty of any crime.

It wasn't until the heat of his rage passed that he'd come face to face with what he'd done. He'd slaughtered those who hadn't deserve it, those who had only been guilty of knowing the men who had gone on the raiding parties.

To know a monster wasn't a crime. Many of the people in the raider's villages had been victims themselves.

But that hadn't stopped him, had it?

He'd slaughtered his way through one body after another until he found answers and now that all the men were dead, he found he could no longer sleep without the blood on his hands binding him as if shackling him to the earth.

Screams woke him in the night and although he'd give anything to turn back time and undo some of his actions, he could not.

He'd planned to end his sorry existence once he'd found vengeance. But he couldn't. His guilt, the choices he'd made, he couldn't leave this world until the scales were balanced and it would take more than just his lifetime to make amends for the wrongs he'd done while chasing vengeance.

Asrel was primed for the ritual, the hilt wedged between two huge rocks, strong enough to take his weight.

Until the wrongs are righted... He lifted his eyes skyward, searching for the star that must hold Fael's soul.

Our souls cannot be together, my love. My pride, my fear, it cost you your life. Then, in my rage, I took innocent lives. My actions will forever be a barrier between us, but I can't leave this world without trying to balance the scales.

Be at peace, my love.

He'd hoped she *would* find peace. He would never know it. He didn't deserve it.

Such a powerful enchantment, he'd never known its equal.

It had taken him well into the evening hours to make the preparations.

The circle of salt was as thick in width as his thigh, and the diameter was easily the span of a lodge tent. He slashed his wrist deeply with a spelled knife, one that would keep his own enchanted body from healing itself as he paced the blood circle thrice.

"Until the wrongs are righted, inside the sword I dwell." He said the words three times as he made the circles.

Then, inside the circle of salt and blood, he rammed his body home on the blade.

As his body died, his soul was trapped inside the sword.

His final fleeting thought as the ties to his mortal coil fell away were about Fael. He'd missed out on a lifetime with her. How could he have been so foolish?

He drifted on, but this time to a place he had

not traversed before. And to a face he had not seen in all the millennia that he traveled the earth—not since that night had he seen her outside of his memories.

"Fael..." he whispered hoarsely.

"Irian." She lifted a hand. "Come...sit. It's been ages since we shared a fire at night."

Confused, he looked around and found they were in a lodge tent, one that bore a striking resemblance to the one he'd called home...eons ago.

Drawn to her, he crossed the thickly woven mat until he could kneel in front of her.

"So sad," she whispered, studying him. Her husky, warm voice stroked over him like a satin caress and her inky-black curls fell over his body as she leaned down to kiss his stunned face. "You have become so sad. Love, why must you torment yourself? Have you not chained yourself to your own guilt long enough?"

"Fael? Are you really here?"

She smiled and lifted his hands to her face. "I am really here, love. Lover. My heart. This is madness, you know. Clinging to this guilt. Can you not let it go? Isn't it time you released yourself from these shackles and came to me?"

"I..." Swallowing, he shook his head. "I cannot. I made an oath. I'm bound."

"Bound to your guilt, lover mine." She brushed his hair back, the gesture achingly familiar even after all this time. "So many years you have walked this earth, buried inside a metal body, carrying out vengeance for those who cannot do it themselves, with your broken heart and your aching loneliness. You made mistakes in your grief. But it's time you let them go."

"No. What I did...the lives I took, those are more than *mistakes*." The warmth of her hands was a soothing balm on the ragged, open wound of his still grieving soul. He didn't deserve her touch, or her comfort. But when he tried to pull away, she stopped him.

Her soft hands had become like velvet braces and he couldn't break free. But, he didn't try very hard.

"You're right. You did horrible things," Fael said, her thumbs rubbing the backs of his hands. "And you've spent thousands of years in limbo, trapped in that sword, going from one master to another as you tried to make amends. You've done *enough*."

"It will never be enough." He shook his head, staring past her while memories flooded him. "You left because I refused you. I threw your love away and you left. You never would have been out there if it wasn't for me," he said, rage blinding him.

"Untrue," she said quietly. "I would have gone as escort and bride witness to Mele. She'd asked months earlier and I'd agreed. She was my cousin and dearest friend." Her eyes softened even more as she stroked his cheek. "Because I was there, she didn't die alone. Because I was there, neither did the others. It's...a small comfort, but a comfort nonetheless. And you came for me, as I knew you would. So I wasn't alone in the end, either. Again, my warrior...let this guilt go. My death isn't on *your* hands. And the death of the innocents...you gave up thousands of years helping others find vengeance, protecting the lost. Your scales are balanced. More than balanced."

All around them a gentle silvery light glowed and pulsed, and a soft wind played with their hair.

"'I cannot change the enchantment," Irian said, the weight inside him so heavy. But it was...different now. Was she speaking truth? *Was* he perhaps guilty of less than he believed? *No.* "The enchantment was spoken and cast. It must be fulfilled. The wrongs must righted, the balance found, Fael."

Her lips, soft, warm, sweet as celatier wine, covered his and Irian groaned roughly, burying his hands in her hair and crushing her tightly to him.

But she broke the kiss and pushed him back when he tried to bring her mouth back to his.

"Your own guilt has affected the scales." She shook her head. "If you'd just surrender that guilt and let it go, we could be together." She touched his cheek. "Let it go. And come to me. Find me. Please, my warrior. Come to me. I long for you..."

* * * * *

Irian was jerked into awareness.

It was morning, the sky still gray in the pre-dawn light.

Around him, the others slept.

"Come to me...find me. I long for you."

Fael. Sweet Fael. Ahh, so long. Is it possible? Was it possible that after this was all done, he could be with her?

Slipping out of the metal casing of the sword, he prowled around the camp before coming to a stop near the swordsman and the lovely Wildling-fae.

Like Fael, Tyriel had captured a piece of his heart without trying.

Unlike Fael, she wasn't for him, never would be, never had been.

He settled on the ground, keeping his presence concealed should anybody waken as he pondered the sleeping woman.

"We find a way to fight for her. Or...we let her go, so she can find peace."

Jaren's words echoed in him, a burr in his brain he couldn't dislodge.

Fight for her. Irian considered that. Peace was something he had no experience with, although he longed for it.

But fighting? Well, that he understood.

Tyriel was drained, her body empty of the resources and magic she needed to survive.

Irian's mind began to race. He could do nothing about her depleted resources. But the magic...well. Enchanters collected magic, hoarding it throughout their lives, in objects or charms, sometimes within themselves. A very few could even pierce the veil and step into the ether plane, where magic was rampant and wild.

Irian had been able to do it by his third decade, the summer before he lost Fael, crossing into that ethereal space between life and death, dreams and waking. He'd lingered for the span of an evening without suffering ill effects.

Over the centuries since, he'd sometimes retreated there until he had to emerge or risk forgetting everything and becoming a creature of magic entirely — forgetting *everything* ... including Fael.

In that plane, he'd created a cask, storing his own magic, since there was no way to carry it in a physical body he no longer possessed.

He could be a conduit, but nothing else. Often, it had seemed a thankless task, because no human could ever hold such raw magic and all his bearers had been mortals.

Now, though, as a plan began to form, his eyes studied her pale face.

Too much raw magic for a mortal.

But what about a Wildling-fae?

Chapter 18

Aryn was exhausted.

Even the elvish steeds with their seemingly endless stores of reserves seemed to be dragging after nearly five days of hard riding. The past night, after a quick meal and break only long enough for the steeds to rest, they'd continued on, straight through the night, because Jaren said he sensed a storm on the horizon.

Tyriel had fallen asleep almost the moment Jaren had handed her up to Aryn and she hadn't woken even when they stopped for a quick repast in the morning, the change from dawn to day only apparent by the lightening of the clouds, for no sun penetrated that heavy blanket.

It had grown colder, too, and Tyriel shivered. He'd never known her to be cold and Jaren now rode his mount bareback, wearing only his leathers, leaving his saddle behind at their last stop so he could give Aryn both his saddle blanket and his cloak in hopes of helping Tyriel find warmth.

Aryn knew a few small enchantments that would work to warm or weatherproof a temporary lodge—such little magics had been useful enough over the past year. Tyriel used to be the one to lay protective, warming spells over their tents in wintry weather and he'd once teased her about it. She'd loftily informed him that he was welcome to sleep in the cold and rough it all he liked.

He didn't know anything that might work to help warm a *person*, though.

"Irian?"

There was no answer from the enchanter, just as their hadn't been one in the past two days.

Swearing under his breath, he started to pull back on Kilidare's reins, but the steed tossed his head.

"*Faster*," the steed demanded. "*We race.*"

Aryn scowled and looked up.

That was when he realized they'd pushed through the heavy forest growth of Appan Wood, the final barrier between them and the outer mountains guarding the High Kingdoms. Those white-capped peaks rose tall and majestic in the air before dipping low to give way to deep, mysterious valleys.

Aryn drew in a slow breath, his skin already prickling from the proximity to what was rumored to be a land where magic was embedded in the earth, down to the very bedrock.

The hair on the back of his neck rose and under his skin, he itched.

Wards, he realized. Powerful, *powerful* wards guarded that kingdom, so strong, he felt them even though they were still some distance from the border.

The screech of a predatory bird echoed around them and Aryn looked up.

Kilidare surprised him by coming to a smooth stop, tossing his head back and whickering, as if greeting the hawk when the bird dipped a wing at them.

"Scouts," Jaren said at Irian's puzzled look. "They know we're coming. Let's not keep them waiting."

The itching under Aryn's skin grew progressively worse, but he ignored it stoically, focused on the mountains and his own desperate hope that they can find help for Tyriel there.

"No! You didn't want me when I was strong and healthy and powerful. Now that I'm broken and weak and dying...well, I don't want you!"

Her words haunted him. At night, as he lay as close to her as he dared, he lay awake, staring at her face and committing every line of it to memory.

He'd been such a fool.

Tyriel stirred in his arms and he looked down just as her lashes lifted. For once, she had a faint smile and her voice, though weak, was warm as she murmured, "I'm home."

Then her gaze swept to his.

He dredged up a smile for her.

Hers faded almost as immediately so he didn't think his effort was very convincing.

"What's wrong?"

What was wrong? Aryn didn't think there

was enough daylight left to list all that was wrong in his world. He struggled to find a believable excuse that wouldn't add to the weight her now frail shoulders carried.

He came up short.

There was nothing he could say, or offer, that would sound believable, and he didn't want to lie. His lies and refusal to admit the truth was part of the reason she'd left to begin with.

Some part of him stood braced, ready for Irian's castigation but it never came and his frown deepened, turning his focus inward.

"Irian?" he murmured.

"What's wrong?" Tyriel asked a second time.

Shaking his head, he met her gaze. At least now he had an honest answer. "I'm not sure," he said quietly. "But I can't find him. He's not..." He reached for the right way to explain the bond he shared with the enchanter. "*There*."

Tyriel's brow furrowed, confusion sparking in eyes that had gone dull. For a brief moment, she almost looked like herself.

But then her lashes dropped and she turned her face into his chest. "Probably up to no good, then. You know how he is." She sighed, her words growing thicker as sleep once more chased her. "I'm glad, you know. That you still have your bond with him. I..."

She lapsed into silence as sleep overtook her once more.

A howling wind came whipping down from the mountains in the next moment and Jaren brought his mount around, lifting a hand. "We should wait a moment," the elf said, voice grim.

In that moment, the mountains began to tremble and overhead, the skies darkened while the wind grew ever stronger, until Aryn's hair was torn from its queue and all but blinded him. and the wind howled furiously through the trees.

Squinting a look up at a sky that had gone from clear and blue to a leaden gray with thunderheads piling up over them, Aryn shouted, "What the hell is this?"

The wind stole the words from him the moment he spoke, but Jaren was close enough to hear nonetheless.

He brought his mount closer and leaned closer to Aryn before he spoke. "My lord Prince has sensed something terribly amiss with his daughter. It's shaken him, and his control. Give it a moment. He'll rein it under control."

Aryn balked, not believing what he'd just heard.

The sky opened up and lightning struck down mere yards away, cleaving a massive boulder in half.

Both Jaren's mount and Kilidare sidestepped, tossing their heads in agitation, but neither panicked.

"It's not safe out..." Aryn stopped mid-sentence as the winds went silent. They didn't fade. In the span between one blink and the next, the winds just *stopped*. The clouds overhead melted away and the brilliant blue returned.

If it wasn't for the smoke rising from the cleaved boulder, it would be like the past few moments had never existed.

"Here," Aryn finished, so stunned, he couldn't think straight.

"Let us carry on," Jaren said. "My lord will not cease worrying until he sees her."

Looking down at the precious burden he carried, Aryn said, "I don't think seeing her will allay his fears, Jaren."

"No. It won't. If you think what happened now was bad..." Jaren's face went grim and he shook his head. "There may well be an earthquake once Lord Lorne sees his beloved daughter."

* * * * *

Aryn hadn't ever spent much time considering Tyriel's fae relatives, her home in the High Kingdoms, or what it was like in Averne, where she'd lived for the first half of her life.

Even if he had, anything he imagined would have fallen short. He knew that within moment of riding into the village of Averne, the heart of kingdom where Tyriel's father, Prince Lorne, had lived for nearly two millennia.

The word *town* didn't seem adequate to

describe the oddly elegant sprawl of courtly homes and charming shops.

The hair on the back of his neck stood on end as he followed Jaren down the main road. It was as quiet as a tomb, unlike any town or village or city he'd ever seen. It looked like the entire population had come out to see them on their journey to the castle where it perched on a slight incline at the town center, its walls a pale ivory that gleamed in the sun.

Nobody spoke or even made a sound, not even the odd youngling he saw here in there, a toddler holding his father's hand, or the babe likely still feeding at his mother's breast he was so small. All of them, even the few animals they passed, stared at Jaren, then Aryn—no. Not Aryn.

Their gazes were locked on the woman he carried.

Their prince's daughter.

The castle gates were thrown open wide to receive them. As they passed by, guards in armor of a metal polished to a high shine bowed their heads and crossed their left arms over their breast in a sign of respect.

The salute was echoed by everyone they passed until they came to the wide stairs case that led to the castle doors.

At the top, a woman waited, alone, golden hair twisted into elegant spirals and twists, a gleaming coronet at her brow.

Jaren dismounted and came to Aryn, arms lifting to take Tyriel.

Once Aryn was off Kilidare's back, he took Tyriel back into his arms. He waited for Jaren to readjust the blankets and cloak that kept her warm, eyes still on the woman watching them.

"Who is she?" he asked quietly.

Jaren didn't bother looking. "My Lady Alys, Consort to Prince Lorne."

"His wife?" Aryn finally looked at Jaren.

The fae shook his head. "No. She's his consort and sits beside him at the High Counsel, helps with matters concerning the kingdom. But he only ever married once—Tyriel's mother."

Aryn wasn't sure what the difference was, but he didn't care enough to ask.

"Why isn't he out here?"

Jaren gave him a narrow look. "He's likely contained himself in a controlled environment for now." Lifting a brow, he added, "Earthquakes."

Aryn turned his gaze once more to the lovely woman waiting for them, her expression poised, save for the way she clasped her hands at her waist, her fingers so tight, her knuckles pressed white against skin a warm, golden shade of honey brown.

Tyriel stirred once more as they passed into the castle and although she smiled at her father's consort as Alys led them inside, she said nothing.

"Prince Lorne awaits in the iron chamber," Alys said as she led them past the grand hall and down a long, narrow passage.

Aryn shot Jaren a puzzled look, but the fae warrior had his gaze fixed on the other woman.

They came to a stop outside a heavy wooden, decorated with a lattice work of thin iron strips. It was an elegant piece of art, but Aryn knew that iron was deadly to the fae.

Tyriel pushed against his chest. "Put me down," she said.

He tightened his arms.

"I'll greet my father on my own two feet," she said, her voice as hard as the iron decorating the door.

Setting his jaw, Aryn carefully eased her to the ground, the cloaks and blankets spilling around her.

Jaren quickly gathered them up and a servant emerged from seemingly nowhere to collect them.

"If you even look unsteady, I'm picking you up again," Aryn said.

Tyriel simply glanced at him. "Let's enter. Neither Alys nor Jaren can't tolerate the press of cold iron, so the longer we tarry, the longer they must wait out here alone."

Aryn bite back a pithy response about how every other soul could get stuffed for all he cared. Instead he offered his arm and was relieved when she took it. Then, reaching for the latch, he opened the heavy door and stepped inside.

White silk draped the walls, swathes of it. Yet Aryn sensed the feel of iron beneath the silk, and the weight of spells—very old, very complex magic—that lay inside those walls. He felt the same under his feet and over his head and wondered at the insanity that lay behind constructing such a room.

But then he looked at the man standing before…well, a throne.

Hell burned in the man's gaze.

Eyes of pale, luminous gold traveled over Tyriel's face. Aryn knew what it was the fae prince saw—had committed those frail lines to memory.

"Da," Tyriel said, moving forward.

Aryn moved with her, but before they could take a second step, the prince was in front of them, moving at a speed Aryn had never seen to catch his daughter in his arms.

"My precious daughter," Prince Lorne said.

Magic exploded out of the prince.

Aryn felt crushed by it and clenched his hands into fists as he fought to ride it out.

The wild magic hit the iron walls where it was nullified, but more kept coming from Lorne until Aryn felt like he'd been flayed raw from it.

It ended in seconds, just like the wild burst of wind from earlier.

But now Aryn understood why the walls and floor and ceiling were all made of iron. This man's rage could level a kingdom.

As Lorne wrapped his daughter in his arms, Aryn met his eyes over her head and gave a short nod.

He understood that wrath himself, all too

well.

* * * * *

"Her magic is gone."

"How does an elf survive such a loss?" Lorne murmured to Alys some time later as she entered their chambers, her body aching and weary.

Her mind was troubled, very troubled. The girl had suffered too many torments, and she could not tell her father all. Alys knew Tyriel, had watched her grow from babe to child to strong young woman and she knew without asking that Tyriel wouldn't want her beloved Da to know all that had been done to her.

Lorne would want to know.

Alys smiled, although there was no humor in it. Her Healer's vow would allow her to keep Tyriel's secrets at least. And this concern, her magic, it was no betrayal to address that.

"Her mother's bloodline is what saved her, love. The iron poisoning alone would have killed a full-blooded fae. And then to rip out her magic...that was an of such desperate courage, I can't imagine the fear she must have felt to take such a step." She sighed and sat beside him, taking his hand in hers.

After they'd helped Tyriel to her quarters—along with the brooding, quiet mortal swordsman who wouldn't be removed from her side—Lorne had retreated so his Consort could do whatever Healing she could.

But he'd known when she came to him that

she didn't expect her efforts to bear much fruit.

"She's dying," he said in a flat tone, the words all but ripping through a heart still bruised from the loss of his Wildling wife.

Alys took his hand, saying nothing.

Friends since a childhood that had long since faded into the past for both of them, they'd come together nearly three decades earlier, both of them grieving for loves forever lost to them. Theirs wasn't a love match, but they did have love for each other, and a respect born of both time and shared experiences.

"The human," Lorne said. "What did you learn..."

The words stopped as both of them sensed the new presence—someone who'd invaded their private chambers.

Alys drew the dagger from her waist while Lorne pulled a blade that he carried at his back, hidden by a small personal glamour. The moment he touched the hilt, black flames leaped to life along the blade. He whirled, placing himself and the blade between the intruder and the slim figure of his consort.

What he saw took him sent shock reverberating through him.

Prince Lorne of Averne, Prince Regent of the High Kingdoms and Protectorate of the Western Gate, had seen many oddities in his lifetime and very little took him aback.

But the spectral form of a Jiupsu warrior, who ached with the weight of age, standing in his personal sanctum had him momentarily at a loss.

He'd seen his second millennia come and go, and yet, in this being's presence, his own age felt like nothing—he was like a stripling in the presence of a forest giant, one so old, its age seemed immeasurable.

The figure glanced at the sword, then back up, quirking a brow. "A blade forged in Myrsae, imbued with the magic of the First Guardians. Impressive. It might even hurt if you were to run me through with that."

Lorne narrowed his eyes. Myrsae, a land forgotten by time to much of the world and attributed to myth by the few who still remembered it. Yet this man spoke of it with easy knowledge. "You're the one who cast the enchantment over the blade carried by the mortal swordsman."

The specter inclined his head.

Slowly, Lorne lowered his sword. "Who are you...and how did you so easily step past my protections?"

"I am Irian." He smiled, a brief flash of his teeth in a craggy face. "And your protections are impressive, princeling. But they aren't as effective as one who no longer relies on the trappings on flesh and blood."

"The trappings of flesh and blood," Alys muttered as she moved to his side. "Such small, inconsequential things."

The warrior gave her a small smile.

Taking his Consort's hand, Lorne looked the enchanter over with a jaded eye. "Now we know the *who* and the *how*. Tell me the *why*."

Irian's eyes fell away and the eerie luminescence of his form dimmed. "Tyriel."

Chapter 19

Tyriel felt so empty inside.

The painful, vicious aches from so many beatings was gone, thanks to Alys' wondrous healing abilities.

Her father's consort had also purged the lingering effect of iron sickness lingering in her system and after a long night's rest and a light meal, the pounding in her head had retreated somewhat, letting her think clearly for the first time in months.

It wasn't an improvement.

Without the constant pain, she was acutely aware of the emptiness inside her, acutely aware of her ever-waning strength and the grief she could feel all around her.

She was mostly aware of Aryn, though.

The way he watched her, as if he feared she'd disappear. In the recesses of her weakening heart, the love she'd had for him almost from the first still burned and it hurt, knowing that he suffered, knowing the guilt he now carried on those strong shoulders.

She wished she had the strength to send him away. There was no reason for him to linger and watch her fade. But it was an arduous task to even speak.

She'd slept away nearly an entire day after

Alys's first healing session, rousing only when driven by thirst or a need to use the personal chambers. Each time, Aryn had been there, waiting by the bed as if he could sense her needs.

Now, on her side, she watched him through her lashes.

He had yet to realize she was awake so his expression was unguarded. She took in the fine lines of strain fanning out from his eyes, the hard set of his mouth, his jaw a rigid line.

The bleakness in his gaze made her want to weep.

"If it hurts you so, then why will you not fight for him?"

Tyriel closed her eyes, Irian's voice in her mind feeling oddly foreign after so much time had passed. *Leave me be,* she thought, not bothering to establish a true link with him.

It didn't matter.

"No. I did that when you ran from us in Ifteril. I let you be even though everything in me said we should follow. Look at what has happened."

Tears burned. I don't know what you want from me. I'm dying, Irian. My heart is failing and everything in me hurts. Just breathing hurts. All I want is peace.

She felt a phantom hand stroke her hair gently and she opened her eyes, half-expecting to see his familiar, ghostly form.

But she didn't.

"I want to know this: if you had the strength in you to keep going, if your heart wasn't failing you,

would you fight?"

She wanted to scream. Hadn't most of her life been a fight of some form or another? *What am I supposed to fight for, Irian?*

Aryn stirred and his tired eyes focused on hers.

For a brief moment, naked longing burned there.

Then he blinked and when he leaned forward to take her hand, his blue eyes were unreadable.

"For him, love," Irian murmured from within her mind. *"For the life you two could still have. If you had the strength to fight for it...would you?"*

Aryn lifted her hand to his lips, unaware of the enchanter's presence. As the sweetly intimate caress, Tyriel squeezed her eyes shut.

Yes.

She didn't even have to consider it.

If she had the strength, she'd fight.

But I don't, enchanter, do I? And fuck you for reminding me of that.

* * * * *

Aryn tried not to think about the frailness of the hand he held as he sat by her side.

She rested against him, thin fingers wrapped around a mug of tea her father's consort had brought.

"Drink a bit more?" Aryn asked.

She heaved out a sigh. "You said you'd drink a cup yourself if I'd drink mine. You've had even less than me."

Aryn grabbed the mug from the table next to the bed and tossed back half of it. "There."

Tyriel glanced at him before straightening, weight propped on a quivering arm. With her free hand, she brought the cup to her lips. Her fingers shook but she took three healthy drinks before lowering it.

"That's enough for now," she said, voice thick with exhaustion. "I want to lie down."

Aryn took the cup and placed it by his own discorded one. As he turned back to her, a yawn cracked his mouth wide open.

"You should rest, too," Tyriel murmured, her lids so heavy it was a strain to keep them open.

"I'm fine," he said, tugging back the covers before helping her settle on the bed.

But when he went to pull away, Tyriel caught his hand. "Lie with me. Please."

A muscle pulsed in his jaw, but he nodded. "I need to take off my boots."

He yawned again halfway through the routine task, mumbling, "Maybe I do need a lie-down."

When he turned to Tyriel, she was already asleep.

Careful not to disturb her, he pulled her into his arms, then covered both of them with the thick, warm blankets.

She snuggled into his chest.

Exhaustion pushed ever closer.

He heard the door open and he tried to look

and see who it was.

But lethargy gripped him, all but dragged him into the darkness.

His last clear thought...had the royal consort drugged the fucking tea?

* * * * *

"Enchanter." Lorne looked over the still body of his daughter and the man who looked ready to follow her into death itself. "This had better work."

"I've already told you I can make no promises." Irian approached the sleeping couple, reaching out with his mind to ascertain that both truly, deeply slumbered. "But this is one way I know that might give her a chance. The sword, Prince Lorne."

After looking at his consort, Lorne picked up the sword from where Aryn had put it when he removed his boots and a few other weapons. After pulling it from its sheath, he offered it to the specter.

He didn't look surprised when Irian was able to take the blade in hand—although he *was* startled when Irian's form flickered, and for a brief moment, looked solid and whole, flushed with health and life.

The change lasted only seconds and with a *pop*, Irian reverted back to his normal, spectral state and the air went tight with magic.

"You must see to it that no one enters the room while I work."

"Of course," Alys said with an incline of her head.

"How long will this take?" Lorne demanded.

"A few days? Perhaps a week?" Irian shook his head. "I do not know."

He placed the sword on the bed next to Aryn, the hilt brushing the sword's arm.

Then, after a final look at Tyriel, he put his hand on the blade.

And disappeared.

* * * * *

Tyriel was lost.

She had no idea where she was.

When she'd first come to awareness in the utter, complete black emptiness, she'd nearly panicked. It had taken forever to get her limbs to move and she'd thought perhaps she'd find herself trapped—had nearly expected it. She'd find herself shut away in some close, airless space and eventually, Tainan would reveal himself, showing her this latest cruelty.

But after endless moments, she'd managed to move. Step by careful step, she'd realized she wasn't in any sort of room or prison that she could deduce.

Beyond that, she knew nothing of where she was or even how long she'd been there.

Her last memories were of Aryn, his arms around her, a cup of Alys' tea in her hand, the flavor of it sweet on her tongue. Then the soft, warm blanket of sleep.

Had she died?

Was this the afterlife?

If so, either she'd failed to live up to whatever expectations the Nameless One had of her or the supposed paradise that was meant to wait for the faithful and true-hearted was an absolute lie.

The endless maw of darkness stretched out around her as she walked. She had no way of knowing just how long she'd been walking, for although it seemed an age, her body wasn't weary, her feet didn't ache—

"Wait..." She stopped and smoothed her hands along her arms. She'd been in her bedchamber back at Averne, in her own bed. Alys had assisted her into a gown of *iferi* silk, soft against her skin but so warm.

But she wasn't wearing the sleeping gown.

And when she touched her arms, it wasn't the spindly limbs she'd last seen.

No, she touched the familiar wool, cotton and leather of the garb she typically wore when outside her father's lands. Inside boots that were coming to show signs of wear, she curled her toes.

"A dream?"

Her words were lost to the vastness around her and she blew out a harsh breath. Once more, she began to walk, but quicker now, with more purpose.

Instinctively, she went to reach out with her magic and the jab of pain that struck her in the chest as she remembered was so sharp, it felt like a blade.

Tears burned a hot path down her cheeks and she dashed them away. It was that action that her aware of the subtle change, a faint lessening of the endless dark.

She could see. Not well, and there didn't look to be anything *to* see.

But she was no longer in a place so devoid of light, she couldn't make out the shape of her own hand before her.

She had no idea when the change had started, either. Not that it would do much any good to pinpoint the change—time and place seemed to have no meaning in this...wherever she was.

But the darkness *was* lessening.

"Am I dead?

The vast emptiness around her seemed to sigh.

And then, in front of her, a pool of light began to coalescence.

With that pool of light took on form, she wasn't surprised to find herself staring at Irian. The light ebbed until she was looking at Irian as he must have looked in life, rather than the spectral form she normally saw.

"Don't you ever grow tired of playing tricks with my mind?" she said, a bubble of anger forming in her chest. Had she just spent all this time trapped in some enchantment of his? *Why?*

"This is no trick, Tyriel," Irian said.

The sound of his voice, oddly more...*real*

than she'd ever heard him sound startled her and the poignant grief in his eyes had her throat thickening.

Tearing her gaze from his, she looked around.

"No? Then what is this?" She was barely able to see much more than perhaps an arm's length before her before the darkness cloaked everything, although she thought the light just *might* be increasing from...somewhere.

"This is...you," Irian said. "I have to admit, it took a long time to come so far. I was starting to worry we'd never find this."

Frustrated, Tyriel glared at him.

"Find *what*?"

"Look." Irian spread his hands out and turned in a slow circle.

There *was* more light, although she had no idea where the source of it was. Her vision, sharply acute thanks to her elvish bloodline, had adjusted to that scant illumination well enough that she could see him without difficulty. He had his head tipped back and she mimicked the movement more out of habit than any real curiosity about whatever it was that held his attention.

"We're within you, Tyriel. In the very core of you, deeper, even, than your soul." He finally spun back to look at her, his dark eyes glinting. "That you don't recognize this hollow hell is odd, but I'm not overly surprised. You've never had a reason to look so deeply inside yourself until you stripped away all your magic—*almost* all."

She flinched. "Stop talking in riddles, Irian."

"This is no riddle." He lifted his eyes once more, a faint smile on his hard, rawly masculine face. "You stripped it all away, save for one faint, lingering spark."

Tyriel shook her head and began to back away.

Irian lowered his gaze back to hers.

"What can a clever, patient soul such as you do with a spark, Tyriel?"

She tried to back up another step, and found she couldn't. She wasn't paralyzed and Irian wasn't stopping her. She just...couldn't *make* herself move. Compelled by something she saw in his eyes, she waited, not even daring to breathe as he advanced on her.

"Sparks can turn into raging wildfires."

He held out his hand.

She looked down, mesmerized by the broad, scarred palm before her.

"You have to take this step, Tyriel. I cannot do this for you," he murmured.

Squeezing her eyes shut, she put her hand in his.

"That's my brave, beautiful warrior."

Chapter 20

"You've always been such a brave, stubborn lass, love."

Irian whispered as he shimmered into view, retreating from her subconscious so he could take the next step.

Behind him, he heard the mutterings from her father and the Royal Consort and while he much wanted to ignore them and move forward in his quest, much depended on Tyriel and Aryn being undisturbed while he finished his work.

Rising, he turned to face Prince Lorne.

For a moment, he was taken aback, surprised by the changes in both the prince and his consort. He was unshaven and wore fighting leathers, as if prepared to go to war, the coronet marking him as a High Prince among the People gone.

Alys, like the prince, had abandoned her regal garb. She wore a simple gown and her hair was pulled back into a plain tail at her nape.

Both eyed with eyes aglow with magic.

Lorne strode forward, a dagger in his hand. When he lifted it, Irian saw the black flames dripping from it.

"When you told us you might have a way to

help, you said you'd need peace and for them to be *undisturbed for a time*—a *short* time. It's been more than three *weeks*, you bloody fool specter!"

Irian eyed the black flames before shifting his attention to the furious fae lord.

"Three weeks is but a blink," he said with a shrug. "It took me far longer to find the last, lingering spark of her magic than I'd thought. Then I had to call her to me. It is not quick work, Prince Lorne."

The prince's lids flickered, his mouth going tight. "What *spark*? Her magic is gone. She..."

He lapsed into silence, catching sight of his consort from the corner of his eye as she approached the bed. For three weeks, he'd hardly left his daughter's side. Alys had spent much of that time with him and after the first week, she'd begun to sink her healer's energy into both Tyriel and Aryn, telling him she could circumvent their natural need for food and water this way for a brief period of time.

Each time she'd done so, she'd expended herself more and more until he sent for another healer, one of her mentors to be on hand to assist Alys, should she need it.

She'd maintained, eating gluttonously to fuel her body as the healing demanded its toll. At the same time, she used her wry humor to keep him from descending farther into his grief.

Alys was not the true love his heart still ached for, but he did have love for her, and there was none he trusted more.

So when he heard her soft gasp, he rushed to her side, even being so rude as to step through the spectral form of the enchanter rather than around him.

"Lorne...do you see?"

* * * * *

"Brother."

Aryn knew he dreamed.

From the first time he'd held Asrel, before he even knew anything about the blade or the soul of a powerful enchanter dead for millennia who had spelled himself into the sword for reasons Aryn still didn't know, odd dreams had plagued him.

Since learning about Irian, and the magic within Asrel, he'd learned to distinguish between his own odd dreams and the ones tied to the man who called him brother.

He sat up and looked around the chamber, turning to see Tyriel—and his own slumbering body. She was entwined in his arms, her cheek on his chest.

Was it the dream or simple wishful thinking that made it appear as though she wasn't so fragile?

He made himself look away. He couldn't afford to hope. The pain of losing her, accepting that he had to let her go, was bad enough, almost enough to drive him mad. If he dared hope, only to lose her...

"Aryn, my brother. *Look* at me."

Tired even in his own dream, Aryn lifted his eyes to Irian.

It was a disconcerting sight, though.

Irian wasn't the ephemeral vision he'd always been.

He looked to be a man of flesh and blood.

The enchanter crossed to Aryn. "If she fights to live, will you be her bridge?"

Aryn had no idea what Irian meant, but the only words that mattered were *if she fights to live*...he went to say *yes*, but that painful specter of hope hovered between them. Hesitating, he looked back at Tyriel.

"Answer, brother, *now*. I don't have much time. For this, I cannot just take control of your body—you *must* be willing."

The intensity of Irian's voice shattered Aryn's fears and he focused on the enchanter. "Yes. Her bridge, her lifeline, her everything. Whatever it is she needs, it's yours. You don't even have to ask."

A broad smile broke over Irian's face and for once, the shadow of sadness that forever haunted the man fell away.

"Be well, my brother." Irian placed his hand on Aryn's chest. "Live a long, happy life."

And blackness fell.

Alys had moved to the other side of the bed to check on the human merc who had brought

Tyriel back to Averne. Both she and the prince spoke softly, one or the other pausing to look around for the enchanter who had disappeared without warning.

When he abruptly appeared at the foot of the bed, Alys jumped, pressing a hand to her furiously racing heart. Glaring at him, she said, "Can you not give us a *warning* before you come and go like that?"

Irian, once more nothing but a spectral form, shrugged. "This will be the last time you see me, Lady Consort." He held out a hand.

For three weeks, save for when Alys herself changed the bedding, the sword Aryn carried had laid in the bed next to the man. Now, answering some summons from the enchanter, it rose into the air and settled between the two sleepers.

Alys went to argue, her every healer instincts appalled.

But then the blade started to glow, burning brighter and brighter until both she and Lorne had to look away.

The brightness reached a crescendo, shattering the quiet of the room with a faint hum as Lorne and Alys flung their arms up instinctively.

Blinking away the blindness caused by the bright light, they looked at each other as sparkling motes, like a magical dusting, filled the air, centered over the two still forms on the bed. As the glittering particles sank lower and lower, Lorne held out a hand, capturing one tiny spark on his fingertip.

Power jolted up his arm and he hissed.

"What is it?" Alys asked.

"It's...that blade. Or what remains of it."

The faint dusting continued to drift down until it coated Tyriel and Aryn. She was still thin, but there was a flush of color to her cheeks even now. "Alys..." Lorne whispered, not daring to hope.

His consort reached out and touched the sleeping woman. Her eyes, when she looked back at Lorne, were filled with dismay and a wild joy.

"She is...filled, Lorne. That hollow void left inside her psyche when she stripped away her magic...it's *full*."

Lorne looked at the foot of the bed.

But the enchanter was gone.

* * * * *

Tyriel was so, *so* warm.

Strong arms held her and when she breathed in, a familiar scent flooded her head, filling her with a deep ache.

Aryn...

As if she'd summoned him, the arm around her waist tightened, pulling her even closer to the source of warmth—a hard male body.

A dream, she thought.

And a lovely one.

Abruptly, he moved and with his arm around her waist, she had no voice but to go with him.

The bedclothes fell away, exposing her ass to the air. After being cocooned with him and his warmth, the cooler air felt like an insult, jolting her into surprised wakefulness just as a big hand landed on her rump.

She blinked in confusion as she looked around, then down.

Her mouth fell open when she saw Aryn, his head turned to the side to give her a look at his profile. He was unshaven, several weeks worth of beard growth darkening his face and the normally silken skein of his hair was a mess, tangled around his shoulders.

And he wore...a night shirt.

"I'm...not dreaming," she whispered.

Aryn grumbled under his breath and rolled again, still clutching her to him like she was naught by a ragdoll. A much loved ragdoll, though, for his grip on her was very tight.

She wiggled and squirmed until she could peer into his face, her mind racing as she took stock. She felt...weak. Weak, but not frail.

Closing her eyes, she tried to focus. It took several moments to calm her racing mind enough that she could center her thoughts on the rapid beat of her heart.

A *strong* heart.

And...

"No," she whispered, tears flooding her eyes at the shock of the other discovery.

Magic *burned* inside her.

The shock of it flooded her, wiping away every last vestige of sleep. She still felt weak but now, giddy with joy, she whispered, "Aryn."

His brow furrowed but he didn't waken.

So very unlike the swordsman. He wasn't as light a sleeper as she—under *normal* circumstances—but there was nothing normal about the pulse of magic inside her, as sure and steady as the heart that no longer failed her.

Scraps of memory came to her as she stroked Aryn's cheek.

"Sparks can turn into raging wildfires."

Irian's voice, strong and certain as he spoke to her in that unrelenting vastness.

"You have to take this step, Tyriel. I cannot do this for you."

"Sparks," she whispered.

She was tempted to reach out to the enchanter and ask him, but the man in the bed with her was far more important than any questions she might have.

Echoes of that conversation with Aryn when she'd realized her path in life had come to its final destination.

"Feel this heart...it beats only for you."

"I'll fill the cracks. I'll fix the edges."

She'd been so *angry* at him when he'd spoken those words. The love she'd felt for him had flared to life inside her, only to sputter and fade. Her death had loomed before her. *That* was when he'd told her what she'd longed for.

And now...

The short beard growth was silken under her hand, his lashes long and spiky as they hid his blue eyes from her.

Moving closer, she pressed her mouth to his, her heart clenching like a fist as she did so. "Aryn."

The arm around her waist tightened and she felt him tense, but still, he didn't waken. She caught her breath as he rolled onto his back again, one more taking her with him.

But when the movement exposed her naked bum to the cool air, she didn't have time for a chill to settle in. Aryn clamped a possessive hand over her hip, his fingers spread wide to curve over her rump.

She kissed him again, his mouth soft under explorations. Wiggling until she had one knee on either side of his hips, she kissed a line down to his neck and pushed aside the soft material of the nightshirt he wore.

She might have laughed at the oddity of that if she hadn't been so needy, so desperate to keep touching him...and to have him awaken and touch her.

The hand on her hip squeezed and he sighed, his body flexing under hers.

Ah...there you are, my beautiful man.

He came awake in the next instant and Tyriel yelped at the suddenness as he flipped them so she lay under him. He stared at her with wide, startled eyes.

She smiled at him. "Hello."

"Tyriel...what...how?" Shock had chased away the sleep from his eyes and he looked at her as though he feared she'd disappear from his sight.

"I don't know." She forced a smile and laid a hand on his chest where his heart pound like a Wildling festival drum. "Can we figure it out later? I seem to have this vague recollection of you claiming that this heart beat only for me."

His only response was to crush his mouth to hers.

She moaned into his kiss, twining her arms around his neck only to release him a moment later so she could fist the material of his nightshirt in her hands. Breaking the kiss, she said, "Off. I want this *off*."

Aryn shoved up onto his knees and went to peel it away only to pause a moment to study the fine material. He cocked a brow at her.

"Likely Alys's doing." She looked down at the silk covering her to her waist. Between her wiggling and Aryn's incessant movements as he clung to her while sleeping, the gown was in a tangle around her waist. "While I'm sure my father is pleased I wasn't in here naked with you, I doubt he had any hand in...that."

His lips twitched as he yanked the offending material off, then came down over her. "If this is a dream..." he murmured, his lips against her neck.

"It's not. *Oh!*"

He'd slid down and caught one silk-covered nipple in his mouth and the pleasure of it ripped through her, savage in its intensity.

"Aryn..." Her lashes started to close, but she forced her eyes to stay open. She didn't want to blink, want to miss a moment of this—an impossible dream somehow made real.

"Are you attached to this gown?" Aryn murmured, kissing a path upward until he could murmur the question in her ear.

"Attached...? What? No."

"Good." He shoved up once more and Tyriel's only warning was the glint in his eyes as he curled his hands in the laced-up vee of her sleeping gown. It ripped.

She was just a decade shy of her first century.

She could knock a fully grown human male across the room with one blow if she chose.

There was simply no reason for her heart to leap into a mad race at what Aryn had just done. But race, her heart did.

He curved his hands over her waist and tugged her upright, wrapping one muscled forearm around her waist to hold her against him as he brushed the remaining shreds of her sleeping down again.

Then, as his eyes blazed bright with need, he bent his head and pressed his mouth to the center of her chest.

Tyriel's bones melted and her head fell back, spine arching as the heat of his caress turned her muscles lax.

"Now that's a beautiful sight," Aryn murmured.

She started to lift her head but he closed his mouth around one nipple and the raw pleasure laid her low.

Distantly, she heard a thud but it had no bearing on what was happening here and now, so she ignored it.

It was harder to ignore the next sound—crystal shattering against a stone floor.

But of them jerked in reaction, but Aryn moved far quicker as the two of them looked over to see Tyriel's father and the Royal Consort standing in the doorway, both wide, arching doors thrown open and several servants at their back.

As Aryn yanked up a coverlet from the bed to tuck around Tyriel, she gaped at her father.

"*Da!* A bit of privacy would be nice! Haven't you heard of knocking?"

Prince Lorne blinked, the look on his face one of sheer amazement.

"*Knocking?*" he asked in their native tongue, his voice raspy. "You have lain unmoving in this chamber for nearly a *month* and now you fuss at me to *knock?*"

Tyriel gaped at him.

Alys, her lovely face aglow with a smile, stepped up and took her consort's arm. "Prince, perhaps we could...discuss this matter after the princess has had time to...bathe and dress."

Lorne looked over at his consort, then back at Tyriel, and finally, at Aryn, who held Tyriel against his chest, the coverlet wrapped around her thin frame.

"Yes," Lorne murmured, shaking his head as he turned. With a wave of his hand, he dismissed the servants and strode away.

Alys winked at Tyriel and caught the door latch. "I'll send servants who can help you bathe, beloved child." She conveniently chose not to acknowledge the ones the prince had just dismissed. "I find I'm famished, though, so it might take some time as I plan to stop by the kitchen and find myself a light repast. Perhaps expect them...a mark or so before we would normally gather for the evening meal."

The door closed on the Royal Consort and Tyriel turned her attention back to Aryn.

Questions danced in her mind.

But they all faded as Aryn closed his hand around her neck and brought her back to him.

The coverlet felt away as she gripped his sides, his hard, sleekly muscled form warm under her hands. His cock pulsed between them, a brand against her belly and she rocked forward.

"I need you," she whispered against his mouth.

Rainbows blossomed behind her eyes as he gripped both of her hips and lifted her, the head of his cock brushing against her wet, aching core.

She tensed, painful ugly memories trying to creep up on her. Shoving her hands into Aryn's tumbled hair, she pulled his mouth to hers.

He kissed her sweetly and when she tore away to breathe, he trailed his lips across her cheek, her jaw, then to her ear.

"Open your eyes, love...see my face," Aryn

whispered.

She did, refusing to let the fear or shame take hold. Not now.

His eyes holding her captive, he lay back on the bed, bringing her with him until she sprawled across his chest. Then he let her go and clasped his hands behind his head.

From under heavy-lidded eyes, he stared at her.

"You lead this dance, Tyriel."

Licking her lips, she nodded. Nervous still, she shifted into place so she straddled him. His cock nestled against her intimate folds and she shivered, then moaned as his length jerked in response to the feel of her wet heat.

"You're entirely too beautiful a man, Aryn," she murmured, stroking her hands across his muscled chest, noting the scars she'd seen hundreds of times. Now, though, she had the right to touch them, to trail the tips of her fingers over them, a ragged, twisting along his right side just below his ribcage, another one, this one a thin long line where he'd narrowly escaped death when he stepped between a man he'd been hired to protect and a would-be assassin. There were other scars, some older, others still baring the faint color of healing flesh.

She bent her head to kiss one, then another, then gasped, her torso straightening as Aryn's cock pulsed heavily against her slick entrance.

He watched her with a slitted gaze, his jaw a rigid line.

"Am I teasing you horribly?" she asked softly, bracing her hands on his chest.

"Terribly." He groaned as she slid against him, the caress tormenting them both as the wet heat between her thighs made everything slick. "I'll be sure to pay you back when you stop." He arched up, biting off a curse, then panting as she ground against him harder. "Please...don't ever stop."

She laughed, the sound rising up and escaping her before turning into a long, broken moan as her machinations began to affect her as much as him.

"I need you inside me," she said.

She was still weak, though, arms and legs shaking as she went to take him. As if sensing her frustration, Aryn caught her waist and lifted her slightly. "Wrap your pretty fingers around my cock, love," he said, voice rough and broken. It turned jagged and savage, a stream of curses escaping him as she followed his direction, gripping his cock in her fist.

She needed no direction now, holding him steady as he tugged her closer.

Her lids felt heavy but when she started to close her eyes, Aryn said, "No. Tyriel...love...look at me. See me. Only me. *Feel* only me."

Focusing on his face, she focused on him— *only* him as she slowly sank down onto him, the hard length of his cock filling her.

When she'd taken him fully, she swayed forward and braced her hands on his shoulders, shuddering as her body adjusted to him.

Aryn's hands tightened on her hips and his cock jerked inside her. Tyriel whimpered, her muscles tightening around him in reaction. He swelled, growing impossibly harder.

It was so *good*, but she needed more.

Slowly, hesitantly, she began to move, circling her hips against his. His hands tightened, then with a groan, he let go and brought his hands back up to rest beside his head.

Tyriel covered them with her own, twining their fingers until their hands were as entwined as their bodies.

"Aryn..."

He shuddered, sweat breaking out across his body, his eyes locked with hers. "Tyriel...love..."

Tears flooded her eyes. Wild magic escaped her, slipping past her grip with ease because she had no control left, barely any strength.

Aryn pulled her closed and took her mouth, arching beneath her as she tightened around him, climax racing closer. Tugging his other hand from her tight grasp, he reached them, clever fingers seeking, then stroking the pulsating knot of her clitoris.

She jolted, her spine going rigid as she jerked upright. Aryn arched beneath her, his powerful body pumping hard and fast, driving into her as she clenched around him, her orgasm slamming into her with brutal force.

He muttered her name, swore, then again,

in a low, awed whisper, "Tyriel..."

As he climaxed inside her, she cried out his name.

Magic, wild and unfettered, escaped them both, choking the air with light, while Tyriel's skin glowed from within.

She sank down, still shuddering to collapse against his chest.

The glow of her skin didn't fade for a long, long time.

Chapter 21

"You are thinking so very loudly," Tyriel mumbled.

"Am I?" Aryn stroked his hand down her back, far too aware of how thin she was. But the energy, the inner strength that was her core, *that* filled her.

He could sense it, all but taste the sheer life of her.

So many questions tumbled inside his head. But he pushed them aside. If he was thinking loudly, as Tyriel had put it, he was keeping her from resting. She might not be able to see inside his head as he'd once accused her of doing, but she had the most sensitive soul he'd ever encountered. That she'd picked up on the turbulence inside him was no surprise.

She sat up, the movements far slower than he was used to seeing from her, and her normal fluid grace wasn't there. But her cheeks glowed with color. Her eyes no longer reflected screaming darkness he'd seen in the days after they'd taken her out of the miserable hole where she'd been held captive. Her dark, tumbling mass of curls was a wild tangle as she tugged a coverlet around herself, her chill another sign she still had healing left to do.

"I think I know part of why you are so quiet while your thoughts are so very loud." Tyriel cocked her head, gaze watchful.

"I guess it's time for those questions," he muttered. He sat, adjusting his position until his back was braced against the elegantly carved headboard. "Will you come to me?"

Her lips curved in a lovely smile and she came just as he'd asked, throwing one leg over his so she sat astride him. The coverlet started to fall and he caught it, securing it around her before the chill could return. "You're still weak," he said quietly.

"Yes." Her nose wrinkled, her disgust at her state quite clear.

He cupped her cheek. "You survived a monster. That you're whole and sane at all is a miracle. You can always rebuild your strength. Be kind to yourself...give yourself the time to heal."

"Since when did you become a speaker of wisdom?" But she smiled as she said it, covering his hand with her own. "I thought you humans had to become graybeards before you started tossing out such sensible advice."

"That may well be the only useful wisdom I ever impart," he said solemnly, even as the sight of her smile made his heart clench. "It's a good thing you didn't have to wait until I was a graybeard to hear it, considering that it's likely I'll live centuries now. The magic..."

He lifted a hand and breathed into it, watched as flames lit there.

And he was acutely aware of the silence within his own mind.

"Irian has long said his power was settling inside your skin." Tyriel's eyes were watchful.

"It's no longer his power, but mine." He closed his hand around the flames. As they extinguished, he looked back at Tyriel. "He's gone."

She drew in a slow breath, but there was no surprise in her eyes. "I thought he might be."

Aryn placed his hands on her thighs, thumbs stroking restlessly.

"Aryn, about Irian..."

He slanted a look at her, reaching up to press his thumb to her soft mouth. The shadows in her eyes confirmed something he'd long suspected. "I know," he said simply. When she started to look away, he cupped her chin and brought her face back to his. "He was the smarter of us both. Yes, I know he's taken my mind over, used my body as he lay with you. A part of me hated him for it, even when I had only suspicions. Now..."

Her cheeks were hotly pink and her gaze kept sliding away.

Aryn pushed his fingers into her hair and brought her mouth to his, kissing her as he longed to do for so long.

"I don't know what he did," Aryn murmured after ending the kiss. Brow pressed to hers, he sucked in a rough breath before continuing. "But as I slept, I *felt* him. I know the feel of his power, his magic, Tyriel. It surrounded me. I could feel it, almost drowned in it...and then it was flowing *out*. From me, into you."

Her mouth fell open on a gasp. She leaned into him, trembling.

"He came to me as I slept," she murmured, the words so quiet, he could hear them. She pulled back then and met his gaze. "He told me there was still a spark within me, a spark that was my magic. I'd been...lost." Shaking her head, she looked past Aryn's shoulder, but he knew she wasn't truly looking at anything. She was remembering.

She continued to speak, the words a hushed whisper in the silence of her room. When she finally lapsed into silence, Aryn simply wrapped his arms around her. "He came to me as well. Nothing quite so...strange, but he asked if I would be your bridge."

Tyriel said nothing so he continued.

"I didn't know what he meant, but there was...something about the way he spoke that told me how urgent this was. I'd told him I'd be whatever you needed. Everything went dark after that, and I slept. That was when his magic began to flood into me. It was far too much for me to hold inside, but then it spilled out." He waited for her to look at him once more. He was right—he felt it in his bones. Slowly, she lifted her head and met his gaze. "It flowed me into you. His power..." He stopped, unable to explain anymore.

"Enchanters can carry a great deal of magic inside them," she murmured, resting a hand over her chest. "Even human enchanters. But eventually, it becomes too much and they have to store it—sometimes in objects, like swords." She glanced at him before continuing. "There are some who can actually pierce the veils and merge with the ether plains—the lingering place between here and eternity. Rumors say to linger there long is to court death...you'll lose your anchor to reality and slip away until you've merged with the ether plains and become naught by a shadow of magic, void of memory. But some enchanters are powerful enough they can walk there, even store magic within the veil, if they can find a way to forge a holding place, like a cask. Irian is...*was* very powerful. And you shared a bond with him."

"A bridge," Aryn said quietly. "He gathered up all the power he's stored over millennia and used his bond with me to give that power to you." He scowled, shaking his head. "But I don't understand. He was an enchanter. You're fae. You have elemental magic, and other gifts. But you are not an enchanter."

"The spark," she murmured, a small smile on her face. It grew as she looked at Aryn. "That *spark* was *me*, the core of myself, my magic...like the embers of a fire. Raw magical energy, in its purest form, is just that, Aryn." She cupped his cheeks, her eyes bright as the puzzle revealed itself to her. "There are places in our world that run rich with lingering magical energy still in the earth. Irian—now you—could easily tap into it for enchantments. I could tap into it as well. But I'd use that same energy to call up water or shake the earth, while you could use it to power wardings or seek a fleeing blood mage. All Irian did was find a way to funnel the raw energy he's stored into me."

"Hardly *all*," Aryn muttered, his head spinning as je fought to make sense of what Tyriel had told him.

"What?"

He traced a line down her cheek. "He gave you back to me—no, he find a way so *you* come back. You were already out of reach, slipping from this world and he threw you a rope when nobody else could."

"You're right." Her eyes closed, she took a deep breath. "Aryn, I'm sor—"

He cut the apology off with a hard, rough kiss.

"No," he whispered against her mouth. "You owe me no apologies."

"You were hurting so badly," she said, the words husky. "I knew it, could feel it. I wanted to stop it, but I just didn't have the strength."

"No apologies," he said again. "Ever. Not over this, not over any of it. I understand."

She looked into his eyes, saw the fierceness there. Slowly, she nodded. "About Irian..."

Her hesitation had him stroking his hands soothingly up and down her arms. "He's gone," he said roughly, struck by just heavily it hit, acknowledging the truth of it.

Tyriel closed her eyes, head lowered. "You're certain? Did he tell you...anything?"

"No." Aryn's gaze focused inward on that strange dream. "But I just...knew. After he told me about the...bridge, darkness pulled me under and my final, fading thoughts were that I'd never see him again."

"I'm sorry," she whispered.

"No." He cupped her face. "He told me more than once that he was bound here until he'd balanced some scale, righted some wrong. Whatever he did to us as we slept... Tyriel, he did what he's been trying to do for millennia." Pressing a kiss to her brow, he murmured, "And more importantly, he helped give you the strength you needed. So don't be sorry."

A brisk knock on the door kept her from responding. She grimaced and glanced down to make sure she was decently covered, but when she went to slide from Aryn's lap, he gripped her thighs. She glanced at him but he was already calling out, "Come in."

Alys peeked around the door, a wide smile blooming on her face as she caught sight of them.

She pushed the door open wide and stepped to the side. "We knocked," she said with a wink at Tyriel. Then, with a quick glance at the tall, slim man at her side, she added, "But I couldn't talk him into waiting any longer, beloved. I'm sorry."

Prince Lorne's throat worked as he stared across the room at her.

"Da," Tyriel whispered huskily. She went to pull away from Aryn, but froze, remembering that under the coverlet, she wore nothing.

Alys bustled over, already talking cheerfully about the meal she'd ordered, set to be served in Tyriel's small, private dining chamber, the doors already thrown open as several servants moved around the room, gathering up the accouterments of a sickroom. "Here's your robe, my dear," she said, tossing it around Tyriel's shoulders and gesturing to Aryn.

He responded automatically, easing Tyriel around to face the Royal Consort before he realized he'd even done so.

"Up we go," Alys said, speaking in the brisk, no nonsense tone of a healer. She tugged Tyriel up and the coverlet fell away, but Alys was already tugging the robe closed, so Tyriel had no time to process her nudity, much less concern herself over it.

"Now." Alys rested her hands on Tyriel's shoulders and blinked back the tears that turned her eyes diamond bright. "Go. Your da is about to lose his mind and if he doesn't embrace you, I fear he'll shake the very castle around us down into nothing but small stone."

With a watery laugh, Tyriel turned.

And her father was right there, hovering at the foot of the bed, the patience he'd cultivated over his some-odd twenty centuries of life decimated under the weight of grief and the keening edge of joy as his beloved daughter was somehow restored back to life and health.

Tyriel took two steps and she was in his arms.

"My beloved child," he murmured.

After long moments when she didn't even try to hold back her tears, the High Prince finally eased his grip and Tyriel drew back enough to meet his gaze. "Hello, Da."

"*Hello, Da.*" He closed his eyes and lifted his face as if praying to the Nameless One. "Silent all these weeks and you tell me, *Hello, Da*? Is that all you have for me?"

He was smiling when he looked back at her, though.

She grinned, a remnant of her normal mischievous humor glinting in her eyes as she looked back at Aryn.

"Well, I could introduce to the only other man who has a hold on my heart."

Lorne's smile took on a bittersweet edge as he glanced past her to look at Aryn. The swordsman had climbed from the bed while they were distracted and accepted a pair of trousers from the ever-resourceful Alys, so at least he wasn't bare-assed as the High Prince looked him over. "I've met the man, beloved daughter."

Lorne tucked her against his side, one arm offering casual support in case her strength waned. Shrewd eyes of pale gray, like fog on the mountaintops, locked on Aryn.

"This...human has a hold on your heart, does he?" Lorne murmured, still staring at the man with tumbled, tangled blond hair and a scruffy beard, his naked, scarred chest bared for all to see.

Some might see a ruffian.

Lorne saw a warrior, and a man in love.

Letting go of Tyriel, hesitating only long enough to make sure she was steady on her feet, he stepped forward.

Aryn didn't move a muscle, but Lorne sensed his wary alertness.

With a faint smile, he offered his forearm. "I am forever in your debt, Master Aryn. If there is anything you desire, anything you need, if I can offer it, you need only ask. And it will be yours."

Aryn accepted the offered forearm, grasping it in a strong hand as Lorne grasped his in return.

"There's only thing I desire, one thing I need, Prince Lorne," Aryn said with a faint smile. He glanced to the woman standing just behind the fae lord before meeting the prince's eyes once more. "But as Tyriel alone is control of her heart, she'll have to be the one to decide if I may have that particular boon granted."

"Hmmm." Lorne released Aryn's arm and stepped aside. "A wisely worded choice."

As the two lovers embraced, Lorne met his consort's gaze. "Let's give them a bit more time alone."

Alys lifted a brow.

Lorne smiled. He'd seen his daughter, touched her face, seen the vitality he'd thought forever gone. She was alive. Her strength would return.

And he remembered being madly in love.

"We'll have the servants bring your dinner up shortly," he said, holding out a hand for his consort. "Tomorrow, we'll sit down together for a meal and celebration. Tonight is your own."

Whether they heard him or not, he didn't know. With his consort on his arm, he turned for the door.

The servants fell in behind him, all of them smiling.

The doors closed as Aryn wrapped his arms around Tyriel's waist and lifted her, spinning in a slow lazy circle before falling back on the bed.

She smiled down at him as he threaded a hand through her tumbled hair.

"Tonight is ours," he said gruffly. "What should we do?"

Tyriel's smile took on a wicked edge. "Oh, I can think of a thing or two to keep us occupied, lover. Would you like me to tell you?"

"Please do."

So, after kissing him senseless, she did just that.

When she lifted her head from his ear, it was to find him watching her with hot, gleaming eyes.

"What an excellent plan."

Epilogue

Irian followed the music.

Fael...

He could hear her, laughing playfully, tauntingly, teasingly...as he drifted. He had no longer had any form. Not Aryn's, not the steel casing of Asrel's, not the borrowed body of another bearer. None.

He was lost, entranced by the promise he sensed in her song but he had no true hope of really finding her.

Would this be his eternity then? Trapped in endless nothing, surrounded by her voice?

Well, he mused, his own thoughts so loud in the vast empty void. *There are worse ways to spend eternity.*

And it wasn't like he hadn't done plenty to earn his torments.

But the darkness ahead of him...was it fading?

A fire. Irian tried to move quicker, but with no form, it was hard to do anything more than drift.

In the next moment, the familiar scent of crushed grass surrounded him and he looked down, saw the plains of his youth beneath his feet and spreading out all around him.

He moved quicker, all but running until he finally reached the warmth of the campfire.

There, just a few paces from the protective stones of the fire, stood a lodging tent.

Lamplight from within highlighted a woman's body and when she approached the flap, then pushed it aside, Irian squeezed his eyes shut.

"There you are."

Fael...

Irian opened his eyes as she stepped out into the night.

Falling to his knees, he stared as Fael came to him.

When she cupped his cheek, he whispered, "Please...don't let this be a dream."

She sank to her knees before him and leaned in to kiss his sweetly.

"In a way, it is. It's the final dream—*our* final dream, my warrior." She cupped his face in her hands. "Our forever dream. Welcome to our eternity. I've been waiting for you for so, so long."

She kissed him again.

And Irian let himself believe. After millennia of wandering, of loneliness and emptiness, he sank into Fael's embrace and finally found peace.

Made in the USA
Columbia, SC
12 October 2024